CHILD

CHILD

A novel
by Gina Strad

Child
Published by Gina Strad
with Castle Publishing Ltd
New Zealand

© 2021 Gina Strad

ISBN 978-0-473-60316-8 (Softcover)
ISBN 978-0-473-60317-5 (ePUB)
ISBN 978-0-473-60318-2 (Kindle)

Production & Typesetting:
Lizelle van Antwerpen & Andrew Killick
Castle Publishing Services
www.castlepublishing.co.nz

Cover Design:
Sam Stradwick

Scriptures quotations are from the Good News Bible
© 1994 published by the Bible Societies/HarperCollins Publishers Ltd., UK
Good News Bible © American Bible Society 1966, 1971, 1976, 1992.
Used with permission.

For Marriette

'The soul is healed by being with children.'
Dostoevsky

'Children in wonder watching the stars,
is the aim and the end.'
Dylan Thomas

CHAPTER 1
Mid-October

Bright from the sky they fell, the first spits of the chill autumn rain. The child lifted up his cupped hands, his short triangle fingers pointed upward to touch the falling water. He opened his little cupid mouth, poked out his tongue and tasted the tiny droplets.

The boy stretched his mouth into the widest smile. He giggled as he ran in circles on the wide expanse of moistened grass. On his third circuit his big sister swept him up into her arms and carried him, resisting and arching his back, twisting and pulling, trying to escape, protesting, all the way up the stone steps until they were inside.

Meadow put him down on the narrow red strip of Persian carpet. He sped from room to room, until he found his darling Papa and raised his pudgy arms again, hoping for a cuddle and a twirl.

The child was too young to make sense of the changes that had evolved in his world over the last few weeks. All time was now to him. No past; no future, only contentment or discontent, according to the moment.

The sister, frowning, stared hard at her laughing brother. She was puzzled. She was miserable; why wasn't he?

The child's father and sister had no mechanism to help them rise above the waves of sadness. There were dark semi-circles under their eyes. New creases and lines on their pale faces hinted at the pain and anxiety they were living through. Nathan leaned over to Meadow, 'It feels like we are living *like dead men walking*. Just doing the expected, rising and sleeping, breathing only to stay alive, doesn't it?'

'Yes, I know, Dad.' She squeezed his firm hand.

The little child bound the small family together. Everything they did; the routine, the shopping, the daily rituals, was because he needed to be kept *normal*, shielded from sorrow. This very need for normality had also helped to protect the man and his daughter from the full horror of their loss.

Meadow looked at the little one. *Oh I need to hold your small warm body.*

'Come here funny Felix. Come and sit up here.' She patted her thighs. 'I'll read you a story before you have your bath.'

He scrambled up on her lap with a book. 'Read it! Read it!'

She held him very tightly, wrapping her fingers around his little cold hands, and was comforted.

Being needed helped to stop the emptiness in the house from overwhelming her heart. The boy eagerly turned the pages before she had finished reading the words. This didn't bother the girl now, as it used to, only three weeks before.

The smell of his damp clothes and hair, like a living animal, brought unexpected happiness to Meadow. She slowly inhaled and closed her eyes while Felix twisted Meadow's light brown hair with his fingers and cuddled into her little female body. She felt a little bit like Mamma.

'Choose another one then.'

Felix wriggled then jumped down to bring her a new book.

His father watched the pair, his grey eyes soft. Nathan wanted the warmth of the child's arms and the clammy touch of skin and sound of breath easily as much as his daughter did. Nathan gazed at his children and turned his head slowly from side to side *My God how real they are. Now time is going slowly my eyes begin to open. I've been unseeing. Well, blind really. Busyness is such a curse. I've been buried in my work, I've never had time to really look at them, hardly even noticed the wealth that's in these two.* He stared at them with a puzzled squint, his mouth slightly open.

Nathan had not meant to buy into the message much of the modern work place sends via media and business success mantras that one needs to work smarter and climb the ladder to higher positions and greater security. That message, though, had embedded itself in his thought patterns. The sudden shock to his planned and prepared path forced him to stop in those tracks and wrenched his thoughts in another direction.

He looked upwards and tugged on his ear.

These kids are not a distraction from my work. They are the reason for my work. A sentence he'd read had popped into his mind. Having time to read anything at all was another novelty.

Nathan had a dawning sense of a different type of prosperity when he watched the two youngsters. He followed them into the lounge where Felix found space to caper and prance about. Nathan grasped their hands. *I've been an utter idiot,* he thought, swinging them in a circle, *missing all this simple joy, planning and saving to be financially secure and safe, when I have, or rather had, true riches here at home.* A shudder caught his breath and tightened his arms to his sides. *That was a fat lot of use planning to be safe.*

Three weeks before, in late September, Meadow had collected her little brother from kindergarten on her way home from school, as she always did. His eyes lit up when she came in the door. He trotted over to her. As his sister bent down to pick up his lunchbox, collect his water bottle and tiny backpack, he put his arm around her neck and hugged her.

They walked home hand in hand. The door was unlocked. They went in and called to Mamma. 'Mum's not around but we can find her. Let's call her loudly. Mamma!' Felix liked the game.

They called 'Mamma, Mamma' everywhere, under the table, in the cupboards, in the fridge, the washing machine and even down the toilet. They rolled together on the lounge carpet, laughing and giggling. Meadow held Felix by the foot, little-piggied it then just lay there quiet for ages.

But it grew darker and later and it didn't seem very funny anymore.

'Me hungwee,' the boy whimpered.

'I'll ring Papa now. Don't worry.'

'We can't find Mum. The door was unlocked but there's no clue where she is. I've tried Gran's and Nan's.'

Nathan left work early and drove straight home. They retried Sarah's mobile, it was on answerphone, searched the house again, the garden, phoned her friends, their gran again and then the police. It was evening by now, and very dark. The search would become difficult.

The police car drove past. It turned and parked outside the gate, the yellow lights glowing in the blackness. Two officers knocked at the door. Meadow flinched. Nathan, holding Felix, let the pair in. The family stood mute as the police checked the house.

The constable said there was no sign of a disturbance. They found no messages. There was nothing unusual on the laptop and no response from the phone again.

Nothing seemed to be missing.

'Yes, Dad, her bag.' Nathan couldn't describe it; he didn't even know what colour it was.

'It's tan,' Meadow told the policewoman. Then she remembered a small detail that could be helpful. 'Mum has a brown birthmark on the back of her neck. You can see it if she wears her hair up. It might help you find her.' The police lady smiled and gave Meadow's hand a little pat.

'Thank you, I'll make a note of that.'

The woman sat down next to the child, holding his hand.

'You can ring me on this number anytime.' She handed Nathan a card. He pocketed it without a glance. As he lifted his hand from his coat, he looked at his watch again. 'Oh my God, it's so late.'

Father and daughter, already stressed and anxious, now became frantic. They rushed about and searched in stupid places under cushions and bedclothes, pulled out drawers, checked everything for the umpteenth time for clues or messages. Nathan was white-faced and shaky, his heart hardly beating, hoping he wouldn't find a terrifying note.

He had thought of kidnappers, suicide, a dreadful accident, swinging wildly between all three. Vivid pictures of a strangled Sarah, Sarah caged, or her body lying by the roadside, her hair matted with blood, rolled on her side like a run-over cat, loomed in his mind like black shadows. He closed his eyes fast shut, shook his head, then opened them quickly and moved his eyes around, hunting for something wholesome to look at to replace the morbid images. He forced himself to stare at the ceiling. It had a centre-piece made of plaster, shaped like acanthus leaves. That worked for thirty seconds. *No. Action is better.* They called every clinic and the hospital, but no one of her name or description: tall, thin, brown hair with red tints, large brown eyes, had been admitted.

Nathan stared at the police officer sitting there, in his house.

'What was she wearing, sir?' Nathan had no idea. The pair had no recollection. The policewoman asked the little child.

'Mamma home soon,' he said.

'You must be very hungry.'

The boy nodded.

'I'll get some food brought in soon.'

Nathan and Meadow continued the search. Looking through Sarah's wardrobe, they could find nothing missing; they had never really looked in there closely before. Well, Meadow had a few times, looking for something pretty for her mother to wear, but hadn't noticed any of the nondescript articles.

There were clothes they had never seen until that moment. A few items they recognized like the midi, navy blue dress Mum had worn to a friend's wedding.

'Her long black coat's not here.' Meadow looked up at her dad. Nathan saw for the first time what little knowledge he had of his wife's current daily life. The missing woman could have been anyone. He could give no clear details that would distinguish her uniqueness. He looked blank and felt confused when trying to describe her. He showed them the photos on the laptop but he had such a meagre amount of information to tell them about her daily life and plans, yet she was a living person – Sarah, his wife.

My God, have I been so remiss to the reality of the life alive right beside me? It wasn't like this a few years ago. But I've been taking care of my family financially. I can't do everything.

That first night Felix moved around slowly, whining and pulling on his father and sister's clothes hoping to be picked up. He cried on Daddy's shoulder and stared open-mouthed at his sister's rolling tears.

'Mamma, want Mamma, MumMumMumma,' he snivelled, tears dripping down to mix with saliva. He watched the strange men in blue uniforms, carrying torches, walking around his home and garden, shining their lights into stairwells and dark corners. His gaze followed them out to the shed where they turned everything over. *Looking for Mamma?* He rubbed his tired eyes with both pudgy hands.

Meadow, shaking, pushed her little brother nearer Papa when the child came towards her. She wrapped her arms tightly around her upper body as if to hold herself together, her heavy heart, like a piece of stone, pulled her thoughts down into darkness.

Felix watched the police go out of the gate, across to the neighbours and then to other houses in his road, his eyes wide, and breathing through his mouth. He fidgeted about and searched for his favourite toy. He found the big rubber brontosaurus, grabbed it, tucked it under his arm and ran calling 'Papa, Papa' until he found him again. Nathan gripped Felix and lifted him up,

'You look forlorn little man. It'll be OK, we'll find her.'

A missing persons was released by the police and Sarah's photo circulated to airports, city police departments, ferry terminals, bus and train stations. No one reported a sighting.

Nathan lay in bed, frightened, sleepless those first few nights, unable to get those vivid images of accidents, suicide, and even of murder out of his mind. The horror pictures appeared in front of his eyes whenever they drooped to close. 'Get out!' he whispered.

The police team visited the family again and offered counselling and support. Nathan declined it. He stood up tall and straight.

'We'll be fine thanks. We've got each other.'

He knew he needed help but mistrusted the police counselling. He had never been able to open up about his fears to anyone – that was part of the problem that he'd had with Sarah. *I feel like a closed up house where I've barred every door and window. I know I've always believed that everything is fine, that's what I just said to the police. What is it that keeps me so isolated and stoic?*

Drifts of foggy thought ran through his mind, *If I opened up one small chink of myself, would that be enough? It would hurt too much right now, I can't do it.*

Nathan checked with the bank after the official missing persons was filed. Sarah had withdrawn two thousand pounds from her account on the day she went missing. She had had to do that in person, her picture was recorded on the CCTV.

He found the card the WPC had given him and gave her the information. They had already checked with the bank of course.

'It looks like this was planned sir,' the police said.

'But she could have been blackmailed or threatened, couldn't she?' He tossed his head.

Nathan refused to believe that Sarah had just walked out of their lives.

CHAPTER 2
1921 – Birth

Albert sat on the top step of the steep flight of wooden stairs, his head in his shaky brown hands. A few tears spotted his broad face. He unwillingly listened to his wife's screams and groans. His body and hands were hot with emotion. It had been many long hours. Rose had had rheumatic fever when she was a child; it had weakened her heart. This was their first child. Could Rose's body endure this huge effort?

Bert got up and paced the upstairs hallway, his long legs striding back and forth. Through the bedroom door he heard Dr Bisson talk reassuringly to Rose, repeatedly encouraging her. There was a massive struggle to birth the baby. Finally, the doctor was saying, 'Push! That's it. Good. Good. Push again! The baby is nearly born, one more big push.'

'Amelia, pass me the forceps, hurry.'

The nurse held chloroform on a cotton pad over Rose's nose to help her over the last hurdle.

Cheers and sighs came through the door, then instructions to the midwife. The baby yelled.

'That's the loudest wail I've heard this year.' Dr Bisson's voice again, and a chuckle. Silence – and so a few more anxious moments. Bert wrung his hands and waited for the door to open. It was 1921, fathers didn't watch their babies being born – that was too intimate, too personal, too private, too real.

'You have a fine healthy daughter, Mr Beauvoir, with excellent lungs.' The doctor smiled. 'You can come in now.'

Albert tiptoed into their bedroom. Rose looked flushed and weak. Wrapped in a white blanket by her side lay a lusty baby girl with plenty of dark hair. Her washed face looked a bit like Bert's. *A perfect baby.* Bert cried a few tears of happiness, kissed Rose and already loved the little creation he stared at. 'Thank you so very much, Doctor.'

He shook his head, 'Ah, but your wife did all the work.'

The bedroom was in St James Place, a terrace of three white stucco houses that had a curved Regency gable and frilly railings flanking the front steps. The middle house stood tall like a loving parent with her arms around each child. The hill they were built on sloped away from St Peter Port on the Sunshine Island. The island lay very close to France. The water was bluer in the bay than in the sea around the coast of southern England. The tide moved rhythmically in and out oblivious to the new life that had arrived on the planet.

When the baby was six months old she was christened Alice Rose and draped in the traditional, white, long, hand-knitted shawl. The vicar sprinkled water on her forehead and made the sign of the cross. The baby winced, Rose tensed, but they continued the prayer for Alice. She was passed around, held and kissed.

'What a beautiful child.'

'She looks a lot like you, Bert, she has your broad forehead and tawny skin.'

Rose carried baby Alice in her arms on the short drive home. The baby then had to fit in with her mother's still Victorian, class-conscious home life. Routine was followed to a T. The maid began work at 7am – she lit the fire then made the beds, served breakfast at 8.30 on the dot. Rose, and the nanny pushing the pram, took their daily walk every evening before tea. Washing day was Monday, fish eaten on Friday.

'What do you think she'll become, Bert? What would you like for her future?'

'Well I hope she'll be brave and loving and adventurous. I don't really care about what sort of work she does.'

'Oh really?' Rose frowned and turned her head. 'I hope she'll be intelligent, elegant, well-mannered and take up a vocation suitable for a young lady. I will do everything in my power to make sure she makes us proud. We have a name to uphold on this island.'

The rocking horse stood in the nursery, the small chairs and table, the porcelain dolls, the tea set, the teddies and sometimes the living maid. It was now 1926. Alice was nearly five years old. She remained the only child for two more years.

She loved one teddy bear especially. He had one ear torn at the top and mismatched eyes. Alice's sympathy reached out to him, the saddest of the toys. She stroked, clothed, cuddled and talked to him.

'Teddy, you'll be all right, just let Alice look after you. Are you hungry?' The much-cosseted, almost hairless bear slept beside her at night, his head on her pillow.

In the morning after breakfast Rose brushed her daughter's unruly hair and clipped it to the side with a big floppy bow.

'Can I go and play with Roselle?'

'Yes, all right, I'll send Renee to fetch you for lunch. Be polite to her grandparents.'

Alice, dressed in a clean blue pinafore walked to the neighbours' house, lifted the gate-latch, marched confidently up the front path and then knocked on Roselle's front door. It opened slowly and Roselle peeped out. Her grandmother stood behind her, her white hair pulled severely into a bun and her drab dress reaching the floor. She didn't smile.

'Please may I play with Roselle?'

'Yes, Alice, but you must both stay outside in the garden.'

Roselle's grandparents brought her up because her parents couldn't for some mysterious reason. No neighbour knew why.

The old couple were strict and merciless, their hard faces hardly ever smiling. When the little girl was given gifts, her grandmother took them from her and hid them.

'You can have this when you're older.' Of course she wouldn't want them then, they were toys for young girls. Alice feared and hated the ugly old woman and hugged her friend when she came running to tell Alice about the latest confiscation.

The garden, like many on the island, had gooseberry bushes and fruit trees growing in the long narrow strip. The two girls watched the old grandpa. He stalked around his plot tying labels onto all the fruiting bushes and trees.

He had written numbers on each label. The grandfather came toward the little girl and thrust his face close to Roselle. His small, cold eyes glinted, 'If you take any fruit I will know because I've counted each of them. And I will give you a beating if I find any gone.'

Roselle, terrified, clutched Alice's arm.

'You are like Gretel and your grandparents are the wicked witches, aren't they?' Roselle was timid and dared not agree. But she let Alice hold her hand. They sat together on the garden seat with their arms around each other. Alice's sympathy overflowed into tears for her ill-treated little friend. Alice was upset by anything sad or unfair and the memory didn't leave her.

Opposite Roselle's house lived three children, Alice's closest friends – John, Martin and Mary-Kate. The following day, Alice looked up at the window facing the street and stared at her three friends. They stared back, their faces expressionless and haunting, their three heads shaved. The children had ringworm and were forbidden to go out to play. That image also embedded in Alice's brain and gave her nightmares.

Every evening, the lamplighter came. Alice, in the darkening night, stood by the floor-length front window and waited for him. The man moved from lamp to lamp climbing a ladder with a taper in one hand. She waited quietly for her lamp, outside their house, to light up, incandescent, like a glow-worm. Then it was safe to go upstairs to bed.

CHAPTER 3

It was now early October, and a whole nightmarish week had passed with no news.

'No news is good news,' Nathan said. It sounded hollow, unconvincing – even to him.

It was a bleak and blustery evening, but Felix was now fast asleep. Meadow was in her parents' room upstairs. She often amused herself with her mother's jewellery. She looked through the boxes and tried different pieces on, looking at herself in the mirror. She looked for her two favourite pieces: her mamma's dangly crystal earrings and great-great Grandma's Victorian ruby ring. She gave a more careful search, but they were definitely not in the silver box.

'Dad, they are missing!' she yelled down the stairwell. 'The ring is gone. The earrings too! Mum never left those pieces at home when she went out, in case they were stolen. She must have them with her.' *Perhaps she is alive somewhere.* Hope, the hope of having her one and only sweet Mamma back, loving her the same as before, life restored to the happiness, security and routine that they had all taken for granted, that hope, rose in her. She closed her eyes, and folded her hands under her chin. *Oh please.*

But that will never happen if she has run away from us. Uncontrollable rage rose in Meadow's chest. She closed the door to her parents' bedroom, locked it and then attacked the pillows with her fists and tried to tear them with her nails. She tore her mother's clothes down from the rack, then kicked Sarah's shoes and threw her bags at the wall with such violence, that Nathan downstairs could hear the crashes, then she tipped all her mother's make-up in the rubbish bin.

'I hate you, you horrible selfish cow. How could you leave us, how could you leave me? I thought you loved me.' It was more heartbreaking that she would abandon them than if she were dead. She believed the thought that flooded her head that her mother hadn't loved her, immediately misery filled her entire being. She wasn't one to succumb to negativity but rather a young person who fought back – the rejection turned quickly to indignation then fury. The bitterness and pain turned to sobbing that lasted hours. The girl gasped for air and rocked back and forth as she wept. 'I'll never forgive you – ever.'

Nathan turned the handle to get in the bedroom to see if he could help her, but the door was locked and bolted.

'Leave me alone,' she managed to express through the sobbing. 'I'll be OK Daddy.'

He stayed outside the door for a few minutes but thought that was unfair as it was private business she was dealing with. *If she doesn't come out soon, I will get the policewoman back.* After another thirty minutes he went back upstairs and told her he was going to ring.

'No Dad! I'll be all right. Please.'

He returned to the lounge but it felt icy cold downstairs. Nathan shivered. *I need my dressing gown.* He walked to the bottom of the stairs and looked up. Meadow appeared there at the top of them, like a cloth puppet, limp, exhausted and pale. Nathan rushed up and hugged her tightly. She felt unlike his bouncy daughter, only the rhythmic heaving of her chest and her damp face reassured him she was still living.

'I came to get my dressing gown.'

He took her hand. They both went back into the bedroom. He glanced at the wreckage in the room and at her swollen eyes, then took his garment from the hook and wrapped the large grey chenille kimono around them both. They each put one arm in a sleeve and stood together, now laughing a little. Meadow smiled up at him. They moved around as one body tied by the gown belt. They laughed a bit too loudly and shushed each other. It was turning into a funny end to the sad hours.

'I'll just go and get into my jamas, Daddy.'

The young girl softly padded over to the rubbish bin, took a lipstick out, hid it in her closed fist, ducked back into her room, tucked it under her pillow, then returned.

'Can it be my turn to sleep in your bed tonight, Papa?'

'Of course.' Their sleep was warm and comforting, interrupted only by the triple inbreathing of Meadow's dying sobs.

Early next morning Nathan's mobile rang. He reached out and snatched it from the bedside table. The police had traced Sarah's cell phone to the airport. It was found discarded in a big pile of rubbish in a skip ready to be towed away. There were no messages on it, except to the taxi company. The police did their forensic work with it but it yielded only ordinary calls made during the week to family members and enquires to the doctor and the school. No clues. Nothing extraordinary. *So she has left us.*

'Oh my God.' It sank into Nathan's heart with a thud of grief. Guilt ran through his mind, then his body, unexpected, like a shower of ice. He shuddered and sat down to steady himself.

It's my fault. It is my fault. I never gave her enough support. If I hadn't ignored her need or I'd taken more seriously the signs I noticed she would be here today. That exact scene had been played out in many broken families. He knew that too well.

At work and in the many phone calls he received from friends and family, each one said, 'We are so sorry. We're sure they'll find her soon.'

Sarah's mother rang Nathan – she was apologetic.

'Oh you poor thing working so hard and being so good to her. How could she be so cold-hearted and cruel to leave you with the two little children? Felix must be terribly upset.'

'We don't know if she has left us, Anne. We're OK. We think something must have happened to Sarah. She's not cruel or hard-hearted, you know that.'

'Well I just wanted you to know I'm thinking of you all. I'm so sorry.'

'And you too. You must be just as upset as we are.'

Poor Sarah – all alone perhaps – maybe held captive or even dead. Now everyone, even her own mother thinks she's rotten – well, Felix doesn't. You'd think Anne would be more understanding considering her own life. Doesn't work that way, each of us in the dark to our own failings. We push them down if we see glimpses of them. We mow them down like daisies in the lawn – pretend we got rid of them.

Meadow drew out of him every thought and fear, asking incessant questions, and openly declaring her inner conflicts.

'Dad, why would she leave us? What was so wrong with us that she would do that? I feel guilty, but I don't know what about. I can almost not bear to think about Mamma. It makes me so sad. What are you thinking, Dad? Please tell me. What do you think has happened? She wouldn't kill herself would she?' Tears started to stream down her young freckled face. She wiped them away with her sleeve.

'Dad let's just think about the possibilities? Do you think we could get a private detective to try to find her? Surely she wouldn't really leave us. Would she?'

Nathan put his arm around the slender body as they sat hunched together on the sofa. He really would have liked to cry with her, but there was a blockage some place inside him that stopped the tears from forming. With sudden clarity, he remembered thoughts he'd had and a decision he'd made long ago when confronted by an overpowering emotional scene – his mother weeping and begging. He would never lose control – he'd decided then to always be strong and unemotional, so he couldn't let go now when he wanted to.

'I'm frightened to talk about it, Pet, because we just don't know the facts. The police won't track a person who has left of their own free will. And it does look like that at the moment.'

When the children were in bed, Nathan turned on the radio to block out his grief. The silence was like an echo chamber filled with sounds and memories. The more he thought of the pain, the more he thought of Sarah, and the larger the ache. The broadcasts didn't help – the music was morbid on every station.

Nathan let the child get into bed with him for the second time when he called out 'Mamma' in his sleep and woke up crying. 'I cried cos I wuv Mamma and I didn't want to go sleep wivout her.'

They snuggled for a while until Felix's continual twitching and the kicking of his short, warm legs became so annoying that his dad put him back in his own bed. He pushed the fair hair away from his face, and then kissed him on his high, rounded forehead and looked into his sea-green eyes.

'Mamma home soon,' the child whispered to Nathan.

Oh God, I hate feeling helpless like this. How long will I be able to keep going?

CHAPTER 4
News – October

Nathan's phone rang. He sprinted to the desk where it lay under a pile of papers. He scattered them about, grabbed the phone, his heart beating fast. *It might be Sarah.* But it was the police again.

'We've traced your wife's passport movements and flights. They stop in Madrid. We have no more information other than that sir, except that the tickets were bought three weeks ago from the Travel Agency.'

'Thank you very much.'

'Will the police help us to find her, Dad?'

'They will try.' But he knew they wouldn't waste police time searching for a wayward wife. They would hear from them if she had an accident or was found dead.

Nathan didn't tell Felix what the police had said; he wouldn't understand.

'Daddy, I know Spain is famous for bullfights, guitars, and certain food? But what else?'

'Er, well, sunshine and warm weather, Flamenco dancing and it's had an interesting history of wars. You've probably learnt about some of them at school.'

'But what could Mummy be doing there? Why Spain?'

It seemed very far away, an unknown country. *How could we ever hope to find her?* Meadow was hatching a plan in her mind of she and Dad becoming private detectives.

'Couldn't we go to Madrid and look for her ourselves?'

'I think that's impossible, Med, let's leave it to the professionals. We wouldn't know where to start.'

But who will look for her really if we don't?

She may have gone off with someone, though there is no evidence of that at all. Perhaps she has a Spanish lover. These worries flashed through Nathan's mind before he fell asleep that night.

Felix woke early and tiptoed to his parent's room, still no Mamma. He ran to Meadow's and jumped on her sleeping form.

'You little rat. I'm still asleep.'

'I hungwee.'

'OK, wait a minute.' *Why must I be responsible for everything now?*

'I want to go out.'

'Well you have to have your milk and cereal first.'

She helped him put on his little green gumboots and a hat and jacket and wrapped herself up warm too. They went out before Papa was even awake.

'I'll have to leave a note or Dad will think we've run away. Wait here.' She darted in, scrawled a note.

Dad, it's OK. We're in the garden or gone for a walk.

She left the note on the table and raced back outside. Felix was gone.

'No!'

Meadow tore down the street then around the block, all around the garden and back into the house. She did another quick look around the house calling 'Felix' over and over. Nathan came running up to her in his pyjamas.

'Whatever is the matter now?'

'Felix has gone too.' She was out of breath and barely able to speak from panting. Nathan pulled on a jumper and stepped into his slippers, held Meadow's hand and joined in the call, 'Felix. Felix. It's Daddy, come out, come here.'

'Might he have been kidnapped too? What do you think Dad? What shall we do? I can't stand anymore of this. Will we have to call the police again?' She was hysterical – couldn't stop rubbing her hands and shivering. 'They will think we are criminals; first Mum and now the child. They will think we…'

'We'll have one more look for him.'

They left the house again, Meadow gripping her father's hand. They turned, pulled each other, confused, not knowing whether to go right or left. A lady drove up to their gate in a tiny white car. She had a small boy sitting next to her. He waved to them.

'Oh, thank God. It's him, Dad.' Meadow wept – half laughing with relief this time. A speck of sparkle, one tear, a diamond, rested on her bottom lashes. Her chin trembled, her teeth chattered, her white skin ghostly as pallid as eggshell. Nathan's heart tore again as he noticed her delicate state.

The lady opened the car door.

'Hi, I'm Judy from the library. I tried ringing the house but I guessed you'd be out looking for the child.' She hopped out. 'I have a little lost one here.' She looked at the boy. 'I know Sarah and Felix very well. They often come down to the library together. I guess he must be looking for her.'

Meadow, emotionally raw, yelled at her little brother, 'What were you doing, Felix? Why did you go down the road? I told you to wait.' She boxed the air with her fists.

'Sowwy,' he said. 'Gone to Mamma.'

Then his sister felt overwhelming pity for him – reached down picked him up and pulled him tightly against her chest.

'You're so heavy. How does Mum carry you around sometimes?' *I haven't got ladies' hips, she'd better be home soon.*

Nathan thanked Judy, gave her a warm handshake and went inside.

'Promise never to do that again,' he said to Felix, squatting down to look him in the eyes, 'Meadow was very, very sad.'

CHAPTER 5
Alice

On her fifth birthday, Alice got her first bike – a fairy cycle. She learnt to ride it easily. She had excellent co-ordination and a reckless attitude towards danger. Saturday was fine weather. She hopped on it confidently. She rode faster and faster around the edge of the lawn, wobbling and turning, her pink face wild with delight. She saw the gooseberry bushes rushing towards her as the bike tilted sideways and fell. The gooseberry bushes bordered the lawn and of course she fell into one. Alice lay there, unmoving, screaming and calling for help – already a habit of hers. Thorns stuck out of every limb.

'Ha!' said her grandfather as he helped her up – still screaming, 'You look like a gooseberry yourself.' No one could touch her to remove the little spines except him.

On the lawn was a fragrant lilac tree. Alice breathed in the gorgeous heady perfume as she played underneath it with her teddies and dolls. Her favourite toy was not the dolls or teddies now, but a big golden bear on wheels, which she rode on and preferred it to her fairy cycle. After all, it had a face you could love and a personality if you used your imagination.

At the end of the garden, in spring, was a bank of primroses and then later on, bluebells. In the old Victorian stories her mother told her there were always fairies at the bottom of the garden. Alice searched for them every fine day. She turned up each flower head and moved every stalk to try to find the tiny folk. Whenever she returned to the house she found a bluebird toffee on the back door step. She knew the fairies had put it there for her.

Every Friday, Alice's grandfather hired a horse, cab and uniformed driver with whip, from Perchards Livery Stables. Grandfather had been a coachbuilder by trade so he hired one of his own coach designs. It was difficult to climb into it and the seat was hard. It had two large spoked back wheels and two smaller ones in front. There was a curved over-hang to protect from the rain and everything was painted black.

Grandpa had snow-white hair, a long snow-white beard and piercing, bright blue eyes. Alice rode on his knee for what felt like hours, while he told her stories or sang to her. The horse walked its way through the rural lanes, the steady clip-clop making a soothing backdrop to the stories and songs. As Alice sat, her shiny light brown hair cut in a bob bounced as the carriage moved along. Her eyes danced with happiness. Grandpa loved Alice in a way her mother never demonstrated or had time to do.

When Alice was almost six, her darling grandpa died in the bedroom next to hers. There was the sound of running feet, the door knocking, the doctor going into Grandpa's room. Alice rushed into the hallway.

'What's happened?'

'Shush, go back to your room and wait.' Alice couldn't understand why. Why would no one talk to her?

It was a day of dreadful sorrow. The sounds of weeping heard from every room. The maid's crying, Albert's sighs and then Rose's wail of grief loaded Alice with frightful thoughts. She shivered alone in her room and mopped up her tears with a white hankie, while she held the sad bear close to her heart.

Grandpa had lived with the little family even before baby Alice was born. Rose was devoted to him. She always called him the formal title of 'Father'.

When Rose wandered through Candie cemetery in her black crepe dress, she stared at the large marble angels and the beautifully carved books and roses that marked the graves. Alongside her father's plot were headstones belonging to the rest of her family too. Rose traced her fingers over the words. *In loving memory of Frederick who died aged 10 months, February, 1877, Stella Maude dearly beloved child, June, 1877, aged 5 years, Minnie loved daughter who fell asleep in Jesus aged 10 years, 1888, Annette, aged 38 years.* There was grandpa's wife Jessie too, loving mother of the above, September 1915. *And my mother too, of course. I am the only one still living. I'm completely alone. The only one left of my entire family.*

Later when she stopped wearing her mourning clothes, her smile returned, but there was no wild happy laughter. Her father had been part of her; they had lived so long together. He was gentle and loving to her, unlike many parents of that time. She felt half of her was dead – Like a stroke victim.

Rose's mother, Jessie, had been against her marriage to Albert.

'He is not of the same social standing that we are. He is a businessman not a proper gentleman,' she had said. Rose and Albert had not dared to disagree. Within six weeks of Jessie's death, Albert and Rose were married in Devon, in 1915, during World War One – four days prior to Bert's departure for Egypt.

Rose had returned to the island and lived with her father in the rented house in St Jacques, the house where Alice was born.

Alice's Diary
Looking back, I can say I loved that house, every inch of it. It had enormous rooms but no modern facilities, no electric lights. We had to walk down the steep stairs with a candle; it gave me the creeps. The lavatory was at the bottom of the stairway. I hung

on till the last minute to go. There was no flush. The maid initially, then Dad, when he returned from the war, would roar into that awful room with a bucket of water. There wasn't a bathroom either, just a galvanised tub in the kitchen. Dad had to empty it, of course. No running water, it all came from the pump at the bottom of the garden.

At the front of the house were twelve, shining white, entrance-steps scrubbed to a polar brightness. There was a hole in the top one where the coalman dropped sack after sack of the black fuel.

Inside the house I was just as entranced. I thought the sitting room was as beautiful as a queen's home. We had green floral carpet and black chintz curtains with pink roses on the print. Of course there was a piano and a green, buttoned stool on which mother sat to play 'Roses of Picardy' and other songs taken from a music cabinet like those that stood in all other good Edwardian parlours. Grandpa had painted a flower bouquet in oils on the door of the cupboard. I stared transfixed at the room every time I entered. I felt so wealthy and contented. Even more so glancing at the hearth with its brass rests and long brass tongs glinting their mirror surfaces. From the attic of the house we had a small glimpse of the sea at Grandes Rocques. This attic was where I used to look at the stars through Grandpa's telescope.

In 1929, Alice's brother Oswald was born. He was a huge baby. Rose almost died giving birth to him.

Alice had watched her dad sitting on that top stair praying and crying. Alice was puzzled. 'What's wrong Daddy?' she asked him. He couldn't reply. He was choking with fears but he reached out and drew her near. She sat by him for a few moments till the nanny dragged her away.

'What's happening?' She looked up into Nanny's face but no one told her anything. 'They don't want me – they leave me out. I should know what's going on. I ought to be told. I am seven years old now.'

'Shush,' Nanny said.

Rose recovered slowly. Nanny was needed to fill the place of mother. 'Mother, why can't you come into the garden and watch me play? Why don't you come to my room and read me stories?'

Nanny took the new baby for walks in his white cane pram. Alice always went too on the weekends. They often walked to Candie Gardens laid out in Victorian bedding flowers. Alice ran around the flower clock madly yelling 1, 2, 3 to 12. She wasn't trusted to push the pram or look after her new brother.

'She is too flighty and capricious.'

'Can I hold him?'

'No, not yet.'

Why not? Alice wondered.

Is a boy more valuable than a girl?

She may have had natural sibling rivalry – but the fuss made of him grated on her much-criticised and self-obsessed soul. Already, aged seven, she felt nothing she did was quite clever, smart or good enough to please a mother who was desperate to keep up with the outward success of her neighbours and friends. Her dad, she knew, would always warm to her, hug and kiss her and encourage her with words.

'You are lovely, little daughter – you will do great things when you grow up.'

'What things, Daddy?'

'Brave things, adventurous things.'

Alice smiled and looked up dreamily. She had no idea what sort of adventures, but was contented with the answer.

The brother and sister were happy together in the sunny anxiety-free periods of childhood. Oswald was so much younger than Alice so through all those days of childhood, she had someone to care for, protect, and lavish attention on. She became close to her little blonde brother in spite of his being the favourite.

But Alice watched carefully, counting out the sweets or birthday presents Oswald was given.

'He has four and I only have two, but I am the oldest.

Mother, I wish you loved me as much as Oswald. That's really all I want. It's not fair.'

'Nonsense, of course we love you as much.'

But it doesn't feel like it.

CHAPTER 6

It was already late October. In the mornings, the child ran to greet his friends at pre-school like he always had. Hugged some, made faces at others. He laughed and played as usual but now, sometimes, he hid in corners until the carer coaxed him out. In only a moment he was over his loneliness and out again riding a tricycle round and round, bumping into tyres and playground obstacles, shouting and making car noises.

When Meadow went to fetch him, she watched in wonder. *He has forgotten about Mamma. He enjoys every minute without a thought of the past or a dread of the future. Oh, I long to be like that. I wish I could just forget our worries for a time. Actually, I'm going to try because I'm so sick of sadness. I can't bear it anymore. I think it's all his physical activity that helps him to forget.*

When they returned home and their father had come in too, she decided to put the physical actions idea into practice.

'Felix, get your toy box and we'll make a city out of Lego.'

'I weally love Mummy 'cause she gave me the pirate set and the wobber's jail set.' He scampered off sparkly-eyed and grinning madly. They tipped out the blocks and other odd toys onto the lounge carpet. The fire was ablaze and crackling. It already made Meadow feel better. She breathed in deeply and then breathed out with a great sigh as she sat down on the carpet with her little brother.

Two minutes later, the lounge was flooded with the smell of Sarah. Meadow startled, looked around the room to see if perhaps Mamma had walked in. The perfume bottle she had given the child to play with was unstopped and had leaked a few drops into the toys. That was all. But the aroma brought a sense of security. It conjured warm images of life before the disappearance.

The siblings created a miniature town with a school, jail and a harbour. Meadow made minuscule books from paper that she illustrated. Felix placed them on minute block desks in the schoolhouse then he put the pirate ships by the edge of the sea wall. Their dad took photos so they could preserve the tiny town. The child would demolish it all before he went to bed.

With no one else to run the house, Nathan had had to leave work at 5 pm every day. This was very different from his normal diligent routine, staying late to tidy up loose ends. He felt guilty and apologised profusely to the senior manager.

'Take as long as you need to, Nat, we can't afford to lose such a valuable and reliable staff member as you.'

Nathan closed his eyes and sighed with the reassurance.

But life was no longer easy for father or daughter. They had to fill the positions of carer, cook, cleaner and companion.

'Dad, could we get someone in to do some of the housework?'

'Can't afford that, Sweetie; costs a lot to hire cleaners.'

Meadow became overloaded with new tasks and complained bitterly to her friends at school.

'I'm finding it hard to keep up with my own interests and things and my homework is always rushed. I have to look after my little brat brother and do half the housework now my mum's disappeared. I'm fed up with it all. You don't know how lucky you are.'

Not much of what she said was true. She adored Felix and she also knew many of her friends only had one parent.

'And on top of that we're eating too much fish and chips and too many ready meals from the supermarket. They're revolting and it's so unhealthy. I can't cook dinner and look after Felix. Besides, he needs to eat his dinner early.'

With a jolt, Meadow remembered just before Mamma disappeared she'd given up cooking interesting food. It had been plain, tasteless mashed potatoes, peas, sausages – not even any fried onions or gravy – the same thing several days in a row. Meadow had turned down her mouth. 'Not the same thing again.' *Mum looked at me blankly with sort of staring eyes. She must have been ill, trapped in her own world. I guess we all live in our own worlds a bit. I never thought about how she felt. I thought it was just a few bad days. We have some good times, some bad times, like a chessboard. Good – white, black – bad, but what if more and more black squares appeared and the whites began to fade? All blackness. That could have happened to her. Oh poor Mamma.*

She thought about this for a few minutes, gazing upwards, her head turned, her hand holding her chin as she recalled the time. Then a sudden frown and a look of determination appeared on her face.

That's selfish though – unless the black comes from outside of you. She needed help to let the light back in. But if she'd thought about me, I could have helped. She's so mean, not trusting, not reaching out for me – her little girl – for nine years before Felix was born, her special darling – then – the beautiful baby boy. Meadow had gawped at her newborn brother when he was brought home from the hospital. She had held his hand, the fingers were wrinkled and perfect replicas, like an old man's, the fingernails like the minutest transparent shells. She had felt a bit sick *with reality.*

'Life can be way too real.'

But Daddy's always loved me the same as if I were the only one. I'm still his special girl. Oh I just love the way he brushes my hair for me before I go to bed – like Mamma did before she left.

Shutting her eyes, she could feel the gentle tugging.

CHAPTER 7
The last day of October

During late autumn, the child delighted in every flickering and falling leaf and in crunching them under his feet. His sister mimicked his leaf stamping and then sat among the piles of brown and yellow watching him. Though she was nine years older, she began to see the world through the child's eyes and it charmed her. Animals became strange and wonderfully exotic creatures even when they were only the neighbours' cats. And the song of a common thrush became magical music from celestial lands. They had to stop perfectly still and listen. Whoever moved and disturbed the enchantment was given a friendly punch.

Felix loved the patterns of sun through the trees moving on the walls of the house. He tried to grab the shadows, but they always eluded him. The sun shone behind Felix's head, the fair hair formed a halo of light. *Now that is too stupid,* thought Meadow, *but maybe we all looked like that when we were very small.* Milly the cat trotted beside him, even she with the sun behind her looked angelic. *Whoa, stop right there.*

Inside, the child would lay stretched out like the cat, in front of the blazing fire. He fingered through his books, saying some parts of the stories, in his sweet way, to himself.

These moments of joy seeped their way into the outlook and attitudes of both Papa and Meadow. The evenings before Felix went to bed turned into times of simple enjoyment when the three drew or read or listened to music.

'This is much like families from a century ago might have spent their evenings.'

'But we have electricity, and a thousand other inventions, Dad.'

As Felix was undressing to get into his pyjamas, Nathan picked him up and threw him down onto his bed. He blew raspberries on his doughy tummy – well he was way too big for this now, but Nat felt so light and free at that moment he wanted to make silly noises. Felix giggled wildly, the boy's eyes creased into little almond twinkles. The happiness in those eyes met his father's gaze – pupil to pupil. The whole person of Felix was contained in those happy, shiny dots. Nathan was overcome. 'Oh my son, my boy, Daddy loves you.'

Having to be mother too to the child, father and daughter became deeply involved in every little bit of progress Felix made. When his counting got to ten correctly they clapped and cheered, when he collected weedy flowers and dandelions and brought them in for the table, they saw them as exquisite and when he wanted to wash the dishes on a tall stool beside Dad they laughed with the boy at the bubbles, the sloshing, the water that drenched his little shirt and ran down the cupboards. Nathan could feel himself changing – he didn't fight it. It felt good.

'Dad, you see how Felix is so simple, I don't mean thick you know, but he doesn't overthink and toss ideas around and around in his brain. He doesn't try to work out the answers or think what might happen in the future. His child's mind mercifully spares him all the anxieties that we bear. How could we take on the same way of thinking? How can we do what he does? Is it possible?' Meadow looked up into Nathan's eyes to see if he was listening properly. 'We can't just make our brains empty, I know. He doesn't sit passively, as we often say. He reads, draws, makes little inventions and uses his imagination in games, runs around and gets excited about stuff like going out, dinnertime and so on. Just real simple stuff. Can't we be more like that?'

'I know exactly what you mean but I don't know how we can, we know too much.'

'Can't we unlearn some of it and sort of become kids again?'

'That's been the human dream, Med, from ancient times until today.'

'Really, Dad?'

'Well, anyway, I think we are trying to be more like him, aren't we? Trying to live more interested in the here and now. To start with, one reason he's such a contented little thing is because Mamma was so strong on not having too much TV time and no electronic stuff while he is young.' He sighed deeply, remembering Sarah's resolve. 'Apparently it makes kids jumpy and also stops them doing the things that make them truly happy like building cities with blocks and playing outside making huts and imagining stories with characters and acting out parts.'

The girl fumed silently, biting her teeth together, her eyelids down, a small frown on her forehead.

'We have her to thank. She was a good mother to you two.'

Meadow spat out, 'Good mother? You must be joking. Then where on earth is she?'

There was an interminable silence.

Nathan couldn't think of any sensible answer so he sat, his face unmoving, his lips pressed together.

'And another thing, Dad, Felix is really quite grateful, when he gets a treat he says thank you and gives us a little hug.'

'Mamma taught him to do that though, Med.'

'He puts his trust in us and...'

'It's not all positive. He gets very naughty at times.'

'Hey Dad, if we are learning from him that means we can be naughty too! Oh I've been doing that a bit at school, I'm sorry to say.' She blushed and put her fingers over her mouth, breathed a big breath and continued, 'But mostly he expresses himself very freely when he's upset, you know his tantrums, kicking, stomping and yelling.' Meadow stomped up and down to express her point, '"No, I don't want to, I won't," when we ask him to eat more dinner, or try some new food and especially when we tell him to go to bed, eh.' They held hands and snorted with laughter, remembering some of the recent episodes. Yesterday the boy hadn't wanted any salad. Meadow had put one spinach leaf on his plate. Felix shook his head slowly – 'no tree!'

'He used to make me frustrated and angry, but now he just seems hilarious.'

Sarah had told Meadow to walk away when the child was in the middle of a tantrum.

But you see, I wasn't having any tantrums, but she actually did walk away from me. Every time she thought of this her eyes smarted and she had to run off to tidy up or ring a friend and find out what they were up to. Sometimes she didn't manage to get away quick enough and the abandonment felt like the betrayal of a best friend, more painful than grief. Nothing stopped the ache in the chest or the tears falling then.

If I only live one day at a time, I can exist.

Nathan woke at 4 am. This was a new unwelcome habit – too many thoughts. He couldn't control them. *I've lost control of my life. It isn't fair.* He'd planned each day and step so perfectly. *What have I done to deserve this? One action from someone else and my world is upside down.*

To an accountant, loss is the worst thing that can happen. It must be balanced. Life must be balanced; always steady growth, receivership the threat. To be taken into some other hands – the fear. He turned on the electric blanket. Warmth – even at a cost. Of course the heaters came on finely adjusted timers to save waste. But Sarah had had her way; a lovely warm patch on her side. He rolled over onto it and pulled up his knees to his chest, then clutched them with his arms, clasping his hands together. He closed his eyes – hopeless – he woke up ten minutes later. Looked at the clock: 5 am. *How can I do my job if I'm tired all day?*

CHAPTER 8

Alice had started dancing lessons. She loved them at first. She fussed over her pretty dancing clothes, holding them up to her body then laying them out on her bed and moving them around into different positions. She ran her hands down the fabric, feeling the satin and the rough tulle, then held them up in front of the window to show anyone who might be passing by.

Alice was already an outgoing people-person – a young drama princess. She loved being with her friends, couldn't bear to be apart from them when she had to go to her classes. When the dancing interfered with her friends' playtimes she cried piteously.

'I miss my friends. I want to play with them.' When she was dragged off to lessons she wailed. Each time it brought a flood of tears. The lessons were stopped.

It was different when Alice turned ten.

'Can I start my ballet classes again? I really, really promise to practise and listen to my teacher.' She now developed her own passion for dance, her mind burned with the desire to be like her ballet idols, Pavlova, Nijinsky and the very young Margot Fonteyn. The lessons began again.

'You have a natural ability Alice.' The teacher, Miss Cumber encouraged. 'You're a gifted dancer.'

It was a competitive hobby. There were parental fights, hot tempers, trophies to be won or lost and the fear of failure haunting Alice's mind. Jealousy between girls, and their mothers, fuelled catty words, which spoiled the beauty of the ballet. But she wouldn't stop now. *It's who I am. It's my identity. I'm a dancer.* The dancing broadened from ballet into classical Greek, tap and even cabaret.

But there was still school – that was compulsory.

At eleven Alice was forced to try for a scholarship to an exclusive private school.

'I haven't a hope of passing the exam, Mother.' Alice wasn't an academic student at all. She failed. Her parents made her try again the next year.

'I hate this exam, I can't do it – it's too hard. Why won't you listen to me?'

They didn't listen. 'See I've failed again.'

She was sent to the College anyway, but the fees were steep. The students: daughters of officers and gentlemen.

'Edith has invited me to stay in her posh house, Mum, can I go for the weekend?'

She didn't tell Rose that her school friend's parents were away in Europe. Edith and her brother were left in the care of two maids. The boy sprinkled cornflakes all over the lounge carpets in the morning. Then he called the maid. His smile haughty and his chin tilted upwards.

'Amelia, come and pick these up!'

He must have learnt that arrogance from his parents surely. I don't think I fit in here either. Where do I belong?

The old feelings of inferiority resurfaced. They dogged her throughout childhood and only abated when dancing. Here she was excellent and confident.

Alice's Diary
1934. Yesterday I decided to buy a real diary and record every

day of my life. It will be a reminder when I'm older of everything I've felt and done. So I've been out and I've bought a very small red leather one. This is my first entry. It's a short poem written by ME.

Lament
You wanted me to be top
In everything I did
But I couldn't be
Top of the class
Top in music
Top in dance
Open your eyes dear Mum
Look at me
I have to become someone else
The stakes are too high.
I fear I'm falling.

September. Right from the start of his school life, my brother has shone in EVERY subject. It isn't fair — he's the brainy one. I feel tormented by my parents' dissatisfaction with my results. I'm a disappointment to them. They only approve of Oswald. In my head, when I lay it on my pillow at night, I can hear my mother's praise of Oswald's academic success and see his face beaming as he hands her his report card. Mine always has, 'Alice talks too much. Doesn't concentrate. Disturbs the class. Is competent at sport.' So then I will dance brilliantly to be loved and successful and prove them wrong in their opinion of me.

Alice put all her efforts into practice. The academic study blurred and faded until it disappeared completely. But she won the big ballet trophy for the inter-island competition, the first person on the

Sunshine Island to have won it. 'Now Mother will be pleased with me,' Alice said aloud and smiled at herself in the mirror.

After the glow of winning had faded she talked to her best friend, the only person she dared to share her true feelings with, and mused about the dancing future mapped out for her.

'You did so well.'

'Yes, but I think it's useless to society. What help does it give to anyone?' She looked at Mary-Kate. 'How does this prepare me for the future – for service, and will it give me a sense of satisfaction? I really, really want to be a nurse. It's a noble caring profession just suited to my personality. I love what Florence Nightingale did. I would like to emulate that. It thrills me to think of helping the sick like Florence did with those wounded men. She was an amazing person actually, so determined and sacrificial.'

'Well you should talk to your parents about it again.'

Alice tried several times, but each mention of this dream was shut down instantly.

'That is not a suitable job for a young lady. There is nakedness, blood, death and it's really not very different to being in service as a maid. No, Alice you must go in the direction you have triumphed in.'

On the shelf in Alice's bedroom were many silver trophies bearing her name, won in various ballet and dance competitions. These cups were fiercely fought over between the islands in the Channel.

Truly she was a talented performer and it was a possible future. But the burying of the nurse dream was done resentfully and sorrowfully.

Why can I never choose my own path? I think it's because Mother can become very proud of a winning daughter in an area that the privileged class admires.

'Who would admire a nurse? A common job for common people.'

Still, her island home remained a blissful place to her. Her happiness enhanced by the jade sea, the almost ever-present sun, the wheeling gulls and the little fishing boats chugging into port loaded with a variety of fish species plus huge lobsters and peach-coloured crabs. One of her strongest impressions evoked by the smell of seafood was walking through the beautiful brick fish market near the quay as a young child. The cast-iron columns and complex timber ceiling with its central roof lights, its great iron sliding doors and its six entrance archways were indelible in her mind's eye.

The uneven cobbled surface of the streets made them difficult to negotiate safely. Those narrow and winding streets led out of the port into open countryside flanked by high, stone walls. In the spring, honeysuckle rambled over them and veronica bloomed in the hedgerows. There were cows on the verdant, lush pastures swatting themselves with their tails. The island was only 24 square miles but there were 600 miles of crisscrossing lanes, originally cow-paths.

The granite cliffs around the island hacked into crevices formed uncountable numbers of bays to frolic in during the summer months.

Alice's Diary

1936. At Ladies College, I'm finding it very hard to concentrate on study. Latin I like, but mostly I'm rebellious and cheeky – so the teachers say. I'm out of place. My mother and father made me come here. It wasn't my choice.

The headmistress and Mother have given me permission to leave school when I'm fifteen, I think because of my behaviour.

August. Madame Espinosa came to judge the dancing festival. She's invited me to come to London and study under her. Mother is happy to let me go to learn from this famous teacher. Of course I'm going.

May 12th, 1937, London. I dodged dance school today. I had to. It was history in the making – the coronation of George the Sixth and Queen Elizabeth. (I've always loved that name, that's what I'll call a daughter if I have one.) The king was crowned with the nine hundred year old crown that was first on the head of Edward the Confessor.

I stood for hours and hours. The people were jumping up to see over the heads of the crowds to get glimpses of the pageantry and glory, but I had a good little spot and saw most of the miles-long parade, the horsemen with their flashing breastplates, the golden fairy carriage carrying the royal couple, drawn by four pairs of horses. The streets were hung with scarlet banners. Such cheers of devotion, the crowd's roar was like the sound of a giant waterfall – jubilation! One hundred thousand faces, eyes wide and hearts glowing, the music of the Scot's guard and the navy bands marching, the wavy white plumes on the helmets of the mounted guardsmen, the glints of hundreds of swords – God save the king! I couldn't believe this wasn't heaven, I'll remember this day as long as I live.

I passed my exams and can put M.R.A.D. after my name. Mother is finally satisfied with me.

CHAPTER 9
November

As autumn turned slowly into winter, the cold weather froze parts of the father and daughter's hearts. They began to give up hope of Sarah's return or discovery.

'Dad, we have to pack up Mum's things and put them away somewhere. I can't stand seeing all her stuff, it hurts too much.'

'OK, Sweetheart, if that will help. I'll get boxes from the supermarket and we can store her things away tonight when Felix is asleep.'

That evening they packed each article in boxes. Some things they had never paid any attention to or even looked at with interest before. Her favourite books: romances; historical and modern, her precious ornament; the little porcelain pot of china flowers she had had as a girl, her hair decorations; slides, clips and ties for when she wore her hair in a chignon, her shoes, her pewter trinket box; full of things Meadow had given her over the years. Looking at this box made Meadow wild with anger.

'Why didn't she love me as much as I loved her dad?' Again he had no words in answer. Then they stored her bags; summer and winter, her hobby materials; mosaic-making books and little boxes of broken old-fashioned china, her scarves; given and collected which she wore so gracefully draped around her neck, her lingerie; given by Nathan for birthdays or Christmas; here he had to wipe his eyes and blow his nose as he gently packed the delicate pieces away. These articles called up a terrible tenderness, a memory of deep intimacy. Father and daughter stopped every few minutes for a hug.

They both felt better taking some action. When every one of Sarah's personal possessions was hidden away, they solemnly carried the boxes downstairs into the study and stacked them up. They shut the study door. *Maybe she never existed? Of course she did, how stupid.* But it was easier to forget, without all the daily reminders.

The next day, after Saturday's fry-up breakfast was cleaned up, Meadow noticed there was an unusual stillness – things were ultra silent.

'Uh oh. That's strange. Too quiet.'

She ran to look for the child. She enjoyed being a substitute Mamma. 'Coming, ready or not.' There was a scramble upstairs. She bolted up, taking two at a time. Felix had found something they'd forgotten to pack. He was under Mum and Dad's bed hugging a small white rectangular cushion that Mamma often tickled the child with. He wasn't crying, just clutching the little pillow close to his body and gazing with vacant eyes.

'Come on out you scamp!'

'No,' he screamed, and kicked his legs. 'Won't.'

She let him stay there to get over his dreamy thoughts.

In half an hour, he came jumping down the stairs with the pillow. He could never be separated from it from that moment. It had to go with him everywhere, even in his kindergarten bag.

Felix's other comforter was the cat, 'Milly-the-cat.' She wove her way around his stumpy legs, her tail sliding gently around him. He tickled her under her chin and she rose to meet his hand, her front paws off the ground. She followed him to the letterbox or into the garden, even tried to get into the toilet when he was there. Of course when he opened a book or put out paper to draw on, Milly would leap on it purring loudly. He couldn't push her off without his sister's help. Milly didn't seem to notice Sarah's absence.

Meadow came home from school fuming *As if we came from dots in the ocean – unplanned and purposeless.* 'Every effect has a cause – every action has a reaction.' Meadow had learnt that during the science class that morning. *Adults are pretty stupid – as blind as bats – well, I know bats can see brilliantly just in a different way. If we are alive, a human, then there is a cause. Adults are so stupid – I'm not swallowing their rubbish anymore – even bats are more intelligent.* She was feeling hot and wound up again. For a moment she felt a bat's horrible waxy skin and the hairy feelers sticking to her face, the miserable webbed wings and scratchy thin toes.

'Get off you dirty creature!' She hit out in front of her, then tore it off her face with her hands. It was like the piece of bubble gum that had stuck on her skin when she'd blown the biggest bubble ever. It had popped on her face and bits of gum hung in her hair for days. 'Not this time!'

Then she glanced up at the shelf where she displayed her prize possessions. *You stupid doll with your insipid smile.* 'I know you were my favourite.' Meadow grabbed it down – her arms wildly pulling at it. She ran into the bathroom where the floor was good and hard. The attack wouldn't have much impact on the carpet. With her school shoes, she jumped on the doll's pretty face – crunching and stomping over and over until it was eggshell in hundreds of pieces. Both tears and laughter escaped while the frenzy lasted. The doll 'Freya' was gone – nothing recognisable. 'Now see the effect? And I know the cause – it was a person.'

The girl charged down the stairs holding the railing, flung open the cupboard, grabbed the dustpan and brush scrambled back upstairs, she swept every tiny fragment of Freya into the pan then tipped them into the bin. She sighed and her breaths slowly returned to normal.

November 7th. Nathan sat staring out the window, his shoulders slumped, his head tilted. Meadow edged closer to his side to have a good look at him. *I suppose losing someone you love in this way is a bit like post-traumatic stress syndrome. Daddy's gone a bit funny, but he'd better snap out of it and do something about tracing Mamma.*

Nathan felt deeply humiliated by being forsaken by his wife. Of course, it still might be more sinister than that so it might not reflect on him so badly. He imagined others saying, *Oh he couldn't keep his wife happy. We know what that means.*

He also knew when a person commits suicide how terribly guilty and helpless the rest of the family and friends feel. Such shame. Such sadness. And it was probably preventable, and then the wondering about how they must have failed the dead person.

His friend at school had killed himself. He remembered the blackness he felt looking at his friend's family going through the rigours of the funeral. They were so hurt, so puzzled, and there was no way to end the misery. They never knew what they had done or not done to cause it.

The women at Nathan's workplace had fussed over him when they found out that the awful story of his missing wife, the police search, and her flight to Spain, were true.

One in particular, Jess, asked him to come for a drink, to get his mind off his troubles. She was tidy, neatly dressed and kind. Attributes Nathan admired. He liked her. She'd always been good to work with. He was feeling lonely and would have enjoyed adult company, but his heart smote him. He felt such compassion for his children, a new sensation that he was adjusting to, that he refused.

'Sorry, but I can't leave them so soon after the shock. Maybe later, thanks.'

But Jess was persistent. 'All right, she said, I'll just pop in to see you at home, if that's OK?'

That weekend when the doorbell rang, Meadow and Felix raced to get there first, the sister only pretending to go as fast as she could so Felix could beat her. She opened the heavy front door. Meadow stared at the attractive lady, looking at her with narrowed, cold eyes.

Felix said, 'Hello, what's your name?'

'Jess,' the woman said. 'Is your Daddy home?'

'Yes.'

'I'll get him,' his sister said.

'Dad, there's a lady at the door asking for you. Who is she? I've never seen her before. She said her name was Jess.'

'She's a colleague, from work, a nice lady.'

He came to the door, 'Come in. These are my children, Meadow and Felix.'

Nathan led the way into the kitchen, Jess followed. 'Nathan you look so much more handsome at work in your suit than in your jeans and sloppy old jumper. I might not have recognised you!' She smiled. 'Can we have a coffee do you think? I'll make it for you if you show me where everything is.'

Meadow was incensed. *What is this stranger doing in our kitchen, without Mum, asking where to find things? Mum wouldn't like that at all. And besides, that's Daddy's favourite jumper.*

She was jealous for her mamma, because maybe she hadn't left them and was being held somewhere against her will.

And it felt like her sacred closeness, her newly found intimacy with her dad and Felix had been invaded.

I've only just got really close to Papa and Felix. They need me now more than before. You are not welcome here. Go away you horrible woman.

The child went to his dad and hopped up on his knee. Felix smiled at Jess. Meadow left the kitchen, went into the dining room and started scribbling words on a pad.

Maybe this is the reason Mum left. Maybe Dad and this woman have fallen in love.

CHAPTER 10
Late-November

Meadow was in bed unable to sleep, anxious thoughts running through her mind that mutated into anger. *How could Mum torment me so? I would never ever do this to anyone I loved. It's the cruellest, meanest thing a human could ever do to anyone. I hate her. I hate her! But I long for her smell, her hair, to be in her warm hug.* She closed her eyes, her face distorted. She felt her hands damp with perspiration. *I can't remember her face or exactly what Mummy looks like. She is all blurry, indistinct. I think I'm losing even the memory of her.*

Meadow could hear her father's snores and there was no sound from Felix's room. She very quietly climbed out of bed, silently padded down the beige carpeted stairs, opened the door to the study, switched on the light and quickly but softly closed the door. 'I'll have to look in those boxes for that framed photo of Mum that we packed away – the one where she looks so happy and beautiful. NO! The stupid boxes are taped too tightly.' She spoke softly to herself.

She had been furious and had wound metres of parcel tape all over the cartons so no one would ever be able to get her mother's things out. That had been the best way she knew of getting rid of Mummy. But now she fervently wanted the picture. It wasn't the same as the ones on the laptop, you couldn't take that to bed or hug the photos close, you couldn't touch them, or put them down the front of your pyjamas next to your heart. *But the dumb boxes are impossible to open without scissors or a craft knife. I can't even remember which box I put the portrait in.*

She was whimpering again. *I'm so sick of hearing my own crying.* She gave up looking for the picture, turned off the light and climbed the stairs to bed. *Maybe there'll be something of hers we forgot to pack away, in the bathroom.* Meadow slipped into the room, in the dim half-light of the night lamp she felt around in the cupboard drawers surrounding the basin. She opened one drawer after another, feeling objects. The perception that perhaps Mamma didn't exist returned. 'I must find something of hers. Oh,' she sighed, 'here is – her favourite soap.' Meadow held it up to her nose and breathed in. *Ah lovely – the smell of peaches and almond, Mamma's favourite.*

Instantly she could see her mother's face, every feature of it, the soft brown eyes, the creases around her cheeks, the ears she used to play with as a small child, the hair she had endlessly brushed, twirled and tried to style. Comforted at last now that her mother's reality was a certainty, she got back into bed, the soap clasped with both hands close to her neck. Breathing in its perfume, she fell asleep.

November 24th. The next morning Felix brought in a minute feather to show his sister. It was soft, green and brown with tufts of down attached to it. They stared at its structure, its shape and the charming colours. They felt it, taking it in turns to hold it and then blow it up in the air. *Such simple pleasures, I feel so free when I focus on tiny miracles. This must be what it's like to be a little child. I can't remember being that young. But maybe if I can really learn to see how Felix sees, I will learn to be happy again like he is.*

'Felix, let's be detectives, let's detect beautiful objects in the garden and along our street. Felix, let's look for pretty things.' She rephrased it so he would understand her. 'We'll have to look really hard.' The wind was biting and the sky almost ink so they wrapped up, wound scarves around their throats then put on boots so the puddles wouldn't worry them. Felix pursed his lips into the shape for whistling, pushed out air in an attempt to make the sound, small puffs of white breath escaped but no shrill notes. He didn't mind, he kept it up for the entire long hunt. They looked in their garden first. Felix found a few interesting stones, some seed heads and various leaves in shades of orange and brown. In their street they saw a few brave wildflowers trapped in the evergreen hedge, looking like gemstones in a green blanket.

When they came inside with their collection of treasures and displayed them on a big white plate, they looked as wondrous as any objects they had ever seen in a museum. A transparent seed head, a tiny yellow leaf, a shiny stone with a line of white running through it, a large, spiky orange leaf, a mauve flower, a small piece of blue eggshell. They sighed with satisfaction. *My friends might think I'm nuts,* she thought, *but I'm calling this joy hunting. I might not tell them about our secret games in case they laugh at me and break the magic.*

Then, later, Felix asked Meadow to write to God, 'Write letter to God, please Meddie.'

Oh, he means like a letter to Santa.

'Please God, tell Mamma come home.'

So she wrote a short note:

Dear God, please tell Mummy to come home.
Love, Felix.

He drew a big wavy letter *F* on the bottom and folded it over. 'Now what, Felix?'

'Put it up.'

'Up where?'

'On dat picture.' Pointing to a framed painting on the wall.

She climbed up onto the top of the sofa and placed the little note on top of the picture.

'Yes! Yes!' he said.

When he woke up in the morning, he jumped out of bed and ran to the painting. The letter was still there. With sad eyes and fallen shoulders, he plodded to Meadow's bed. He shook her awake and dragged her out of her cosy, warm duvet. 'Look.' He pointed and sounded very disappointed.

'Look at what?'

'Dat letter.'

'Maybe He has answered,' she said to cheer him. 'I'll get it down and look.' As she got it down, she had to think fast, she lied to him. 'Yes, God says, "I read your letter, Felix. I will do it."'

The child jumped and clapped, a huge saintly smile on his face. 'Yes, yes cool.'

Maybe the hope inside Felix will be a homing beacon, a flare sent up in the darkness.

CHAPTER 11
Louis

Alice's Diary

1937. Returning from crowded and noisy London is like coming back to paradise for me. I love the cliffs of the south coast, the sea air. Ah, the sea with its tumbling waves, the beauty of the yellow gorse and the mauve heather. I think Pine Forest Bay is my favourite spot.

Bunty and I have started the Island Dancing Academy. It's already thriving. Can't believe it, we have over fifty students. It's dreadfully hard work but we are so very pleased with ourselves, and the little pupils.

Our family are great friends with the Robilliards and have been for several years. Dad knows Jean from business meetings. The two families are growing very close as we spend so much time together. Mr R, as we call him, and Dad sit on a blanket together smoking their pipes, discussing business and the state of the world. Mum and Estelle chat about their children and their hopes for us all. I know the children from school. The picnics and outings with the Robilliards have brought Louis, their son, and I into constant contact. We are only a year apart in age. And we both love swimming. We competed ferociously in the school swimming galas and cheered each other on at sports days. Our family go with the R's every Sunday, weather permitting, to Portilet or to another little beach to swim and share our picnic.

The tide is high by the Portilet harbour. So Louis and I can have little swimming contests. He always wins. Louis Robilliard is the island swimming champion. In fact, he is a great all-round athlete who is brilliant at hockey and football and everything else. He's a very popular young man with tons of friends.

March 1938. My friendship with Lou, which is a good wholesome boy and girl friendship, could be called going steady, I think, although nothing formal has been said about it. He often comes home to see me. The Robilliards' home is only a ten-minute walk from ours. In the winter we play billiards on a half-size table or the game of sardines where you turn off all the lights and hide. If you are found, the finder has to squash in with you. We love it. Last week Lou tried to climb into the copper used for boiling clothes. It was filled with freezing cold water and did he yell, a dead giveaway, hah.

Lou enjoys dancing too – it's a really popular pastime with nearly every young person here. Many evenings we go to the Royal or the Hotel de Normandie. Lou borrows his dad's car and we feel like swells arriving in style. We often go with Emile and his girlfriend, Amy. We make a fun foursome.

April 1938. I'm nearly eighteen, but I think more like fourteen as I have had such a sheltered and old-fashioned upbringing.

The realisation that Lou is a handsome and desirable young man dawned on me in one flash as I stared at the familiar figure swinging me around in his arms last night!

It was at that moment that I realised I loved him in the romantic sense not only the friend sense. He has become my first love and I believe what they say, my first love will be the sweetest. (Maybe he will be my only love, who knows?)

I see him nearly every day. We go for long walks, cycling trips and also canoe around the bays. At times we are quiet – when we are exhausted, then we hop off our bikes and sit under a tree reading books, holding hands. We stay very fit through our sporty pursuits, but we also see every film that comes out at the Regal. Sometimes Amy and Emile come too. Life seems very easy now with almost no responsibilities except for my part in the dance school, which I love, so that isn't a hardship.

Alice was nearing the end of her teenage years. She had a strong body and legs – she was very proud of them, nicely shaped from the dancing and tanned from the sunshine and beaches. Her wavy mid-brown hair stood up from her heart-shaped forehead making a natural frame for her face. She was attractive in her vivaciousness, but not classically beautiful, her posture and movements graceful and athletic from the ballet practice. Louis found her boisterous laughter compelling. She was perennially cheerful.

Alice continued to enter competitions in every dance category. The outfits and drama were as much a part of the items as the choreography. Always posing, always smiling, fixing the camera with her saucy smile and effervescent eyes. 'Rhythm of the Rain' was danced in a short, shiny raincoat and sou'wester, little tap shoes and bare legs. The Mexican Dance costume had a gorgeous bolero over a white puff sleeve blouse and a full paisley skirt with petticoats. Alice's head tilted coquettishly while her shapely arms held her skirts Spanish style. Character was her favourite genre.

Many studio portraits were taken of the dozens of parts she played. She was also part of the chorus line of girls from shortest to tallest in line, in sync, in 30s mode, hair and shoes adorned with the huge bows so fashionable in that era, who danced and performed to the well-patronised local show-goers. There was Alice in the middle with the confident and happy smile – catching the eye of the judges. She surely was made for all this showmanship – Miss Personality. Alice kept all her newspaper reviews and pasted them in a scrapbook. She underlined her name. *Miss Alice Beauvoir came first with her attractive dancing that so delighted the audience that they gave her the only encore of the evening.*

Alice's Diary

These years are halcyon times, gentle and unworried. On New Year's Eve, my parents and our friends went to the Royal Hotel to dance the night through. I was introduced to Henry, a graceful dancer, but of course he means nothing to me. I only have eyes for Lou, whose warm smile and serious ideals captivate my heart and mind. What a brilliant night – all of us together laughing and changing partners – dancing with Dad and my brother and Lou and his dad. 'Get a wiggle on!' They yelled at the band if the break was too long between numbers.

On the news we hear that Germany is pushing quietly into new parts of Austria now. I try not to think about it. I don't think they will try any tricks on us.

CHAPTER 12
December 1st

At work, Jess called Nathan over to help her with a problem that she could easily solve by herself. She wanted him to feel special and useful.

'Oh thank you so much. Now I understand how that works.' She looked up at him and blinked. She was aware he was emotionally vulnerable.

Jess had worked with him for over two years. She found him soft and co-operative. She liked his steadiness. He almost seemed unchangeable. Jess was well-organised and quick – Nathan liked these qualities, being a methodical and thorough person. They easily became friends. *His wife leaving him, or she might have met with an accident – I don't think! Is a wicked thing to do to such a nice man.*

Nathan didn't want to tell Jess that his wife's disappearance could be half his fault. That was much too personal and quite unprofessional. Anyway, he had only just realised it himself and still couldn't see clearly where he had missed it.

Jess was relentless. She had called in nearly every weekend to see if there was anything Nathan needed. Meadow was scheming, but couldn't think yet of a way to get Jess to leave her dad alone. *I guess he does need a friend – but not her.*

'Dad, why don't you ask some men mates to come over for a drink? I know you must be a bit lonely. I'll look after Felix and put him to bed.'

Nathan came home from work with some news. He looked cheered. 'Med, my two colleagues have asked me to go fishing for the weekend. Jess said she would come over and stay with you two to make sure you're safe.'

I know she is worming her way into Dad's heart. Now he will be grateful to her. She doesn't want to help him; she wants to have him.

'Dad, I'm sorry I can't accept that. I don't like her and it's too soon after Mum's disappearance for us to have another woman in the house.'

In the end, Gran said she'd come. It was nice getting a bit closer to Gran. They talked a lot and Meadow found out information she'd been thinking of asking her about for a while. What Sarah's mum's childhood had been like, and what she would have done if she'd had the opportunity. She would have liked to train as a florist, she said. *Well she certainly could have done that at any time. Why hadn't she? It's true what Mum said. She does seem a little fogged up, but underneath that mist there's a person who had hopes that have been buried or dashed completely. Such simple ones too.*

Meadow unpacked the dishwasher and found that Felix had put the mug in they hadn't been using on purpose. It had Best Mummy in the World written on it. The slightest thing started the water falling, but this time the tears just stood in her eyes and didn't drop. *I think that's some progress.*

Time was going incessantly slowly for the girl. Nathan was sitting on the sofa gazing at nothing in particular. Meadow frowned at him. 'Dad what's wrong with you? You should be hunting after Mamma,' she said under her breath.

Meadow was disappointed in his lack of gallantry. She wanted her father to be an adventurer who would risk everything to go and rescue her 'Mother-in-distress'– if she could be found.

'Slow and steady wins the race,' he muttered like a robot.

'Oh, shut up Dad,' she mouthed, 'and get off your chuff won't you!'

Early December. The rain on the roof and windows sounded like frying oil, cracking, splattering. It woke Felix. He was a heavy sleeper but the noise was sudden and loud. He opened his eyes wide and stared at the darkness. The door was open – it always was at night. The light from downstairs glowed through the doorway like a beam from a lighthouse.

The child's books fell to the floor as he scrambled out of bed. He grabbed his cushion and padded towards the light. Quiet voices speaking, monotonous and low.

He took the stairs one at a time, holding the rail. The last step was opposite the lounge. He didn't call out. He was just curious. *Who is it?* He gently pushed open the lounge door. Without his slippers, he made no sound.

He slowly walked up behind the sofa. Papa and a lady were sitting there quite close to each other. Felix blinked his sleepy eyes at the light, dropped his cushion then crept nearer. 'Boo!' The two adults jumped, startled by the voice. Nathan stood up. The lady turned – it was Jess.

Felix swivelled and ran for his little pillow, snatched it up and darted back upstairs, jumped into bed, and pulled the covers up high so only his eyes were uncovered. He closed them tightly. In just two minutes, Nathan was standing over him in the dim light, examining him for tears. No tears.

'What a funny boy. Good night.' He bent over and kissed the child on the top of his head. For one second his ruffled hair smelled like Sarah's. *Ridiculous.* He smiled, for one brief moment he was free. Then anxious thoughts flooded back like a surge of water.

Nathan went back downstairs and turned on the CD player. Bad idea, it was dance music that was still in the machine. He hadn't bothered to check it. He was a good dancer, probably rhythm and the ability to move gracefully inherited from his grandmother. He had danced to this before with Sarah.

'Nathan, can you dance?'

'A little.'

'Well, come on then. It'll cheer you up to get moving.'

He slowly moved toward Jess, tense and awkward. 'I'd rather not if you don't mind, I'm really quite tired.'

'You boring old thing.'

'We have work in the morning and I have to get up very early because of the kids' lunches and school bags and so on.'

'All right. I'll be off now.'

She kissed him on the cheek as she left. He didn't respond with as much warmth as she would have liked.

December 12th. Jess came around for coffee as usual on the weekend. Nathan still looked forward to her visits. He just needed another adult to talk to – someone capable. She greeted them all with a smirky smile.

'I'll hang the washing up in the garage for you.'

'I can do that,' Meadow said without returning the smile, taking the washing basket from her. She hung the small clothes on the little airer and ran back to fire the sheets into the dryer. She dashed back to the kitchen so she could get back to her position as watchman. Meadow kept her eyes fixed on her father's face.

What are his eyes saying? Getting nearer the pair. *What is he saying to that interloper?*

She watched him being manipulated by flattery, his face flushed, his eyes lowered. *Daddy is naïve to it,* she thought.

'Nathan, it's not good for you to be at home so much. You're a young man. You need company. I'll cook dinner tonight. We could nip out for an hour, couldn't we?'

The whole time Nathan was out he thought about the kids. *It's a cold night – are they warm enough? What if they need something? Does Meadow know my cell phone number? Of course she does. It must be scary for them without Mum or Dad – it's too much responsibility for a young girl.* He sighed. Then he smiled when he looked at his watch and the hour was almost over. It had been a kind of torture.

Jess looked pleased with herself. The wry smile was easy to interpret. Nat wasn't able to read the subtleties.

'You don't mind if I come in for half an hour, do you? I'll just check the dishes have been dried.'

'If they haven't been, it isn't because Meadow is lazy. She is a reliable girl and very thoughtful.'

The dishes had been dried. Meadow sat at the table in her pyjamas feigning interest in her schoolwork. Jess turned to look at her with a perfect smile.

'It's good to see you being helpful to your dad.'

She nodded at the clear bench-top.

That woman is so condescending she makes me feel like a complete idiot.

Although I can't forgive Mum for walking out on us, if she has for sure, what would happen if Dad paired up with Jess? I don't trust her at all. Not one bit. I won't let it happen. We haven't even got any proof that Mum is dead. We at least need to find her body before Dad gets any new ideas. It's me he should be thinking of. It's bad enough to have no certainty about Mum, but Jess. I'll have a long talk to Dad and tell him how upset all this is making me. It's hideously mean of him. What about us, Felix and me – we are what's most important right now.

CHAPTER 13
Books – December 14th

The light on the horizon – silver platinum like a precious metal, intensified. The sun pushed partway through and shone a blinding white. There was no heat in it of course – it was December.

The three were getting used to amusing themselves in the winter season. How Felix loved reading books, or rather looking at them. Nathan and Meadow had watched Felix's face and seen the expressions of happiness grow as he had stories read to him. His eyes widened, his mouth smiled or tensed, his hands clapped. It seemed to take him away to another realm. They mutually decided that if it worked for him it would work for them. Every other one of the child's joys had given them ways to cope successfully. Here was another way. Nathan hadn't read a complete book for months, maybe more like a year. The three would go to the library together and hunt for treasure. Felix was obsessed with pirates so the treasure would be real to him.

They decided to walk there; it might be like old times. Nathan was happy going there in his old jumper and jeans; he hated that suit he had to wear for work. Meadow thought she might bring a friend, but then thought, *Dad will want Jess to come,* so she gave up that idea.

Felix grizzled halfway because of the long walk, so Papa stood him on a wall and then piggybacked him the rest of the way.

'Stop Dad! Felix, look – the yellow button plant.' Meadow

pointed at the tansy growing wild behind the wall. The siblings gave each other a secretive look.

What on earth is that about? he wondered.

In the library, friends waved at the little family. They gave them sympathetic looks and kept away.

Felix flung off his puffer jacket and left it lying on the carpet. In his red and white striped T-shirt, dressed for the pirate search, he rushed to the children's section. There were puzzles, a bead counter, and mini beanbags. He rolled around on the bags, flicked the counter, looked at the jigsaws, grabbed about six books off the shelf nearest to him, picked two and hurled the others away. Meadow frowned at him. He went to gather the thrown ones and returned them, pouting his lips and squinting his eyes. But he put the books back nicely and then said, 'Ha!'

'You cheeky boy.'

Nathan hunted for a long time, walking through the aisles trying to find a topic that interested him. *Accounting, no I get enough of that at work; a travel magazine featuring Spain and cooking for young children, mmm a bit boring. Could be useful.* Then he drifted to the psychology section that he poo-poohed. *Actually, there are some absorbing topics right here.*

Meadow loved reading, especially Young Adult mysteries.

She could never work out who-done-it though, until it was revealed at the end.

They found their minds taken into other places when they read. It was a wonderful, easy solace. A place of escape where they let their imaginations go right into the story. It set them marvellously free.

In the world of a story, thought Meadow, *I have the ability to be quiet and alone, two rare states in the hectic life I'm living at the moment.*

Nathan read on the library wall: *Books help us to understand our behaviour and our friend's actions. They show us how to live and how to die.*

Horrible, he thought, *but true.*

Other quotes around the walls were more encouraging: *We read a few words of a good novel and then begin to see images and to forget ourselves.*

'Wasn't that just what we've been talking about?'

And the last one he really liked: *I can live a thousand lives instead of only my own.*

'Yes indeed.'

Books, well the stories in them, gave the small family somewhere to go when they physically couldn't go anywhere. They took home armfuls of dreams.

That night they all got into the big bed together. Nathan read a couple of books aloud to the child. To make it more fun, they switched off the light and, under the blankets, used the phone torch to see by. Milly sat watching the bed covers move; little toes were twitching. She sprang onto the blanket, pounced on the little feet and bit. Felix squealed. Then giggled as it happened over and over.

'Keep still, Felix, or Milly will never stop.' Meadow rested on her father, her head on his shoulder. It felt strong, manly. She burrowed into safety. Milly purred like an engine. Felix was blissfully still now and Meadow enjoyed the silly stories, chuckling with the boy. Nathan only remembered reading to Felix a couple of times before Sarah's disappearance. He had read to Meadow more as he hadn't been so distracted then with only one child. Sarah was always willing to read to Felix – he'd left it to her. Now he had to do it. He had baulked at first, but discovered another new amusement. He acted out the various characters and animals with strange noises and silly voices.

'Stop it, Dad. That's not wite.' Felix knew when the story had been cut short or altered.

Meadow was crying softly – joyful times at school and at home started the almost daily waterworks too. It was like rain falling inside her – like a waterfall that ran down into her secret sore places, the uncovered raw wounds. The water re-covered the exposed parts, washed them and made them clean.

'I like the new you, Daddy.' Meadow cuddled closer.

A new me? Oh.

CHAPTER 14

The Friendly Island in 1938 was calm, and continued in its same busy, daily routine. Steamers putted in and out of the harbour. They brought mail, papers and goods. They left with tomatoes, fruit and flowers. You could hear some of the islanders speaking in the local French patois, like they had done for over a century, as they loaded their produce onto the boats.

If you walked a way up the hill you came to Saumarez Park, a broad green meadow surrounded by massive trees. Cattle shows were held here, followed by lobster luncheons in large tents. Nearby were glasshouses where grapes were trained along the walls, hundreds of metres of them, thousands of bunches of luscious grapes hung just within touch. A one-hundred-year-old fig tree bore three crops a year, under glass. The produce sent to Covent Garden Market in London. Fruit was plentiful; nectarines, peaches and raspberries. Guernsey biscuits, jams and conserves covered the tea tables. Bees droned in and out of the flowers growing on the edge of the field.

The cross of St George flapped in the sea breeze over the Royal Courthouse when the court was sitting. Martello towers, a hangover from Napoleon's day, watched over Fermain Bay as a passenger boat arrived. On this day, a dense pea-souper fog covered the waters, a heavy swell rolled the ships back and forth. The bell on Castle Cornet rang, a clear sharp note.

Houses, churches, shops, crammed the steep slopes rising from the harbour. The grinding and moaning of winches and the screeching of gulls mixed with animated human speech.

The sea stretched hazy, blurry to the horizon. When the fog lifted, France was a black smudge in the distance. The wind pushed the waves eastward, making ruffles on the surface of the sea. Here and there a crest of white flashed. The sun pushed its way through the mist and cleared the last tufts of haze.

Picnickers soon dotted the sands, though summer was almost over.

'There is serious talk of us being at war with Germany.'

'I don't think it will come to anything really. We've only just got over the Great War.'

'It doesn't affect us.'

'No, nor us.'

The military and the politicians felt it very differently. It was indeed serious, so serious that a few families were making plans to evacuate to the mainland-England.

Alice's Diary

1939. I've seen uniformed members of various branches of HM forces walking and driving through St Peter Port lately. There seems to be an increase in all things military. The Royal Air Force is here too of course.

June has arrived with gorgeous sunshine.

September. Dreadful news, Poland has been invaded and fallen to Hitler's army. We hear the German forces may be heading for Holland and Belgium. They say the Germans will over-run France and eventually come to Brittany.

Schools here are evacuating their pupils already. Families are abandoning their houses, leaving their homes entirely as they are and sailing away on steamers to Britain with nothing but a few hurriedly filled suitcases.

September 3rd 1939. Today the radio broadcast a gravely spoken announcement by Neville Chamberlain.
'We are at war with Germany.' It left us stunned. We looked at one another. Mum held onto the back of a chair to steady herself. Daddy knows what war is; he turned a sickly white, his usually tanned face faded. It seemed fantasy to me. But Louis knows how grave the situation is – he's been a member of the Guernsey Militia for a while now and is commissioned as a second lieutenant. He looks so manly in his battledress with the pip on his shoulder.
Emile is already in the army and stationed in Hampshire. He too is a second lieutenant now.

May 1940. Germany has attacked Belgium and Luxembourg. In Holland, the Dutch army was defeated in only five days.
We have a new prime minister – Winston Churchill.

June. Louis has transferred to the Hampshire regiment on the mainland joining Emile. Lou and I are no longer able to see each other. My head is full of thoughts and prayers that he will be safe. I'm no good at partings. When he left for England, the tears flowed like a river. I don't know if I will ever see him again. I wait every day for the post, hoping for a letter. I've had three so far. I read them over and over and then put them away in my top drawer under my hankies. I've had two phone calls – one of them lasted seven minutes. We have sent each other our photographs too.

The war has progressed – the Allies were swept back to Dunkirk and the evacuation of our troops from France was accomplished with amazing bravery but also with the loss of many young lives. Our island's geographical position puts us in grave danger. During May, in spite of the war, we were at dances and enjoying ourselves at the Royal Hotel and at Café Central.

Now it's June, the RAF and all military personnel have been ordered to leave. The evacuation of children and mothers has continued. More than half the population have left. Dad doesn't want to leave. He has just bought a new house. He is fifty-two. He is not panicking. He's calm and keeps his head. He says we will stay and face whatever comes. No running away. He has worked hard and doesn't want to leave his home and business to the looters. We are very united as a family and are prepared to face come-what-may together.

My brother did not leave with the rest of his school friends, as Mother could not bear to part with him. Many children have stayed on the island, but only a few of them are fifth and sixth formers.

June 26th. Lou has been away for 12 weeks, can't believe it. I got a letter from him today – very sweet of him to write.

June 27th. We saw the first Nazi plane flying overhead. It circled the island then flew across it and back again for about an hour, the black cross and swastika on its side clearly visible and threatening. The noise became deafening as it dropped altitude.

June 28th. Mum said, 'Why don't we go to the harbour to see the mail boat off to England?' This is an age-old custom for us islanders and a short stroll we enjoy. She thought about it a bit more then said,

'No, I think I'll wait for Daddy to get home first.'

I went upstairs to my bedroom to get my red cardigan, it would be cooler if our walk was to be later, and glanced out of the window. I saw three German planes swooping down – flying over the church; a silver trail coming from the rear of the lead aircraft. I tore downstairs and told Mother. Then, machine-gun fire – clack-clack-clack.

'No! Oswald is at Bobby's house and Dad is on his way home.'

'If we had gone down to the harbour we could have been hit, Mum. Thank goodness you changed your mind.' A few minutes can mean the difference between life and death.

I expected our house to be hit; the noise was so loud. We dashed across the road and down into an air raid shelter. It was actually the coal cellar, there were no windows; the smell of the coal dust filled our noses. A neighbour sitting down there on coal sacks with us just kept repeating, 'Why don't we give in? Why don't we give in? We should surrender like all those other countries.' We wanted her to just shut up. It was adding to the tension all round.

Daddy walked in, white and shaken, but alive, thank God. He had lain on the ground during the machine-gunning and then crawled his way up the street, sheltering in doorways and then against hedges to dodge the bullets.

Clouds of black smoke swirled upwards from the town. The raid continued for one and a half hours. Our nerves were in shreds so no one could sleep that night.

This morning we heard that bombs had fallen without warning down by the harbour, smashing tomato lorries to smithereens. These tomatoes were to be sent to England, food for the German enemy. The Heinkels had come very low over the sea. People had waved to them before the bombs were ruthlessly dropped upon the line of waiting lorries. It was ages before the noise of the explosions and guns stopped. The siren had sounded but everything was already ablaze: smoke choked the air. The beautiful harbour was scarred and wounded. Lorries and carts were left black and boats blown apart.

The drivers of the lorries had hidden underneath them, but the incendiary bombs had torched them or their burnt-out trucks had collapsed on them. The blood of the dead and wounded mixed with the red of the tomatoes to create a crimson scene from Hades. The cries of the injured penetrated the hearts of those who had escaped and were in hiding under the harbour wall. Thirty-four civilians were dead and many injured.

The enemy landed quietly on the other side of the island. The gates have closed on our Guernsey. Last week was the last few days of freedom. Most of us are shaken and nervous. When I heard of the casualties, butterflies swirled in my belly. I could feel vomit come up into my mouth. Some other people, I heard, threw up from fear. The dreaded invader now occupies and rules over our Sunshine Island. What will the future be like? Our familiar world has ended; an unknown one begun.

June 30th 1940. We've heard that there is to be no more mail coming or going between Britain and the Channel Islands.

I'm so glad I got that last letter from Lou.

Lord Haw-Haw was on the radio last night. Germany calling.

Lies, all lies, but many people listen to see if they can hear any news about their sons or to hear the casualty lists read out. The radio said our Churchill had been killed in a plane shot down by the Nazis. More lies.

Fifteen German officials drove in convoy to The Royal Hotel today and were in discussion with the Bailiff of Guernsey. The government house in Queen's Road is where the commandant has installed himself – relishing that it was the one-time resi-

dence of the king's representative on the island. A visitor told us some local 'Lovelies' sat in plush chairs with Wehrmacht and Luftwaffe officers. How have the officers found Jerry-bags so swiftly or did they go looking for the officers?

We know now that it's the end of the raids. We patted each other on the back and gave each other big hugs. We haven't been maimed or killed like those other poor Guernsey people.

The German army wear green, the air-force blue. Both wear high black Russian boots and the officers have pistols.

Two soldiers guard the hotel entrance. The fifty local army and navy personnel had to report to the hotel and then be interned in Castle Cornet.

June 30th. The president of the island's emergency committee rang Whitehall today. 'Goodbye!' he said. That was the last contact permitted.

None of us can guess how long this separation will last.

July 1st. The front page of the daily newspaper today:

*Orders of the Commandant of the German Forces in
Occupation of the Island of Guernsey
All inhabitants must be indoors by 11 pm and must not leave
their homes before 6 am.
All firearms and ammunition must be handed in immediately.
The cliffs are laid with mines. It is forbidden to go there.
Heavy fines will be imposed on those who visit them.
Cyclists must ride in single file.
All Germans have the right of way.
Shops must close at 4 pm.
No fires are permitted.*

All dogs must be on leads or they will be shot.
Houses must be evacuated if requisitioned by the German forces.
Clocks must be advanced one hour to synchronise with German
time.
Prayers for the Royal Family are allowed in churches but
The British National Anthem cannot be played without writ-
ten permission from the commandant.
No gas is to be used after 9 pm. Blackout must be observed
from that time until the morning.
We will respect the population but should anyone attempt to
cause the least trouble, serious measures will be taken and the
town will be bombed.
Signed Commandant Brandt.

July 3rd. Amy rode over by bicycle to my house today. 'Come
on, I want to see the soldiers.' I joined her on my bike. We did a
quick sweep of the town. It wasn't that exciting so we rode over
to the tennis courts to have a game.

Everyone seems anxious to see what the occupying force is like.
Curiously, loads of people are going into town to see them and
get up close to them. Daddy says when the soldiers come into his
shop they are very polite. But they have secured the best cars for
themselves and are eating as much of the produce and meat as
they can. Smart shopkeepers are hiding their goods. There are to
be no more buses. Can't understand that new rule.

August 16th. About 250 German troops, wearing Wehrmacht
helmets and jackboots, led by a band marched through St Peter
Port until they stopped at the Royal. The onlookers were sullen
and mute. This evening the military band will give a concert
in Candie Gardens: Admission six pence for the Red Cross. Are
they mad or am I? 'We have bombed your island home and

invaded your lives now come to a concert as if nothing has happened.' Mourning people in the houses of the dead civilians are outraged as well as grief-stricken. The Germans are under the delusion that we'll treat them as the master race and give them preference in everything. They will learn the truth soon.

August 17th. Many of the tomato growers are almost idle as they have nowhere to export their produce to. So we are inundated with tomatoes – all free.

August 18th. An odd bod local rode through the town today on horseback. Must be a protest of sorts. Hope he isn't arrested. But 'No riding on horses' is not one of the new rules.

August 19th. Apparently there are about one thousand troops here. We had better be careful! There are plain-clothes Germans wearing raincoats and trilby hats. What a laugh no local ever wears those items. So stupid!

August 20th. A Messerschmitt performed stunts like a dolphin over the harbour today, exalting in the German victory. Diving, looping the loop – it seemed impossible but I watched; my heart thrilled. It lasted 15 minutes. Is propaganda beginning to turn my mind?

September. There is considerable activity in the air above our island. The Nazis have been losing between fifty and one hundred and forty planes a day. We heard on our crystal set they are calling this the Battle of Britain. There have been many dogfights; Spitfires and Hurricanes chasing German planes in the sky over the island.

We pin all our hopes on our newly beloved Churchill.

CHAPTER 15
A Note – December 18th

Meadow flipped through the little gold-edged book of Good News quotations that Sarah kept next to the recipe books. A note on blue, lined paper fluttered out and the girl picked it up from the sticky floor tiles and gazed at her mamma's writing.

If anything should happen to me, I would like all my jewellery to go to Meadow and all my money to go to Nathan to bring up the children. I want them to know that I love them as I love my own soul.

'It's dated ten months ago.' *Oh she did think of me.* 'Dad, look at this. Maybe Mum did plan to die somewhere.' As those words left her mouth and the reality of the possibilities hit her brain, Meadow started to shake. Nat held on to her, pulled her close. 'We can really plan a trip to Madrid now. If we take Mum's photo and be like real detectives we can find out what happened to her. Can't we?' She looked up at him, searching his face expectantly.

'I will think about it, Sweetheart. Really I will.'

'Oh, Daddy, hurry up and think – it's taking too long, I can't bear the waiting.'

Meadow grabbed a handful of her hair in a fist.

What is the matter with you? You're so slow and cautious, Dad – I hoped you'd be my dashing hero.

In the quotations book they found two passages highlighted in luminous yellow.

Song of Songs 4-10 How sweet is your love, my treasure, my bride!

This had been written on the couple's wedding service. Nathan remembered clearly the love he had experienced that divine day and was now distraught at the thought of where it had disappeared. *What on earth happened? If we find Sarah alive, I will do my best to bring back that feeling.*

The other underlined quote was

Hear my cry, O God; listen to my prayer!
In despair and far from home I call to you.

Was it a clue? Or just something she'd highlighted years ago?

Felix's birthday was only two weeks before Christmas. He had three friends from kindergarten coming to his small party. They made enough noise for ten. The custom among his friends was to have birthday guests stay over for the night. Nathan couldn't bear the thought and Meadow was too young to look after the other kids. Felix didn't care a fig. He didn't even ask for them to stay.

One young friend had brought Felix a blue helium balloon with Best Wishes on it. It stuck to the ceiling when the boy let it go and Meadow had to get it down by standing on the table. Felix ran like a maniac holding the string tightly and then out into the garden.

'Hang onto it, Felix. It'll fly away.' *This is like my attempts at hanging onto happiness. I think I have some and then suddenly I can't find the string to keep hold of it.* The balloon lasted precisely three minutes before a swirl of breeze lifted it out of Felix's fingers and up, way up, over Mr Clarke's roof and it was gone.

The games were a shambles. No one really knew how to keep order. It had always been Sarah's duty.

Why is Jess singing 'Happy Birthday dear Felix' and not Mummy?

Jess was not much help. She didn't see why she should clear up the mess because it was easy for Meadow to do it.

Anyway, it's her brother's birthday.

The house was littered with paper and food, spilled drink and burst balloons. 'And there were only four small boys. Imagine six or eight, Dad.'

Later that evening at 8.30, when they thought the child was asleep, a cheery voice asked, 'Dad is it still my birthday?'

Nathan and Meadow's eyes turned to look at each other. Neither moved their heads. 'Cute.'

On Friday after school, Meadow wandered into the utility room. She looked around at the piles of washing that were building up, damp and smelly. 'Pooh. Yuck. Two baskets full! Felix, go upstairs and see if you have any dirty wet clothes in your room.' She yelled after him, 'Look on the floor!'

I'm gonna help Daddy. I don't want that hideous Jess telling him I'm no good.

Meadow had helped Sarah do washing before, mostly removing it from the machine then hanging it up. 'It's simple – you just put it in, choose the temp and the time, delicates or whatever.' She piled in the first load – the machine almost full, it was a top loader safer for little kids – turned it on then drifted into the dining room, spread her homework out on the table, shuffled the books backwards and forwards till she found the easiest assignment – her vocabulary list.

Felix stared around his bedroom, looked under the bed and on the carpet beside it. He grabbed socks, pyjamas and his red knitted pullover. With the washing under his arm he jumped one step at a time with both feet, almost coming a cropper on his dangling pyjama sleeve, but he steadied himself holding the bannister. He ran to the laundry, lifted the lid of the washer and stuffed the bundle in. He found Meddie at the table.

She gave him paper and a pencil. 'Draw the cat, Schmeelix.'

'Milly-the-cat,' he said and handed her the picture.

'Oh that's cute. It's more like a horse than a cat but good try. Now draw a car.' The sound of the machine spinning and then groaning to a standstill stopped the homework session.

Meadow went to the utility room to unload the washing. Felix followed. 'I'll pull it out – you put it in the basket. Oh my goodness, how did Dad's white undies turn pink and your white socks too, Felix? Papa will be furious. Ha ha! He's got women's knickers and you've got girls' socks.'

Felix frowned and puffed his lips. At the bottom of the machine was a tiny red garment.

'No! That's your beautiful hand-knitted crimson jersey Gran made for you. Look at it you silly boy – it's so small it could only fit the cat now.' Her eyes pricked with a few tears, then she decided it was wasting good teardrops so she stemmed them. They put half the washing in the dryer. 'I'm going to ring Nan to find out what I can do about the pink clothes.'

Felix ran round the house calling 'Miwee, Miwee-da-cat come here.' She was curled up on a chair by the radiator.

The child put his arm under her stomach and lifted her up, her hind legs hung straight down. She was used to Felix. He took the tiny wet red jumper and pulled it over Milly's head. She bore this well, her sleepy green eyes almost closing. Now the arms. The boy tried to bend Milly's foreleg into the now cigar-sized sleeve of the minute article. She hissed and tried to escape. He held her tightly and felt for the other paw. The claws came out, she batted him with her hind legs and scratched at his face in a one-second attack.

Felix ran screaming, 'Meadow, Miwee skwatzed me.' Blood

poured out of two thin stripes on his small screwed up face and dotted his fingertips. Milly on three legs – one still inside the doll-size jumper, ran in circles mewing piteously.

'Fee-lix!'

Meadow dabbed damp cotton wool onto her brother's wan white cheek. The skin so soft, the cuts so red. He sat perfectly motionless and mute, two drops as big as rain plopped from his swimming green eyes.

The next day when Jess came, she noticed the mini crimson garment hanging on the line. *Sarah should have taught that girl how to do the washing correctly.* 'Utter neglect,' she said under her breath.

CHAPTER 16
Landing

In England, Louis was commissioned into the Hampshire Regiment as a second lieutenant.

After attending a Young Officer's Training Course, a call to Lou came straight away. His reputation as a loyal and dedicated soldier of the Crown was already known. He was ordered to report to the Admiralty.

'What on earth for sir?'

'Can't tell you that, all hush-hush. They need you up in London immediately, Lt Robilliard.' When he arrived in London he went into the Admiralty building, showed his papers, saluted the officer, and was directed to room 104. Captain Waring was poring over a map of the island. The lieutenant saluted. 'In Whitehall, they need to know what is happening in the Channel Islands. The Prime Minister wants to find out exactly what has been going on in these islands of ours since the Germans landed. We need someone to go to Guernsey and get all the details about how the population are coping, the strength of the invaders and their treatment of our people. We need to know the numbers and location of the German forces, curfew hours and patrol times.' The captain looked at Louis eyeball to eyeball.' We will make plans from these details for a military raid. The information is of immense importance.'

Lou immediately volunteered to go.

'Lieutenant Louis, think about this well. You know you will be shot if you get caught and you can expect no help from us at all.'

'I'm happy to go sir.'

'I'm happy to hear it. It's on the south coast beaches we think it safest to land. You will go by submarine. Which beach would be the best for you to be put ashore on?'

Lt Louis searched the map spread out on the large wooden table. 'Le Jouennet looks suitable. I know it very well.'

'But what about this small cove with the almost perpendicular cliffs – Petit Port Bay? Very few people ever descend those uncountable steps I've heard. The inlet is so narrow it's practically hidden from sight.'

'Yes sir, perfect.'

'You will land in civilian clothes. You know what that means! And because it's urgent you have only one night before you leave from Plymouth. Can you handle a dingy?'

'Certainly sir.'

'You will stay three days and be picked up that evening.'

'A fellow Guernseyman, Lt Emile Courbet, is being interviewed. I presume you know each other?'

'Yes sir, a good choice. We were at school together actually.'

Before the journey to Plymouth, Lou bought himself a bottle of brandy to swig if it looked like capture was imminent at any time. The next night the pair climbed on board the Royal Navy submarine. The reconnaissance mission, actually espionage, was titled 'Operation Anger'. Churchill was livid at the invasion of the British Channel Islands.

The submarine glided into the black water but then immediately rolled from side to side in the heaving swell. Lou vomited over the side of the conning tower. Nervousness or seasickness or both, he wasn't certain. The boat remained on the surface for nearly an hour before it slipped below to a depth of 60 feet and proceeded toward the island. They were 20 hours under the sea. The sub surfaced briefly in the darkness to let the men and the dingy off. The two officers were rowed ashore by an able seaman, no need for them to handle the dingy after all. It was painted a dirty yellow, inconspicuous at night. They landed without incident.

It was a low spring tide when the two were dropped ashore. Lou had on grey flannels, a shirt which had a compass on one of the buttons, a Guernsey and sandshoes. As they walked along the wet sand, Lou looked down. 'Hey we're leaving footprints, they'll be easily seen in daylight, even if the tide comes in. We'll have to climb over the rocks.' They had been instructed not to use the steps to climb the towering cliffs, in case the enemy had mined them. Louis and Emile carefully climbed the very steep cliff face using a narrow pathway that was known only to a few. Lou had often shinnied up this track as a child. It was hard to find in the dark, as it was so overgrown now. Louis hid his signalling torch in the bracken. They couldn't carry it with them. It was an obvious clue and cumbersome. They criss-crossed their way up in a westerly direction.

Later, Louis told Alice: 'By the time we reached the main path, I had already drunk my bottle of brandy, the sea breezes were icy. It took us about an hour to reach the top of the cliff. "Stop! What's that?" A scuffling sound in the nearby bushes. We froze. "Only a rabbit!" But I was looking around constantly and often stopped when we heard little noises thinking they may be German foot patrols. We were shaky and sweating like pigs in spite of the cold air from the brisk and cutting wind at the cliff edge.'

They made their way across damp fields in the semi-darkness. The sky was already lightening in the east. They would have to hurry. Emile walked 50 metres in front of Lou to disguise their relationship to one another. They reached the Old Mill and hunkered down there until the sun rose. Then in the same spread out fashion the two continued their trek until they came down the pathway to Louis's uncle's home on the Ville au Roi estate. They were treated to a royal breakfast, after the surprise had died down. Emile fell asleep with exhaustion on the sofa straight after eating.

'Wake up! Lou shook his fellow commando. We must stay alert at all times.' Emile, startled, was wide-awake in seconds.

'Say Lou, I was so scared last night I don't think anything will ever be able to terrify me again. How about you?'

'You know very well. I was scared witless too. But I'm one hundred per cent certain we haven't finished with our fears yet.'

Lou's uncle rang his friend Albert Beauvoir to tell him to come around at lunchtime as he had something interesting to show him.

Albert drove to the estate and knocked. He jumped with shock when he spotted Louis, his favourite young friend, now Alice's boyfriend. 'What are you doing here, don't you know you could be shot if the Germans find you?'

'Yes Mr Beauvoir, but we are on an important mission for our England and our islands.'

'Yes, yes of course. I understand. How long are you here for?'

'Three days.'

'And where are you going to hide out?'

'Well I hoped you would be able to drive us to Mr Sampson's home. It's close to the west coast and overlooks the airfield where we can observe the activity of the German air movements.'

'Us?'

'Yes, Emile Courbet is with me.'

'Just as well it's this week, the Jerries are going to requisition all our vehicles over the next week or so.'

Naturally Alice was told and forced to promise to keep the secret. She managed to sneak out of the house unseen.

She cycled like the wind up to the Sampsons' house, threw her bike onto the hedge and knocked on the back door. It opened and she slipped in, coming face to face with Lou, who hugged her with great warmth.

'Come upstairs and talk to me while I shave. You know I have to go back in three days.' He couldn't tell her any details about the mission – it would be safer that way, he said.

'What a fantastic surprise. How exciting. I thought I might never see you again and here you are so soon,' she said.

'Well it could be truly dangerous if we are seen. You must swear not to tell a soul. The Sampsons think us foolish for volunteering. We would be shot as spies as we only have our civies.'

Bert told Rose about the boys. She immediately rang her best friend Mrs Robilliard, who naturally called the Sampsons to talk to her son. Lou was able to talk to his parents' neighbour who managed the stores that supplied the Germans with rations, so he could find out the amounts of food distributed and therefore the troop numbers and locations. From their hideout at the Sampsons, so close to the airfield, they had found out the aircraft movements too. Emile's uncle was Assistant Harbour Master which was devilish handy as he then received all the specs on shipping movements as well. They had fulfilled their commission so easily.

Three nights after they arrived, just before the curfew hour, the two officers made their way independently to the high cliffs above Petit Port. As Louis walked confidently along the road, the sound of a motorcycle behind him grew louder and louder. *Is it following me? Don't look around, just keep walking but move over so they have the right of way.* 'A motorbike and sidecar passed me with three Germans on it. They ignored me and kept going. My heart pounded audibly in my chest,' he later told Emile.

The two spies moved with caution to their meeting spot, looked around again for any evidence of prying eyes, then climbed down to the rocks below with great care, sticking to the previous route exactly. Louis felt around in the growing darkness for his signalling torch in its hiding place. For several seconds his heart stopped beating as he thought it had been discovered and taken.

'No! Oh here it is. What an idiot to panic. Phew,' he whispered.

They retraced their steps as quietly as they could over the rocks, although they slipped and slid because of the slimy seaweed now moistened by the high tide. The MTB should be there to meet them soon.

Lou signalled the letter R in Morse code as they had been instructed. For three hours they remained on the icy rock ledge, repeatedly sending out the letter R.

There was no sight of the rescue boat. They had a plan in case this happened because of bad weather or unforseen dangers. Lou once again hid his torch in a roll of cardboard under the heath, then they made the arduous climb back to the top. Emile had borrowed a bicycle and had hidden it in a copse for a contingency. Louis went in the opposite direction to a different planned safe house.

For the next two nights the same scenario: the same procedure – signals and no response.

'My arms ache from holding this torch and the tension is killing me.' Lou's hoarse voice was shaky.

'Oh my God, they aren't coming Louis. We're stranded here. Those lousy bastards have let us down. They had better have a very good reason.'

'Well, all the beaches do look similar to mainlanders.'

'No, not that surely. Perhaps it was too dangerous, German boats or searchlights. I need some of that brandy you polished off.' He forced a smile. 'Now what are we going to do?'

CHAPTER 17
December 24th

'Life was so different this time last year.' Christmas was now a confusing and melancholy time for the three. They were used to having Mummy buying the food and presents and organising everything else – making the house festive, sending notes to people or messaging them online. Depression, like a mist, swamped their motivation. Neither Nathan nor Meadow knew where to begin. So they didn't. Nathan just bought a few things as they caught his eye, for Nan, Gran, and the kids. There was no one to mind the child so Meddie couldn't help her dad to buy presents. She was itching to go shopping. *It's my mother's fault that this Christmas will be a lousy one.*

On Christmas Eve, they had their yearly celebrations with Nan – Nathan's mother, Liz, and usually Great Grandma. She was to be there this year too, but they had been told she was unusually subdued and finding it difficult to get around. 'Remember she is ninety-three now.'

This year, Nathan's brother Brett and his wife would be there. Meadow went up to Nan's front door with armfuls of white stock and green chrysanthemums, nearly a metre tall, she thought. They obscured her head so Nan had a problem knowing who it was. Felix jumped up from the corner of the steps where he'd been hiding and yelled, 'Happy Cwistmas!'

'You daft ha'porth,' she said and gave him a huge hug.

It was empty without Sarah, but Papa and his girl had prearranged being especially vocal to dull the effect. He had bought a couple of bottles of Christmas Champagne, and sparkling grape juice for the kids. Meadow made sure everyone felt included and special by repeatedly checking everyone's glasses were full.

They exchanged gifts under the lopsided Christmas tree, giving hugs and thanks at the same time. The Barclays hadn't discussed how much to spend on each other or how many gifts to give the adults. It had become much too tedious and expensive, anyway they were too disorganised to get something for everyone. The children were exempt from this. So they made quite a haul.

'Oh cool,' Felix said to nearly everything he opened. He ripped the pretty paper into bits to get at the secret inside, frantic and tense, almost crying if the package was hard to undo. He held up his cheek to be kissed by the giver.

Great Gran had tried to buy gifts but found the trudging around shops too much for her weakening legs, so had put ten pounds in envelopes for each of them. She had forgotten about Brett's wife, as usual, who simply smiled at the error.

'Funny sort of Christmas this is,' the old lady said, her eyes focussing on her inner world, scenes she remembered of madcap Christmases past. Brett pulled down the sides of his mouth and distorted his face when he noticed her vacant expression.

Meadow gave a gift to Brett's wife first and then sedately sat on the blue carpet to unwrap her presents carefully so as to keep the paper and ribbons for another time.

'Just what Sarah did,' whispered Nathan to Liz. Meadow's favourite gift, although she didn't say so, was a jewellery box made of carved wood with velvet-lined drawers and a little musical piano that played when she opened the lid. 'Oh, I love it.'

'I'm glad you like it,' said Nan. 'I thought it might be too young for you.'

'No, not at all it's adorable and I have quite a few things to put in it now. I might have some of Mum's jewels if we can't find her.'

It went a little quiet for a few minutes, so Nathan suggested Meadow help Liz to dish up the food.

Nan had a little miniature Nativity scene on the bookcase. The child went over and stared at it.

'Baby Jesus looks like a girl – He's got red lips.' Then the silver crackers on the table caught his eye. He was desperate to pull them. He sidled up to them and slid one down into his lap.

'No, wait you sneaky boy.'

Dinner was glazed ham and hassle-back potatoes, with a variety of colourful vegetables. Dessert was Eton Mess with cream and raspberries.

'Where ever did you get them in the winter?'

Great Grandma was forgotten by the children and Nan had no time to spare on her. The old lady sat gazing around and now and then got up and looked at the gifts, then drifted into a spare bedroom for '40 winks'. Mostly she was ignored. *She's had her life*, Elizabeth thought, *now it's the young ones' turn.*

After the feast, while the children were busy with their presents and Brett and his wife were clearing up, Nathan asked his mother 'Please tell me about Dad. I know I've never been very interested before, but everything's changed now. I want to learn as much as I can. I haven't had time either or well, actually, I've been too busy to listen. What was he like? What did Dad have for interests?'

'I'm sorry to say this Nat, but as you know, Dad was a very independent man, cold and unemotional towards me and you children. He was a hard worker for a few years but then got hooked on gambling and wasting money. Stupid things like horse racing and lotteries, always hoping for the big win. He loved playing poker with friends. He had barely any relationship with me towards the end, in terms of companionship or intimacy. And no time for you kids. He was addicted to the hope of winning. He started lying to me and going out at unusual hours of the night. It just tore me apart. I had no control of my life. What could I do?'

Nathan gave her a cuddle while a few tears sprang into her eyes. 'This is becoming a daily occurrence in our house.' They both laughed a little.

Nathan had been broken by his father's disinterest – he dealt with it by perfectionist tallying, useful in his accountancy position.

Oh, so I reacted against what my dad did, as children do, and became very careful with money and very reliable as a man, but I haven't learnt anything much about the emotional side of myself.

'Tell me more Mum, please.'

'You were shocked at your father's behaviour even when you were a young boy. You were a quiet, diligent pupil and always did your homework without me having to nag you. You and your brother were my consolation. But as you know, Brett didn't keep that up.'

This little chat explained many things to Nathan. His slowness to open up, his resistance to risk – the reasons he shut down Sarah's dreams, and partly his attitude to women. He'd watched the way his mother was bullied and despised her for it. It was Meadow who was opening his eyes to positive female attributes. And it was Felix who was causing her to blossom.

The child pointed to an old discoloured photo of Nathan as a boy. 'Felix, Felix, me.'

'Yes, you looked just like him at that age.'

Nathan's father had died of a heart attack when the boy was only twelve, so he'd taken on board the responsibility of the man of the house. His brother was two years younger than him and so he felt the obligation to protect his mother and keep his younger sibling in order too. He was angry with Brett when he didn't study hard at school and often spoke very sternly to him about his duty to their mum. Brett hated this – it was just like his cold Dad all over again. They had big rows and even punched each other a few times.

'You're not my parent! You're only two years older than me. And you are so boring – always doing the correct thing. Do you think this is helping Mum?' He'd looked at Nat with malice, his grey eyes narrowed, his mouth sulky. They hadn't been friends for years. But when Brett heard about the hard time his brother and the children were having, he'd rung Nat several times to offer help.

'We missed that wonderful time we could have had being boys together, all because of our stupid attitudes. We can make up for it a bit, old boy.'

Brett and his wife had driven a long way so they could all be together at Christmas. He wanted to support Nathan during this difficult time. He remembered how fatherly Nathan had tried to be to him when their dad had died even though he had resented it at the time. Brett called Nathan over with a jerk of his head. 'Can we talk for a few minutes?'

'Sure, Bud.'

'I hope you don't take what I'm going to say in the wrong way Nat, but I don't want to see you hurt anymore.'

'Fine, fire away.'

'Well, it's about Sarah. I heard you are thinking of going to Spain to see if you can find her.'

'Who told you that?'

'Meadow.'

Nathan shrugged and rolled his eyes.

'But what if she doesn't want to be found? Of course she may have come to a sad ending, I know. But I'm worried you might get your hopes up and then suffer another trauma. You see Nat, if she has actually left you, well, that's a dirty trick. And she's not worth taking back even if you do track her down. If she's run off once, what's to stop her doing it again? She's unreliable. I think it's my turn to be big brother now and I really don't think you should ever trust her again, supposing you find her.'

'Thanks for your concern, little brother. I'll think about it seriously.'

Jess had gone to her elderly parents' home for Christmas but was miffed that Nathan hadn't invited her to go with him to Elizabeth's. *Why wasn't I invited after all I've done for that family? I bet it was that jealous girl's fault.*

CHAPTER 18
Failure

The two courageous young men found their individual paths back to the Sampsons again. The young spies realised finally and absolutely no one was coming to rescue them. Actually, an attempt had been made; a captain had been put ashore, in his military uniform, at Le Gouffre. He had climbed up the cliff path, which he knew well, but it took him longer this time – he was wary of mines. His plan was to make contact with Louis and Emile. Disaster: At the top in pitch-blackness, the captain tripped and stumbled into a German trench. He landed with a crack as he fell on an ammunition case. A torch shone in his face. He was a prisoner – fortunately not in mufti.

When the young officers heard that the captain had been taken prisoner and that he was their lone rescuer, the reality of their position seemed doubly hopeless. Anxiety crept into their thoughts with its threatening images of death.

'Now if we are captured, we will definitely be shot as spies, Louis.'

'Yup, we have no way off this island. We'll have to do some hard thinking.'

'I heard from my uncle the Germans have become highly suspicious some service personnel are still here.'

'Well we know a few military didn't manage to go with the evacuation.'

'Also Mr Beauvoir was informed the Germans intend making house to house searches this week.'

'Now what?'

'Well I think my friend the groundsman at the cricket pavilion, Frank, would help us.'

'At Elizabeth College?'

They thanked the Sampsons warmly for putting themselves in real danger for their sakes, then the pair, in solo fashion, made their way to the sports ground. They were permitted to hide there as they had hoped.

'It's safe to hide in here for a few days.'

'Anyway, thank you, old chap.' He nodded at Frank.

Frank unlocked the door and re-locked it when they'd gone in. He looked around him in every direction. Put the key into his pocket and sauntered off humming *Jeepers Creepers.*

'We'll have to keep our heads down below the window sills and crawl like crabs so no Jerry sees any movement.'

'That won't be so difficult upstairs because of the balcony railings.'

'What's that animal noise?'

'Just my stomach howling with hunger!'

'Lying here on the floor, I can see all our old sports team's names and the captains'. Look up there Louis, see your name – swimming – cricket. As we have nothing to do or read, I'm going to memorise the team members and the trophies to stop myself going insane with boredom.'

'Do you think someone will bring us something to eat?'

'Maybe not. Hope so.'

'At least we can crawl to the tap for water after it gets dark.'

Alice's Diary

Both Mother and I had the feeling that the boys were still on the island. We couldn't sleep for excitement. A report reached me that the boys had indeed been unsuccessful in their get-away. I found out from Daddy where they were hiding and cycled over straightaway with two grey woollen blankets squashed and tied tightly then hidden under newspapers in my bicycle basket. I rode a roundabout route to confuse anyone, neighbour or German who might be watching. I can't trust anyone but my special friends. I took the hideaways bread and Bovril this morning, but will have to vary the way and the times over the next few days. Poor Louis was ravenously hungry and they are so cold in that old wooden pavilion. They can't stay there – at any minute they could be discovered. This is no schoolboy adventure, every hour in hiding is adding to their danger.

'Oh Emile, you look worried and exhausted.' Alice looked from him to Louis who was curled up on a blanket on the floor of the pavilion.

'Yes, look at him asleep in his clothes, he's dead beat – all in. Of course we can't stay here, like this.'

'The house to house searches haven't happened you know – you can both go to your parents' houses.'

'They will be horrified. They don't know we're still on the island.'

'Yes, probably they will be shocked, because I've told no one, only Frank, my dad and I know you're here.'

Alice's Diary
Louis told me his mother fainted when he walked in the door. Emile's hugged him passionately but then felt sudden terror and rushed him upstairs to his own bedroom, pulled the curtains then talked to him for hours.

'What will we do now?'

September 10th. The Germans have tightened their control. Other islanders have been caught trying to escape. Eight in fact did escape in a small boat. So risky – they could have been shot out of the water. Haven't heard if they arrived safely in England.

More German officers have been put on guard.

I took some books to the Robilliard's – Lou had asked me for something to read. He seems quite happy. I promised him I would never say a word about where he is and crossed my heart and hoped to die and saluted him. He laughed out loud – good to see him smile. I told him he was getting too careless about his safety. He said he'd have to move around a bit and could he stay with us for a while. Oh so excited.

Even Mum and Dad like the plan. Emile will go to Amy's house.

October 1st. The brave lads have been on the island for four weeks already – their parents need a break from all the tension and fear of discovery. Lou stayed with us for two happy weeks, but it's clear the boys can't hide any longer. They are well known on the island. Many people already know where they are holed up. It would only take one collaborator to snitch and then it would be all up.

Monday. Mrs Robilliard is showing signs of a nervous break-down – shaking and recurrent headaches. She may be losing control.

Friday. Mrs R did lose her perspective of the situation. She bragged to the state's supervisor, her friend, about the presence of the two commandoes. This was a huge error. It was his duty to report to Major Shirrif H.M. Procureur as head of the island. He had made a sworn arrangement with the occupying power to tell the truth about all the Guernsey happenings.

He himself was under threat of severe punishment if he didn't keep to his promise. Major Shirrif almost convulsed when he heard about the two lieutenants.

'Oh, I don't want to know,' he replied to the state supervisor. 'I wish you had never told me.' For several nights he lay awake, deeply disturbed and wracking his brains at to what to do. He was a lawyer before being the head of the committee set up to oversee all the legal and military problems on the island. He was used to negotiating and solving complex problems, but he was stumped this time.

Then a thought appeared amongst the confusion. He would visit the German Commandant, Major Brandt, and say that there may be several Armed Forces Personnel still on the island and that if he would grant an amnesty, they would hand themselves in.

The Major might agree to this plan as he wouldn't be wanting any secret forces in hiding, much better if they came out into the open so the occupiers could keep them under guard.

Major Shirrif went directly to the German Commandant to discuss the position of servicemen possibly still being left on the island. Of course he did not mention the unfortunate spies.

He saluted the German Commandant, who saluted in turn.

'I would like to discuss a problem I think we may have.'

'Certainly. Take a seat please.'

'I would like to suggest something which would benefit both of us.'

'What exactly is this about?'

'Well, I have heard from a source that there may be servicemen still on the island. They didn't get away with the others when they were evacuated and now they are trapped here.'

'I see. Go on.'

Well, would it be possible for them to hand themselves in, and any civilians that may have sheltered them, if there was an amnesty, a promise that they would be treated as prisoners of war and that their assistants would not be prosecuted? You see it can't be good for your forces to have these people on the island. It would clear the whole matter up for you and me.'

'What exactly do we, the occupying power, get out of this?'

'A good name, a reputation for fairness and the knowledge that there could be no terror attack from the remaining personnel, if there are any.'

'Let me think it over please.' The commandant walked around the room, his hands behind his back, an expression of total concentration on his face, his mouth firm but his brows and eyes moved continuously.

After five minutes he returned to his chair.

'Well, if this deals with a potential problem, I can see the benefit.'

'The amnesty will have to be printed in the newspaper sir, so that it will reach everyone on the island.'

'Yes, when?'

The notice was to be printed in the Guernsey Press in English and German. It was printed on the 19th of October and then again on the final date, the 21st of October 1940.

It was genius of Major Shirrif to add his little clause in brackets, knowing the truth full well.

Members of the British Armed Forces (if such there be) in hiding in Guernsey and persons assisting them must report at the Island Police Station, St Peter Port at the latest by 6pm Monday the 21st of October 1940. Members of the British Armed Forces obeying this order will be treated as prisoners of war and no measures will be taken against persons who have assisted them.

Any member of the BAFs who may be found after this time must expect to be treated as an agent of an enemy power and dealt with accordingly. Also all those who have assisted in hiding such persons will have to take the full consequences of their actions.

Der Deutsche Kommandant Signed Major Brandt
Signed Major Shirrif – President of the Controlling
Committee of the States Of Guernsey.

But could they trust the Germans to keep their word? They had no choice.

CHAPTER 19

When the boy woke up on Christmas morning at about 5 am, he crawled to the end of his bed and felt around for his special decorated stocking pinned to the end board. He couldn't see much. It was still black outside.

He put his nose inside the big red sock, sniffed, then held the shapes of little gifts he found. Some were chocolate. He pulled the wrapper off one that smelled sweet and popped it in his mouth. Then felt for a similar package and repeated this three times. When he climbed out of bed about an hour later, he went to Meadow's room and stood quietly by her bed.

She opened her eyes then screamed at the strange little boy with blood all over his face. It was chocolate and raspberry toffee – she could see that when the light was on. She hauled him into the bathroom and washed his face, then Felix climbed into bed with her and helped her unpack her stocking. Dad had done his best, but he had no idea really what to get his maturing daughter.

Felix and Meadow laughed together at the pink and melon coloured lip-gloss shaped like a fox and a badger, other cheap gifts: the magic tricks, fake spiders, fake fingers and yet more chocolate. Felix lay back in her bed his head on the pillow. He rolled his eyes back and lifted his chin, frowning.

'Can't see my eyes. Why can't see my eyes?'

'Crazy boy, no one can. Here, look in the mirror.' They both peered in and giggled themselves to tears.

They were going to Sarah's mum's house for Christmas lunch as usual. Looking out the kitchen window, Nathan said, 'Hey it's snowing a smidgen.'

They could scarcely believe it – a sort of white Christmas. Snowflakes fell like goose-down onto the shrubs under Felix's window. He couldn't wait to get outside. The children examined each flake very closely to see if they could find any alike. 'Look at this one.' But the tiny stars melted in their hands before they could notice the various differences in design. The child looked down at his favourite plant, lamb's ears – so woolly and soft. He patted a little clump, but they were glass, iced up and frozen.

Felix in his blue puffer jacket with the hood up, Meadow with her light brown hair tucked under a cerise crocheted beanie against the backdrop of white, looked a picture. So Nathan got out his camera – digital but not the latest model, he would never splurge on something unnecessary, and snapped several images of the kids laughing and throwing tiny snowballs the size of peas. *I must record these days, it might be important for them in the future, or if we find Sarah, or they get a stepmother, they will need to remember this time when the two of them became so very close.*

When they arrived at Gran's, the children tumbled out of the car. They raced to the door and fought over pressing the bell first.

'Happy Christmas you two!'

Felix ran inside. 'We go to Spain find Mamma soon.' No mention of this had been made to Gran! Felix had heard snippets of Meadow's ideas as she talked to Papa. He looked at Gran, his eyes bright, his face excited.

'Not until Easter,' said the girl.

Nathan winked at her as a signal. 'Let's not shatter his dream. We haven't even finalised this, Mum. He's just heard us talking about possibilities.'

Gran still apologised continually for her errant daughter and hardly considered any other possibility for her disappearance.

'We are going to do our best to find what's happened to her.'

'But what if you find something dreadful? What would poor Felix do?'

'He has us Anne, don't worry.'

But Nathan thought back to yesterday when the kids had found a blackbird in the garden, stiff with its legs in the air. Felix had sobbed until they had to threaten him with time-out in order to stop the hysterical wailing and kicking legs.

If he cried about a dead bird, what state will he be in if we find Sarah's body?

During Christmas lunch, their traditional roast chicken, (because the children hated turkey) crammed full of chestnut stuffing, they pulled more tacky crackers, with old jokes that they already knew the answers to, containing horrible plastic animals and garish coloured hats that it was an obligation to wear. Felix's unstoppable talking and the giggling from the children over absolutely nothing helped the small gathering to forget the missing person.

No one mentioned Sarah for fear it would bring a morose atmosphere into what should be a happy family day. The four listened for ten minutes to an old Christmas album of seasonal songs that they'd heard many times. The truth was they were bored. Outgoing Sarah was missing. She would have known what to do to keep the day alive. It fell to Meadow to step in the gap, and she brought up the topic deliberately unmentioned.

'Can we have another look at some photos of when Mamma was a girl? I want to see if she looked like me.'

'Well, yes, I'll get the albums – but I think you do look a lot like her.'

The girl sniffed the old musty books and flipped through the first few pages.

'Felix doesn't look at all like her as a baby and it isn't just that he's a boy.'

Sarah appeared a wistful, vacant-eyed little child, her hair in pigtails, her clothes ill-fitting.

'Were you poor, Gran?'

'Yep, we had very little of anything. That husband of mine spent all his money on booze and did nothing to help around home. Not like your dad.'

Meadow looked up at Nathan, winked and tugged his jumper.

'Sit down Dad, let's look at these.'

Nathan glanced at Felix to check if he was OK. The child was fiddling with the box of new toys he'd just received at Gran's but he quite preferred the old things that were kept at her house for the days when he visited, and was comparing them. He was absorbed.

'Oh, she looks doleful.' Nat had seen these photos before but was much more interested now. He might find some signs or indications of why Sarah had deserted them. *Well heck, she might not have.* He butted into his own thoughts.

'Was she a melancholy child?'

'Some of the time – but she had big dreams. Even when she was nine or ten she knew she didn't want a life like I had. She was going to study and make something of herself.'

Nathan stared into the air, his mouth half open.

'She called me all sorts of names when I got down about our situation – names that hurt a lot. She couldn't understand why I didn't pull myself up and change our life. 'Why does Dad have to affect us so much?' she often said.

'Later, as you know, I became clinically depressed. The therapist said I'd been discouraged once too often by the promises my husband had made and then broken.

I just gave up. Sarah couldn't fathom why I didn't try harder for her and her brother's sake. When she was about thirteen, she threw all my anti-depressants down the toilet and told me to stand on my own two feet.'

Meadow looked afar off. *That's almost the same age as me.*

The inherited problems passed down the line and the same rejection and result were foisted on the children. Pain circuits form patterns in the brain, new research has discovered. These become automatic responses – somehow these patterns are passed down to the children. Nurture not completely to blame any longer.

Sarah had a much older brother who had left home at sixteen and made his own life in Australia. Gran rarely heard from him. That was hard, especially now her daughter was missing. It seemed her children only knew how to run. *The reasons lay hidden in their souls. But I'm sure it's their childhood influences, both James' and mine,* she reflected.

But Sarah's brother did ring because it was Christmas Day. Everyone had to go to the phone and wish him Merry Christmas even though they had only heard about him and seen photos of when he was a boy. Maybe they would meet Uncle Jeff one day. He asked lots of questions about his sister.

'Is there any news? What was she like before she left? Have you found any clues at all?

'Now I'm old,' he joked, 'in my mid-forties, family seems to mean much more to me. If you find her, I will come over for the funeral.'

That was good, thought Nathan, but she could have used a brother when all was well.

Gran went over to Felix to give him a little pat on the back for behaving so well. He stood up and looked her closely in the face. 'You look spooky. You have cracks in your eyes,' he said, then gave her a quick hug and went back to the toy box. She made a half laughing smile and looked tenderly at him.

As they returned home that night, Nathan gave Meadow a quick look as she walked under the hall light. *She has lipstick on, oh my God what next? Wherever did she…* Then Sarah appeared in his sight, almost touchable in reality. He couldn't hold the image of course. But he could whisper to it. 'Sarah, your daughter needs you right now. I miss you so much.'

That night Felix called out, 'Papa, Daddy.'

'What's the trouble now, little man?'

'Someone's wet my bed.'

'Mm, I wonder who that could have been?'

CHAPTER 20
January

'Daddy, "we cannot become what we want to be, fearless and brave, by staying where we are." That's what the headmistress said today in assembly anyway. You agree, don't you?'

Meadow had convinced Nathan that the three of them would definitely be able to have the trip to Spain. They needed a holiday. The weather would be lovely at Easter and she could take one extra week off school, it wasn't yet the year for her big exams, so it wouldn't hurt. In the February holiday there wouldn't be enough time to travel far. Gran had said she would live in for that time so Nathan could still go to work.

Nathan had holiday leave owing to him. Although he'd taken some time off when it was half term, he had accumulated so much by being what Sarah called a workaholic, a job addict, that he could have the time away without jeopardising his position in the company. What was there to lose? It was all dovetailing nicely. They got quite excited about the plans when they began reading about Madrid and the surrounding areas.

'Madrid at Easter,' they read, 'is quieter than usual as it is the important holy holiday week for the Spanish.' Loads of locals left the city then. Travelling around would be much easier. No big crowds. But looking online they saw the hugeness of the city and it's hundreds of attractions. Fifty museums! They wouldn't even take Felix to one. He would squirm. 'There's a world-famous zoo, Dad, with three thousand animals and a dolphin show, and chocolate shops by the dozen. There is a drum parade called Tamborrada. Felix would love that. And there's a cable car.'

They had decided to take the child with them even though leaving him at Gran's would be easier.

'How could the little mite cope without you and me, there is no one left. We'll have to take him. Anyway, it'll be more fun.'

Nathan looked over at the child and grabbed him by the collar of his shirt, lifted him up then threw him onto the sofa. Meadow threw herself down there too so they could both be tickled until they screamed for mercy.

'We are going to be a mini detective agency, the three of us,' Meadow managed to say after she got her breath back.

They hit a few problems in their planning to be sleuths though. The city was so enormous they wouldn't know who to show the picture of Sarah to. They could ask at the airport, car hire, train station, but who would remember her? It could be months ago, if they had seen her at all. And they couldn't speak Spanish. 'How could we possibly show the photo to hundreds of different people? She might have left the city weeks before. The picture will not be much use.'

'Meadow, we will have to hire a local private detective, either an Englishman who speaks fluent Spanish or a Spaniard who speaks English.'

'But the cost Dad?'

Nathan had become more liberal lately with his savings, but he wasn't at the stage to blow it all on something fruitless.

'I will make some enquiries here at home first.' *We might have to content ourselves with just being in a place Mum had been in. Maybe died in,* he thought.

Nathan was deeply heartsore but not an outwardly emotional man. He had managed to cry several times though not with much drama and nearly always in solitude. Meadow wondered if he was telling her everything he knew. Perhaps he had a secret he was keeping from her, a secret about Mamma or his own secret.

In the evening when it was just the two of them up, 'Dad, you know,' she said, 'you don't seem to be really upset about Mum.'

'I can't see any point in giving in to sadness. I need to keep going at work, I have practical things to do, like earning money and paying the bills and I have to stay positive for you and Felix.'

I wonder if it's Jess? 'Actually Dad, you know it's he who is keeping us hopeful I think. He has been staring out of his bedroom window, just looking at the street and the gate as if he expects Mum to turn up any time. He doesn't get upset; he just looks and then after a while starts playing again. It's as if he knows something we don't know. Could that be true?'

'I hope so, Sweetie.'

'Do you mean Dad, that if Mum was found and wanted to come home to us, you'd have her back? Just like that.' Meadow opened her eyes and mouth wide. 'After all the misery she's caused us.'

'It might not be entirely her fault, you know, Pet. We must consider that.'

Now Meadow really thought there must be a romance going on between her dad and Jess. *What does he mean not entirely her fault, what has he done he isn't telling me?* She felt suspicious of him, but that was disloyal to her now much dearer Papa and she felt guilty.

'Dad, you know how we've talked about how Felix handles our present life better than we do, and that his child brain is so brilliant at not worrying or dreaming about horrible futures? Well, I think we should let him guide us as to how to treat Mummy, you know, if we find her alive.'

'Really Pet? Well, if you're happy with that approach, it makes sense to me. He was the closest to her because he is so young so, OK, let's take our lead from him.'

It was a chicken's way out, but they were emotionally exhausted and Felix had become quite the guide to them in so many other ways.

CHAPTER 21
Surrender

Alice's Diary

*The notice was published in the island paper again on the 21st
of October. The German Major gave his word that any members
of the British Armed forces who surrendered by 6.00 pm on the
day of the 21st would not be shot. No measures will be taken
against anyone who had assisted in hiding any personnel.*

*On the appointed day, the 21st, I sat in my office not able to
concentrate on what I was meant to be doing. I imagined the
boys and their parents on the walk to give themselves up; the
trepidation, the anxiety on their faces.*

*How loud the clock was and so slowly went the minutes until
the hour they had planned for the hand-over. I went home,
thoughts racing in my head. I needed news. Daddy arrived and
told us the boys were in the Guernsey prison. They were OK and
had a full tray of food. Oh thank You.*

*A number of servicemen surrendered themselves. Emile's par-
ents and the Robilliards had walked down to the office, at
separate times to allay suspicion, to hand themselves over to the
occupying power. Both Lou and Emile wore battle dress. Major
Shirrif had got hold of two uniforms from the stockpile stored by
the harbour, in the hope that the Germans would treat then as
bona fide prisoners of war – a gesture carried out at great risk to
himself and his family.*

The boys were to give their rank and number but nothing else. But the next day, Lou was taken to Fort George and questioned continuously for hours.

Louis' Notes

At midnight the Germans stopped the questioning as the inter-rogators were too exhausted to continue. Why are they doing this to me? Do they suspect something? Has someone snitched? The next day the inquisition continued, this time by Herr Stute.

'Why have you come? Who is involved? When did you arrive? What are you really doing here?' The same questions again and again fired rapidly at me. Emile, I found out afterwards, was treated in the same way in a separate location. For me, the questions continued – they just didn't let up. My eyes flickered with exhaustion. My mouth was dry, my head exploding. During a short break I was allowed a breath of fresh air. Oh heaven.

A civilian on the road, who I didn't recognise, ran over to me and said softly, 'Your parents, Alice and her parents, Emile's girlfriend and his mother and father and the groundsman had better be careful.'

How on earth did he know anything? A complete stranger. It was obvious that someone had blurted everything and certainly not kept to the story we had planned. Either that or there was a double agent. I was worried to death then. The Germans certainly did not seem to be keeping their promises. Were we mad to trust them? It had all been so carefully negotiated, made public and signed.

Emile and I were hauled before a German Court Martial. A very polished and exacting judge arrived and interrogated us again. The same questions, like nightmares repeated.

The doors burst open, two of their officers rushed in. 'You have been here a long time. Why didn't you tell us?'

Two days later we were court-martialed again. I sat opposite the judge. A guard sat beside me.

This time the German judge said, 'You are a dirty common garden spy. I find you guilty and sentence you to death by firing squad.'

Emile was marched in. I signalled to him by pulling my finger across my throat. It's all up. The end.

The Germans were very professional and stuck to legal protocol exactly. They wanted to do everything perfectly to show what a great society it would be when they were in complete control of Great Britain.

The sentence had to be confirmed by an even higher German authority in Berlin.

Discipline in the German army was very severe. They dare not break the rules by not following protocol. The punishment they dreaded most was being sent to the Russian Front.

CHAPTER 22
Mid-January

Walking home from school, Meadow stopped to stare at some bare trees. Felix was yanking her hand,

'Come on Med!'

'Wait, be patient. I'm looking at something.' She stepped back and tilted her head upward.

The bare trees – the skeleton trees with still branches, immovable in the cold winds – there are no leaves – how could they move? She felt her soul was like a bare tree, dead, immovable, only worse. With each remembrance of her mother's desertion a piece of protective bark was stripped away. She could hear the clunk as the pieces fell to the ground. It was nearly all gone now – just a hard shiny trunk remained. Nothing could dent it. Bark was soft and impressionable, you could cut initials into it, but the core was impenetrable. Nothing would hurt her anymore. She hardened her face and bit her teeth together. She and the child walked on.

When Nathan arrived home, the girl noticed he had on the same shirt again.

'Papa, you've worn that shirt for days without number. You're getting whiffy.' She waved her hand in front of her nose.

'Oh my goodness, how shameful. Mumma kept us in good nick – it's hideous without her in every way.' *How dependent I was – still am.*

'Bath time, Felix.'

Felix stood next to the bath. He had managed to wrench off his jeans, his shirt and his jumper, but he stood shivering in just his shoes and socks and his underpants, his little white chest accentuated by the still lightly tanned legs from summer. Meadow choked, laughing at the ridiculous image until the tears ran down her cheeks.

When he finally got in the water his entire body was submerged head to toes. He wasn't as long as the bath and could swish from one end to the other, causing copious amounts of water to gush out all over the floor. Nathan soaped his hair, which was quite longish now, with no mother to take him for a hair cut, and pulled it up into a very long peak. He looked as mad as a cockatoo.

Outside, a winter storm was raging. Trees were being blown about and bits of them, little branches and twigs, were hurling themselves at the bathroom window. It was cosy, all three of them in a small, steamy, water-laden room, joking and teasing each other lovingly.

A crack of thunder was heard quite a long way off, then another louder and coming closer. Felix looked out of the bathroom window at the same time that a huge fork of lightning flashed from sky to earth. He stiffened and sat up. Meadow counted one; two, then a huge roar of thunder shook the house. Felix screamed and jumped out, dripping water all over Nathan and hung onto him. The room lit up like a bomb had exploded and the next clap was like cannon fire. Even Meadow ran to Dad. The three made a pathetic tableau of damp figures clinging and dripping.

'Want Mamma.'

'We'll be fine, it's only a storm. It'll be over in a minute.'

They towel-dried themselves and got Felix into his pyjamas. It took a while to settle him down. Dad and daughter took turns reading the child comforting stories – *Maggie in the Snow* and *Harry the Dirty Dog*. He wanted Mamma several more times before he went to sleep.

Meadow looked at Nathan. He looked relaxed and happy. *What's wrong with him that he doesn't need to find out about Mamma? Felix and I are desperate to know.* Her stomach tightened.

'I think we should speed up our plans to trace her, don't you?' The girl didn't say Sarah or Mamma. She assumed her father would be thinking the same thoughts that she was.

Nathan thought logically about hurrying the plans along. He didn't know what to do because his brain hadn't sorted everything into boxes yet. He searched through the compartments in his mind where he filed his thoughts.

Need for adventure was stored in the *High Risk* file – too costly.

Need to Pursue / Go after was filed under: *Done – He'd won her hadn't he? And his position at work was satisfying.*

Need to rescue female in distress was in the *Urgent* file – but Meadow's name was listed not Sarah's. Nathan raised his head and looked up, tapping the table with his fingers, he leant over, grabbed his paper diary – much more user-friendly and concrete – he wrote: *High Risk – costly – trip to find Sarah – worth it.*

He made a *To Do box* and added *Pursue Mummy – good investment.*

In the *Urgent* box – *Rescue two damsels* – Sarah and Meadow, and one small boy and me.

He could see it clearly now it was in front of him on paper, labelled. He highlighted the most important words in neon orange.

January 28th. The police rang again. They had some devastating news. A body had been found that matched the description of the missing woman. There was no identification on the body. She had been dead for several days. They couldn't find the birthmark – the neck was too damaged. *Oh my God, we should have gone looking sooner. Sarah, I'm so very sorry.*

At last Nathan was able to let go and grieve. His sobs so deep and loud, though he was in the bathroom with the door locked, were unmistakable. He couldn't hide them from Meadow.

Finally Dad has realised – he can't bury it anymore – His heart has broken – that's a good thing I think. She rushed upstairs and knocked gently on the bathroom door.

'Daddy, Daddy, I love you, let me help.'

That girl, he thought, *what would I have done without her? She's so very young. Why does she have to suffer like this?*

'Wait a minute Med.'

He waited to get back some of his self control. He slowed his breathing down. In a few minutes, after blowing his nose and washing his face, he opened the door. His daughter ran straight into his arms. This just brought the weeping back, now both of them clung like lovers finding one another after months of separation.

'Has anything happened Dad?'

'Well, yes Sweetheart, the police rang to say they have found a body.'

'But Dad it might not be her, it might not be her!' Loud wails shook her little frame.

Nathan had to drag himself to the police station and leave brother and sister watching a fairy-tale-happy DVD on their big TV. The child didn't notice Meadow's red eyes as he laughed and jumped onto her lap, his eyes riveted on the animation.

Nathan printed off some extra photos of Sarah so they could be faxed to the Madrid police.

'I won't be long.'

The body was in a small gully on the outskirts of Toledo, about 80km from Madrid. He hadn't asked how the person had died. Those morbid details could come later if it proved to be Sarah. Dental records were the most reliable way of matching a body with a person. He had to tell the police the name and contact number of the dentist and look at the gruesome official images to see if he immediately recognised his wife.

Driving to the station alone, he felt utterly bereft. He stared at the empty seat beside him and called out her name in the air. 'Oh please, it can't be her.'

I will have to change our plans for the Easter trip to Madrid and fly there immediately if the dental records prove it is her. As he got out of the car, his legs almost gave way and a wave of nausea swept through his belly.

They always need a formal identification. I can't expect her mother to do it.

The photos looked a bit like Sarah, but the body had been found several days after the death. It looked as if it had been beaten. The features were bloated, bruised and blue. She didn't look clearly like anyone.

They waited three days for the dental records to be sent over and matched. Those three days were like no others in their misery. They were fraught with outbursts of emotion and tears. Felix climbed up on Meadow's knee and hugged her. He cuddled Daddy too when he saw his wet eyes and his sorrowful expression.

'Mamma home soon,' he said.

Where did that come from? Why now at this dreadful time?

Tension and fear played havoc with the girl and her father. They jumped when the phone rang. Now it sounded like an alarm, repetitive and piercing. 'I hate that ring tone Dad. Can we change it? My heart almost stops.' They whispered near-silent words to each other. They squeezed each other's hands as they passed. But the child sweetly played on, laughing and shouting, sometimes being disobedient, all as usual. Of course they hadn't told him anything that was going on. Now they looked at him with deeper pity. He was a lost boy now. They wanted to wrap him up in a soft baby blanket and keep him from sadness.

They tried to brighten up for the child's sake. Making conversation for the sake of covering the dread. It was impossible.

The dental records didn't match. It wasn't Sarah.

The crazy joy that ensued after the news was as emotional as the sorrow had been. The threesome jumped, yelled and danced like young puppies. They put on some dance music, the Bee Gees' *Staying Alive* and leapt about with relief. Felix had no idea why this celebration was happening, but he enjoyed it. He jumped rhythmically, swirled and sprung at an intense speed, shouting 'Staying alive,' until his cheeks glowed. 'Gen Daddy gen.' But they were wrung out and needed a diversion. They decided to go out and buy takeaways as a treat. They could have anything they wanted.

It wasn't Mamma.

CHAPTER 23
October 1940

Alice's Diary

The boys have been locked up in the Guernsey jail awaiting the Berlin decisions.

Went to town and bought gloves for Lou to keep him warm if he were sent to France – knowing their freezing winters. I wrote a letter, rolled it up and inserted it into one of the fingers.

On my way back from the prison where I delivered the gloves to the guard, I met Mrs Robilliard. She said that four officers had come to their house last evening and questioned them. So we weren't surprised when we heard a knock on our front door at 9 pm.

'Go to bed, Oswald, and stay there,' Daddy whispered to him.

The knock was repeated. Five Germans stood on the steps.

They wanted each person in a separate room. I was sitting in the lounge by the bright fire, trembling, biting my nails.

I was questioned by three of the Germans. The first said, 'Tell us all you know. What did Louis Robilliard come for?'

'I don't know.'

'Did the lieutenant arrive in uniform?'

'Yes'

'Then what were their military tasks?'

'I'm sorry. I don't know.'

Officer Stute was seated with his feet up on our stool smoking a cigar. In a fit of rage, he kicked the stool over and stood up.

'Did he come to see if the daisies were growing?' he snarled.

'Did you see Louis on the island before September?' I told the lie that we had all previously agreed on – that they had come only three days before.

'You're a liar!'

Who did we think they were? Our story might have been all right for the local police, but these men were professionals, lawyers in civilian life. At 11.30 pm, two Germans escorted me to my room upstairs.

'We are looking for a revolver.' Me? A revolver? How stupid. They took the letters Lou had written to me from England. They said Louis was an agent and I was his contact! Mummy was questioned. She never could lie. She told them the actual date the two spies had landed. It all unravelled from that moment. All the questions were repeated, then Herr Stute said what my mother had told him. I continued to lie.

'Who is the liar? Your mother or you?'

So I owned up – confessed to the actual date of their arrival. The five left at 1.15 am. We rushed into the dining room and started talking the moment they'd gone. Daddy put his finger to his lips.

'Don't say anything.' He was really scared and thought the house might be bugged. We laughed – it was impossible. The Germans had all been questioning us the whole time. Anyway it was too late; part of the truth was out.

Who else knew that mother had told the true date and I had capitulated?

I needed to think more clearly, so I went for a walk along the top of the cliffs, away from the banned area, to let the wind blow fresh in my face to help me think straight and then strode on up towards the inland tracks. The thistles and nettles edged the puddled road. A kestrel came swooping overhead. It must have seen a mouse. I felt just like that tiny creature, scared, maybe spied on, hoping to be hidden from the big enemy bird.

October 24th. We and the Robilliardss, Courbets, Amy and her parents, went to dinner at Travers Hotel for a little celebration now the boys were in custody and we could all relax because the questions were finally over. It was Emile's 21st birthday – of course he couldn't come.

October 25th. Went to the office as usual. At 11.15, a plain-clothes German walked in.

'Come with me, Miss Alice, at once – the commandant has some questions.' Not again!

I got my new swing coat from the rack then followed him to the grey Standard. I sat in front with him. 'Maybe he is taking me to the prison,' I thought as we were driving in that direction. We stopped right in front of it. He got out.

'Follow me.' With a thumping heart I walked toward the prison door. I was led through a passage into a long stone corridor, the echo of our footsteps ominously loud. I was handed over to an officer – Lieutenant Wulf – the head of the Field Police. He wore a high-brimmed German cap on an almost clean-shaven head, which gave him an air of authority. His strong nose, small ice-blue eyes and thin mouth accentuated his power, yet he spoke to me kindly. Then he took me to my cell. In it was a crude wooden bench and a wide wooden plank covered by a straw-filled sack. That was my bed! A very small barred window high above my head let the light stream in in rays. I walked about a bit and even did some quite strenuous ballet exercises. As I sat there on the bench resting, I heard a door creak open down the

passage then the sound of clattering feet went past my door. I peered out of the grill and saw Amy, and then one by one everyone who had been to dinner last night passed my cell. They were rounding us all up! No Mummy. I later found Lt Wulf had been kind to her and let her rest in the fresh air as she had a nosebleed as she often did.

Before it got dark, three grubby blankets and an enamel mug of water were handed to me. I wasn't aware that the key turned in the lock. Claustrophobia doesn't hit you like a cricket ball. It starts minutely, slowly until you are engulfed. It wasn't until the darkness enfolded everything and the sound of St James church struck the hour that I felt trapped, suffocated, a prisoner. Every minute lasted an hour. I cried myself to sleep.

October 26th. In the afternoon, three officers came to me to say that Louis had divulged everything. And that meant I must do the same. I didn't believe them and added nothing more to what I had already told them.

October 27th. Mummy passed my door with her coat and hat on, ready to go home. She waved goodbye but wasn't permitted to speak to me. It was Mum and Dad's silver wedding anniversary, so I was overjoyed about her release.

October 28th. When my mug of water was given to me in the morning, the guard told me my father had been released yesterday too. Happy tears stung my eyes. One by one, again, the others passed my door dressed to return home. 'Why am I still here?' I paced up and down my small floor space reliving my answers, lifting my head to the dingy ceiling in puzzlement. In the future I would tell the whole truth. It was too stressful tell-

ing lies; I couldn't remember all the details I'd told previously. A loud grating sound and the door was unbolted.

'Your turn now.' I put on my shoes and coat and followed the guard. I felt peaceful knowing I only had to tell the truth if they questioned me again. The officers pushed a piece of paper in front of me. They had written down every detail I'd told them. 'Sign it and you are free to go.'

Oh the unutterable joy of being free. I ran almost all the way home, my feet as light as in ballet slippers. Daddy had come to meet me; I flew into his arms.

Getting home was like being covered in a clean, warm eiderdown. We were all just perfectly content and hugging and crying. Oswald had been fetched from his friend's house.

'To be home again with the people I loved most in all the world.'

CHAPTER 24
February 13th

Early spring brought cold sunshine and another sprinkling of snow. The trio huddled together inside. Loneliness lurked in every corner of the lounge where they sat.

Nathan and Meadow watched the child building a garage out of coloured wooden blocks under the side table. He was contentedly making engine sounds and lining up the models by shape and colour then brrrming them as he parked them.

Meadow was anxiously counting the days off on her calendar until the Spain holiday and needed to fill in the time that was going so incessantly slowly.

She joined her delicate hands behind her head, lifted up her hair and let it drop, repeating this movement until all the hair was pulled together into a neat topknot. With one hand she took a shiny vermillion elastic from her pocket and held the infinitesimal bun fast.

'Maybe, Dad, if we got busy with a few projects we could keep the same feeling of purpose and happiness Felix has. Do you think we could do something in the garden? You know, a little vegetable patch or a flowerbed. He would enjoy watching things come up.'

'Great idea, Sweetie. We could start this weekend if the weather stays fine. It's late winter really, not quite spring, not much grows this time of year. You do some research and find what we can plant, eh.'

She found that it was too cold to plant any vegetable seedlings in the garden yet but they could get the soil ready.

It stayed fine enough to go outside, but they had to wear woollen jumpers, and coats of course. In the garden shed Felix found Sarah's sunhat. 'Mummy's hat,' he said and held it up.

'We hope to see Mamma again,' Meadow told him to comfort him. But she no longer dared to believe it. Felix put the wide-brimmed hat on his head. He became very still. With his broad face and the hat sitting low on his brow, Meadow thought his head looked like a flying saucer. She snickered then covered her mouth to stop the child being upset. *Being able to hold or wear an item from a missing person is very comforting, I can see that, almost like touching or smelling them again.*

'Come and help us dig the vegetable patch.'

Nathan remembered with regret that Sarah had suggested digging and planting vegetables at least ten times, but he had only told her it was a waste of time – they were cheaper to buy in the shops. *I pretty much squashed all her little ideas and plans. What if she is lying cold and dead in some Spanish valley like that other woman or on rocks under a cliff, the salt sea water lunging at her broken limbs.*

He had haunting images appear in his mind and a headline: *Body of Beautiful British Woman Found.* He shook his head and forced himself to think of now and the children.

'What sort of vegies would you like to grow?' Nathan asked the child.

'Mummy likes carrots.'

'But what do you like, little one?'

'Me like peas.'

'I've researched that, Dad. We can sow peas in a couple of weeks.'

Meadow was also having grim mind pictures brought on by the sunhat.

Mummy must be dead. Just because she left the country doesn't mean she isn't dead. Just because that body wasn't Mummy doesn't mean she isn't dead. Tears formed in Meadow's eyes, but she blinked fast to get rid of them and grabbed Felix's little hand and pulled him over to the corner of the garden where the soil needed to be dug over. 'We can't plant any flowers or vegetables till it's nice and smooth.' They dug for a while until Felix started throwing dirt and laughing. 'Stop that you little toad.'

He just laughed more and ran away to be chased and caught and then kissed. He smelled of beetles, mud, moulding leaves, and happiness. Felix trotted over to the snowdrops, which grew in clumps, and hung green and white heads. 'Oh.' He said as he flicked them and drops of dew flew into his rosy face.

The birds turned up to peck over the newly dug earth, looking for worms and insects. The three sat on the back steps watching them and listening to the robin sing. Happiness broke into their hearts like the sun popping out from behind a cloud.

Meadow wanted to capture that contentedness and store it in her memory like a precious stone that could be brought out and held whenever she needed it. Now she had quite a few of different colours and sizes, but it was hard to reach them when she needed them most.

Will I be able to find something precious to keep tomorrow? I will keep a look out every single day, if I can remember.

It rained during the night so she was feeling disappointed about not being able to continue in the fresh air the next day. But the garden was almost dry in the morning. Quite early, Felix escaped by standing on a stool to open the back door, which had bolts as well as the brass door handle. Meadow quickly followed him out. Hanging from the tulip tree were four jewels. 'Look Meddie, one silber, one gold and two blue.'

'Well done! But say silver-ver. Put your teeth on your lip like this-vaa, silvaa.'

'Yes, a silber one.'

His sister just smiled at him and gave up her corrections. 'Felix Schmeelix.'

'Sank you Pot Snoke.' He said.

'You're as batty as a hatter!'

The jewels shimmered, sparkled, gleamed and flashed as they turned in the light of the early sun swayed by the gentle wind currents. Of course it had been raining in the night, they were only water drops hanging on threads of spider webs, but Meddie felt rich, princess-rich.

CHAPTER 25

Alice's Diary

November 8th 1940. Without any presentiment, a plain-clothes officer entered my office in the clothing and footwear department of Education Supplies, now housed in Ladies' College. The staff, all immaculately dressed and proper, stared at me as the officer asked for me.

'The case will be reopened,' he stated almost in a whisper. What is he talking about?

'Come with me. We must leave at once.'

I was frightened now. I started shaking and walked out, unsteady on my feet. A long black car was parked outside my office. Herr Stute was seated in it. Major Max drove the requisitioned Wolseley.

'You have five minutes to say goodbye to your family.'

'Why? What's happened? Only five minutes?'

They drove me to my home and I packed some socks, a jumper, my new camel swing coat with the high waist, to keep me warm, and a hairbrush. Mum gave me some fruitcake in a brown bag. We kissed and hugged like it might be a forever separation. She was trembling so much that her false teeth rattled.

'Oh, this can't be happening. We have just been released. It must be a mistake.'

Herr Stute wore a small tight cap, which accentuated his stick-

ing out ears. His long coat, double-breasted and buttoned, hung on narrow shoulders. One hand was in his pocket; in the other, between yellow-stained fingers, a cigarette burned. His jackboots shone as he stood legs apart, leaning back. His cheekbones striking in his skull-like never-smiling face — a face as hard as granite. His voice sarcastic, 'You are going somewhere by plane,' he said, as I returned to the waiting vehicle.

I'd never flown before so this was scary, but strangely I was excited too.

I got in the car, then Major Max drove to pick up Amy. He had a sneer of a smile on his thin lips. 'First arrests on British soil.'

This time he took us out to the airfield in the basically stolen vehicle. We had no idea where we were going or why. When we arrived, we saw Frank, the Robilliards and the Courbets standing there in front of a plane. Their skin grey in the runway light reflection, worry written along the lines on their faces.

The plane, a Junkus 52, had a dark green-grey design on the body. On the side was the white German cross. Reality made my heart race and stomach turn. It was a ghastly nightmare and I couldn't pretend it was fun anymore. 'We could so easily be shot down.' They made us climb up the wobbly stairs into the small aeroplane, the propellers already whizzing. There was a crew of three. Two of the uniformed officers who'd questioned us were on the aircraft — that dreadful Herr Stute was one of them. The cockpit was open, the controls were visible; we could see everything. The noise was deafening, it blotted out the sound of speech. The plane shook as it took off. There was brilliant light from the sliding sun on the ground below us. Looking out the window, I could see Petit Port like a tiny model bay. Then out and over the sea, soon we were above Dinard Harbour. There were ships down below, half submerged: bombed obviously.

Then, over land we flew for quite some time, the engines roaring in our ears. The descent that I feared was as smooth as a swan.

We had arrived at the Villacoublay airfield. This little airport lay close to Paris. From there Amy and I were driven to a hotel. Naively, I thought we might be put up there for the night. A guard stayed with us while Herr Stute went into the hotel. We waited for more than an hour. By this time our stomachs were groaning with hunger, I felt for my fruitcake, no! I must have left it on the plane. We shivered involuntarily with nervous tension, even huddled together. The air was icy cold as it blasted into the car as he opened the door when he returned. The officer stared at us with the same insincere smile.

'I'm sorry to inform you I have to take you somewhere unpleasant.'

We were driven into Paris. It was 6 pm — already black. We saw the outlines of the familiar buildings we'd seen in photographs. This was wartime Paris, not Paris the City of Lights. Darkness settled over our hearts too. The skin on my face felt cold with sweat as I put my hand to my cheek. With a sense of foreboding, we stopped outside a sinister, grim, monolith building. The main gates opened, the car drove through. We were pushed into an office — the bright lights assaulted our unaccustomed eyes. We had to hand over our watches, jewellery, scissors and money. They were sealed in envelopes with our names handwritten on them. Pictures of Hitler and Goering hung on the wall behind the desk.

'This is the notorious old military prison — the Cherche- Midi, the one that houses French fighters who resist us, before we take them away and shoot them,' said Herr Stute.

Amy and I gave each other sideways glances and held hands when we weren't being watched. Again my heart was racing.

My throat was so dry my tongue almost glued to the roof of my mouth. 'Ice would be good to eat – there's enough of it outside,' I thought.

The keys clanged from the belts of the guards as they marched us to our cells. We were artless. It was just the beginning of the war; we didn't know about the Gestapo's reputation. I had no fear of torture. To me this was a day of firsts, first plane flight, first time in France, now the first time in a Paris prison.

I wondered what had happened to Mum and Dad. Had they been arrested too? It seemed everyone else involved in hiding the Lieutenants had been.

The cell door was unlocked and I was shoved in. I saw three girls in the gloomy half-lit room. Moments later an air raid siren whined loudly. We scrambled under our beds and waited till everything was quiet. We clambered out and introduced our-selves. There were four of us in the cell, three French girls and myself. They looked dreadful. Unkempt dirty hair and wrinkled stale-smelling clothes, they had only cold water to wash in. The girls had little altars and rosary beads by their stretchers.

The guards brought us grainy black coffee, then one hour later two tablespoons of coarse raw sugar on a plate. We licked it up, each granule a delicate treat. In another hour the door was unlocked again and pushed open halfway. Thick macaroni soup was poured onto our out-held plates. We were handed a chunk of black bread. I thought little of this, but should have savoured every morsel, as it was twenty-four hours before we had anything more to eat. The next day I felt dizzy with hunger and weak in the legs.

November the 11th. Armistice Day. We heard shouting, scuffling, blows and groans. Outside in the yard – we watched through the haze of rain, fifty or so young French students being forced to stand at attention. They were some of thousands who had protested against German occupation by singing 'La Marseillaise' beside the tomb of the unknown warrior, and now their punishment. All night those boys stood in the rain, now torrential. They must have been frozen numb with cold. As dawn broke, we heard them coming inside, being clipped about the head, pushed and hit. They had survived. Others had been shot. The Catholic girls in my room had prayed for them for hours, caressing their rosaries and crossing themselves in front of their little shrines. In the sky above the prison, a plane flew over trailing a smoke message: 'Courage Courage.'

Those young students had not been forgotten by their true friends. My cellmates looked into the sky, staring at the little miracle.

We had a view from the window of the prison courtyard. Day followed day. We saw some prisoners being marched around, that was all. 'How long will we be here? What will they do to us?' were constant questions in my mind. My French wasn't good enough to understand the girls when they spoke quickly, so I was completely alone and disoriented.

The men exercised daily, even in the snow. They shuffled around the yard muffled in hats, coats, any article they could layer on, their hands wrapped in rags. Vapour puffed out of their mouths like fog.

We watched them, not really enviously, but what else was there to do? On the fourteenth of November I was startled as I sat watching as usual when I saw my father out there in the yard. I screamed, 'Mon père est la!'

I was mad with joy. I was desperate to let him know I was in the same prison.

'Don't call out!' Simone said. 'We'll be punished.'

I wanted my dad to know I was safe so I jumped onto my bed as close to the window as possible, and sang as loud as I could the popular song, Somewhere Over the Rainbow; I'd just performed a dance to that tune. Daddy looked up. I knew he had heard me. To see his face but not be able to reach out was torment.

November 16th. She opened her eyes a fraction, blinked several times. The blurry scene outlined four rough stretchers. She turned her head, found a body close to her, glanced over to another mound and blinked back the sleep. She remembered, cold with fright, as she looked at the bare brick walls, this is a French prison. It's my birthday. I'm twenty today.

Alice's Diary

I didn't know Louis was in the same prison. Henri, one of the orderlies who brought us our daily rations, told me two British officers were in solitary confinement on the same level as our cell but in separate blocks. The buildings were at right angles to each other. Henri said he would tell them to look out for me. My heart began to beat as fast as a bird's. I sat for two hours by the window. I didn't see him.

Every morning our cells were unlocked so we could go out and fetch fresh water. We also had to empty our filthy latrine buckets in a drain that was in the centre of the courtyard. This drain was now blocked. Sewage and other unspeakable waste started to flow out over the cobbles. The stench was horrendous, not to mention the hygiene — or lack of it, I mean. Of course the muck was on everyone's shoes and brought into the cells. Soon everywhere and everything looked and smelled like a scene from hell. The Germans were clean fanatics; we had to scrub for hours.

One morning it was my turn to empty the bucket. I walked out into the yard, treading carefully to keep my shoes clean. I looked up at the iron fence that separated the men from the women. I spotted Lou and he me. Oh what happiness. What unexpected happiness. I slowly made my way to the fence. Louis made a dash. We kissed through the wire, our lips just touching for a second. Was this a dream?

'Alice, if I don't make it, please remember you're my best girl.'

I wanted to kiss him again but I reluctantly returned to the middle of the courtyard. Had anyone seen us? They had threatened to shoot us for just one little act of disobedience.

Louis' cell, in the block joining ours, could be seen easily opposite mine. Now he knew I was there we could look for each other. If we tilted our tiny fanlight windows a little we could write messages in the dust. Later on we used the soapsuds and water the guards gave us to clean our floors. We sent short notes: I love you. Be brave. Hold on. By standing on my bed, I could make out his replies.

One afternoon, a bullet went whistling through Lou's window, missing his head by a fraction. The guards roared up to his cell and moved him to another in the interior of the prison, a cell with no window.

December 5th. A guard came to tell me the case against us had been referred to Berlin. Now, panic gripped me like a vice. My breathing became tight and irregular.

It was bitterly cold in that old stone building. There was no heating and only the one dirty blanket each. We slept in our clothes, sometimes two in the bed, to keep ourselves from being frozen to death overnight.

I had had Jewish girls in my cell from time to time. The authorities made us all change cells and inmates regularly. A new inmate – a lovely, intelligent Jewish girl – Marcelle Meyer, a medical student, who spoke good English, was in prison because she'd poked her tongue out at a German. We got on well and made lots of noise – danced, joked and sang together like school children. A rap on the door, 'Be quiet, this is a jail not a cabaret!'

A key turned in the lock – German officers had sent for Marcelle. She was summoned to a tribunal.

'They are sending me to a camp,' she said with tears in her eyes when she returned. 'I don't want to go so far away. Paris is my home.'

Added note: No one at that stage of the war had heard of concentration camps so she wasn't scared. She hoped the camp might have better facilities than the Paris prison.

Another pencil note was added to the diary several years later:

N.B. I tried to get in touch with Marcelle after the war through the Red Cross, but no one had even heard of her or her family.

We were given little Bibles by an American padre who was allowed to visit us occasionally.

N.B. I still have mine. It's a precious reminder of those weeks.

News filtered to me through two little notes pushed under my door by the guards. 'Monsieur Pierre Courbet has died.'

Oh, Emile's dad, how terrible! Why?

CHAPTER 26
The Countryside – February 15th

The child saw the sunshine flooding in from the kitchen window at breakfast. 'Sunny today.'

'Yep, you're right. We need to see more trees and fields and listen to some birdsong from the woodland birds. Get coats and hats, it's sunny, but cold.'

They drove towards a little village not too far from home. They could park the car there and not worry about the pay and display fee. There were enchanting walks across slopes down to the river. Along the banks were shiny yellow marsh marigolds in bud. A bright gold brimstone butterfly darted out from some foliage. The child chased the little creature, stumbling through the wet bog. They passed sweet violets and daffodils shooting up, getting ready to flower, standing high in the grasses. The pussy willows were out already. Felix was lifted up to see them closely, but that wasn't enough – he had to have some to take home. He squashed them between his fingers, smiling wickedly.

They crossed the fields by the ancient Saxon church. Around the gravestones were groups of narcissi, snowdrops, violas and a few fading crocuses. It was magical to the child. He felt the petals, smelled inside each variety, bending his short legs he looked in the trumpets for bees or other insects and jumped when one flew out. Meadow had hoped to see forget-me-nots, but it was too early in the year for them to flower. Only their leaves stood in little clumps.

Meadow made a promise to herself that though her mother had forgotten her, she would never forget Mamma. Glancing at one of the gravestones, she imagined her mother's name engraved on it and the date and year. She would write on it, *Forever Mamma. Safe in Heaven.*

Being active, winter was a jail term for Felix. He skipped a while, then tried little flips on the woodland floor. He ran madly through little groves of trees shouting and yahooing. He pretended to hide and jumped out at his sister, who tried to look surprised. The child giggled every time. He wanted to do it fifty times. But Meadow got tired of it after the first few false frights. 'No more Felix.'

Red-winged birds darted in and out of the ivy that clung to the bare oak trees eating the last of the black ivy berries.

'I hungry.'

'As usual.'

They went back to the village to buy pasties and a drink.

They sat on a dry-stone wall to eat. The grasses moved and made tender sounds. Nathan thought he heard her name once when the wind blew the stalks – 'Sarah'– like someone breathing out. He said it to himself voiceless.

They returned to the wooded area. The local vicar passed them, 'There's a splendid lythe if you keep walking in that direction.' He pointed. They kept walking through a canopy of filtered lights. Dots of green light spotted the twigged walled cages of branches, dappled and bright. 'It's quite a way,' the vicar had added.

Meadow's eyes turned to stare deep in the woods. At the base of an ancient oak, *drifts of sunny aconites sitting like yellow cups on fringed saucers of green. Surely enchanted.*

Now Felix would never walk this far without moaning and groaning, but as they were half running he enjoyed it. Then in a moment, he was sitting on the leaves and mud. 'Me tired,' he said.

Nathan lifted him up. 'Help me get him on my shoulders, Meddie.' She gave the child a leg up. The face of the boy shone like a smiling idiot. He was king of the castle – higher than anyone else. They trudged on in the direction of the lythe. It was thirty more minutes.

'This had better be worth it, Dad; we have to return too.'

The branches cleared overhead, the clouded light visible now at the end. In one second they were through and standing in a valley surrounded by woods. Birdsong filled every second of time – so various in sweetness and range. 'Rooks, finches, wrens, chiff-chaffs maybe?'

Then no human spoke. A minute passed. 'Look Dad, there's the water.' His girl indicated with her head.

A long thin organic shape lay in the field below them, silver and still. A big white cow with one bent horn, her feet in the water, looked up at them chewing.

'Is heaven Papa?'

'Not yet, Felix. I'm sure it's better than this.'

'Mamma here?'

'No, Sweetpea, but peace is.'

'Piece of what?'

'Haha, Nutboy.'

'Keep still and just look.'

The lythe was Ophelia's river pond or a ribbon of Shining. It was split in two around a tufted island then re-joined by long silvery grasses and damp hedgerow weeds. There was no one but the three and the only sound, the singing of birds. They stood mute.

'Bah, we have to go back.'

'We can bring Mummy here to the secret valley should we find her,' Meadow whispered into Nathan's ear.

'Yes, Pet.'

He pulled Felix down off his shoulders to run all the way back chased by his sister. The stillness of the place hung over them like a shadow as they sat in the car. Felix was not fidgety. He seemed to sense the mood. Then it was broken by, 'Cold and hungwee – go home.'

'We'll return in the summer when all will be fresh, the birds will be twice as loud, pheasants and the murmuring of wood pigeons, chattering, will surround the whole valley and it will be the brightest green ever with white flowers and yellow flag irises all along the edges of the water. It will be one of our very own hidey places.'

'White cow come?'

Thoughts came so fast to Nathan, he couldn't capture and tame them, but one lingered – then stuck. *It's all wasted, it mustn't be wasted, our lives mustn't be wasted. I can bring up Meadow and Felix well, with love and do the best I can, but still it could be wasted if there's not a better purpose than just being alive. Even living in the moment like Felix won't do. There will have to be more. I will find what that is. I will search and hunt until I reach it, whatever it is. Just like I must begin in earnest to search for Sarah.*

He got out of the car and threw a stick into the air, way into the trees, with angry determination. The birds screamed as they left the branches to wheel in the sky above them. Tears sprung into his eyes, flooded them, then coursed down his reddened cheeks.

The next day was a normal workday. Well, it was supposed to be. When Nathan arrived he bumped into the director.

'I need to see you today if that's OK, Nathan.'

He thought he knew what was coming – a threat to be fired or let go if he couldn't put more effort and time into his career. The kindness of the boss had been stretched, as he saw no end to this arrangement of early leaving and time off for family events. Nat had already put in for, and received the time off, for the Easter break. Surely the boss wasn't going to tell him he could no longer have it.

At lunchtime he knocked on the director's door.

'Hope all is as well as can be expected, Nathan. Sit down. Sorry, but I have to have a chat about something important.' Nathan's stomach tightened and his breaths came a little quicker. He hated displeasing anyone, especially the boss. 'My staff are very important to the company, as you know. I've had some complaints from a couple of your co-workers that they have had to pick up some of your work responsibilities.'

'Yes that's true, though I've been trying really hard, I just can't seem to be all finished by 5 o'clock. It's impossible to stay any later. I haven't got local grandparents who can come and mind the kids.'

'I understand that, but if it's impossible – and I have given you several months to sort this out, then I shall have to' – Nathan held his breath – 'find you a different position in the company. Something less demanding. It will, of course, mean a lower salary. It's a demotion really, I'm afraid.'

The punch felt physical and took the breath right out of him. Another hit. He already felt like a demoralised nothing. He had poured himself into his profession and worked devotedly for several years to get where he was in the company.

Leaving the office, he recited in his head, 'Failure leads to life lessons and future success.' *Everyone loses his or her status at some time, but this hurts more than I thought it would. I'm embarrassed to look my fellow colleagues in the eye even though it's not my fault. All I've worked for all these years, the promotion and the higher salary for the family, gone in one moment.*

In his mind appeared without warning the old worries. *How will I pay the bills? Can I afford the mortgage? Can we still go to Madrid? What will I tell Meadow?*

His daughter noticed his demeanour as soon as he walked in the door at home. He walked in with a little stoop, his chin almost on his chest.

'Daddy you look like a whipped and beaten dog with its tail slinking and its back bent. You should be crawling and whining like Mr Clarke's spaniel. Haha!'

'Meadow, something else bad has happened today.'

'What? What?'

'I've been demoted at work to a less responsible and lower-paid position.'

The girl ran up to him and gave him a giant bear hug.

'Dad, it's nothing – we have each other.'

Tears welled in his eyes. His sight blurred. *She's so brave – braver than me – a motherless child. Get a grip man. What kind of a man are you?*

CHAPTER 27

Alice's Diary

All razors have been removed from the prisoners.

Emile's father was found dead in his cell. An open Bible lay beside him, his head slumped – his wrists slit – he had used his razor. How tragic for Emile and his mother who have to go and identify his body. But this event may help to save us. The authorities do not want to look cruel to the British. The German Major who had given his word about the boys and helpers not being shot, has been informed.

In Guernsey, Major Shirrif had been arrested. He was given one hour to pack before his flight. He was under grave suspicion of knowing all the time there were spies on the island. He was accused of leading the British espionage. The Major had fought and worked for the boys and their families, courageously risking his own reputation and life.

Alice's Diary

December 8th. Once more a rap on our cell door.

'Just to confirm to you, Miss Alice, your case is being taken to Berlin now.' I already knew this was coming, but now shattered and apprehensive, I sat shaking on the bed. My emotions fragile, the slightest noise made me flinch. And then I was shocked again *when I glanced out the window and saw Major Shirrif being marched in across the prison yard. There was no mistaking him. Of course I didn't know he had been arrested. We have no way of getting news in this awful place. Now what chance do the boys or any of us have? Now I know the case is being taken to Berlin and they said we will have to go there for the trials.*

I have been in this prison almost five weeks. I'm wracked with worry most of the time. I fell asleep sobbing again last night.

December 19th. Terrible tension, waiting, waiting and more anxious waiting for the news from Berlin.

December 25th. Christmas, oh Christmas.

The Germans stood in a group in the prison yard. They sung heart-rending songs as a gift to us. Christmas carols in perfect harmonies. They even brought us presents, an apple, an orange and a sprig of spruce. Every one of us tears flowing; it all seemed such a paradox. Any act of kindness made us weep.

December 28th. Our door opened without a knock; a guard stood there; I expected some water or an order to move.

'Pick up your things and follow me.' Not another room change, or the trip to Berlin, please God. But he took me downstairs to the office, where I saw with shock all the Guernsey prisoners assembled, but not Louis and Emile. We lined up as our names were called. We must be heading for the trials or a camp. More tears and trembling, my emotions frazzled, I started to breathe with gasps, panting for air and even finding it hard to get any breath at all. The others looked at me. 'It's asthma,' said Mrs Courbet.

'But I've never had it before.'

'Brought on by fear.' She held my hand for a brief moment.

Then a surprise, we were summoned to the large wooden desk one at a time. The officers handed us back all our personal belongings in the named brown paper bags. We looked at each other, not daring to imagine the best or the worst.

The men looked appalling: unshaven, thin and haggard, their eyes bloodshot. We hugged them all with deep love and affection, but I felt only bones under their dirty coats. I clung to Daddy. A moment later, a great shock – we were being released. Sent back home. Our minds couldn't take it in and we were too weak to shout for joy.

Could it really be happening? In a very short time I was standing on the runway with our friends ready to board. What a reunion, what mixed feelings, sorrow at the state of our friends but happiness at the release.

Would the freedom last this time? One period of hell then suddenly a reprieve; too hard to comprehend. It had been false the first time, what could we expect? And another worry, Mother wasn't with us. I hadn't seen or heard of her those whole seven weeks.

Spontaneously a tiny bubble of hope rose in my chest as my lungs began to work regularly again. I began to dare to believe that bluebirds were real, the rainbow's fairy-tale land too. We would be like Cinderellas going to the ball after all. No camps, no Berlin, the commandants there had agreed to abide by the promise made in the Guernsey Evening Press by Major Brandt. As we flew over the small area of land between the airport and the coast, my heart was singing quietly. But still no Mother – was she alive or dead? I could never be even a little happy until I knew what had happened to her. Dad had no news to tell me. As we were landing, an assisting officer told me something wonderful; my mother had been held at Caen, too ill to stand the gruelling prison in Paris.

From the little airport where we landed we were transported by coach to Granville, where Mother was waiting for us, thinner but alive, her face and ankles still swollen. Oh, her arms around me – that warm cheek – So many tears of thankfulness. She had stuck it out in spite of high blood pressure and head troubles.

At Granville, Mr Robilliard bought as many Camembert cheeses, which he loved, as the money from his envelope allowed. He stuffed them in every pocket of his coat and trousers. He was filled with circular bulges and ponged like rotting fish. Now we could laugh at last.

How grateful we all were, pinching and punching each other to see if we were actually alive and going home. We only needed our eyes filled with moisture, and smiles we couldn't hide to communicate our messages of love and gratitude.

It was so cold our breath was like smoke as we talked. Gloveless, everyone was clapping and rubbing their hands to keep warm – blowing warm breath on our fingers and stamping our feet to stop them freezing.

We found this old newspaper on the boat that took us home:

Jersey Press December 24th 1940.
Proclamation.

1. *The findings of the Legal Investigations have proved conclusively that 2nd Lt Louis Robilliard and 2nd Lt Emile Courbet are guilty of espionage.*
2. *Mr Jean Robilliard and Mrs Estelle Robilliard, Mr Pierre Courbet and Mrs Marie Courbet, Mr Frank Lovell and Miss Amy Vaudin, Mr Albert Beauvoir and Mrs Rose Beauvoir and Miss Alice Beauvoir have given refuge and assistance to the two officers. They are guilty of high treason.*
3. *Major Shirrif acted against his appointed duty of information.*

4. *All the parties concerned have tried to mislead the German authorities.*

In accordance with German Military Law and in agreement with the Hague Convention, the penalties for
Espionage are – the death penalty and for
High treason – the death penalty or penal servitude for life.
In spite of these circumstances, The German Military Authority have given full consideration to the notice published in the Guernsey Press on October 18th.
All the persons concerned will be exempted from punishment. 2nd Lt Robilliard and 2nd Lt Courbet will be sent to a camp as prisoners of war.
The other persons, except Mr Pierre Courbet, who is deceased, will be brought back to the island.
The matter is therefore settled.

All the above measures have been taken in the expectation and under the condition of the perfect loyalty of the population of the Channel Islands in the future. The whole community will bear the consequences of any further misconduct of any individual.

Major Brandt

We were saved from death by a line of ink, and a man who kept his word.

December 30th. It is a very rough and stormy day. Yet this is the day for the boat trip to our homeland. It is a cargo boat and we are in the cattle hold, vomiting and wanting to die. It is difficult to pen these notes. We have to stay down here for eight whole hours. To me it feels almost worse, if that's possible, than the imprisonment has been.

January 1st, 1941. New Year! How true! We picked up Oswald from the Collins' house where he had been for the seven weeks. They own a sweet shop — so he did all right!

It was unreal to be in our own house again. We gazed around at our familiar possessions, picking some up, wiping our hands over the dusty furniture, even kissing the curtains. It was true we were all safe and home again, except Emile's dad of course. If only he could have seen the future and fought those tormenting thoughts telling him all was hopeless. He would have been here with his family and friends safe again.

January 9th. A bouquet of flowers came from the German Lt Wulf to Mrs Rose Beauvoir. She had been with French guards in the French jail — where there were mothers in cells with babies crying all night and it had been freezing. Luckily she had had Bert's long johns in her bag by mistake or she may not have survived. The food was thrown through the door as if the prisoners were zoo animals. Why was this French prison worse than the German-run one? He was sorry she had had to endure that treatment when she was so ill.

N.B. How strange that some of them felt remorse even early in the war.

After being back in Guernsey for only one day we had learnt several of the people involved in the espionage assistance could no longer be employed in civic positions or have any public duties. But the groundsman, my friend Amy and I were exempt.

Had each one of us told the truth? Were we in fact informants? The others involved may have given different stories.

Major Shirrif was returned to the island too, but he had to step down from his role as Guernsey Head Administrator. The Germans felt they could no longer trust him.

The two brave boys – Lieutenants Louis and Emile, we were informed, would be awarded Military Crosses. To be presented at a later date. No one knew when that time would be.

A poem to you: Louis, MC, sportsman, patriot and friend:

War is not glorious
Lads march out superb
And die victorious.
Oh my heart, be still!
You have cried your cry
You have played your part

CHAPTER 28
Bravery

The monotonous dripping rain was followed by a surprising sunny spell. The young pair went straight back into the garden after school to check on the state of the soil to see if it was ready for the planting of the peas.

While they were mucking about feeling the earth, Meadow thought she saw something moving in the garden shed.

Maybe a dog or cat has got shut in.

She nudged the door open a few centimetres and peeped in.

A hand grabbed hold of her jacket and pulled. Soon a person had hold of her wrist. 'Stop it! Stop it! Let go!'

She turned a sickly white and screamed.

'Felix, help me!'

Felix kicked open the door, his face serious, his jaw thrust out, his eyebrows frowning and his body tense.

A frightful, ugly man lurked inside the shed.

Felix kicked the man on the shins and punched his bony thighs. 'Let go!'

'Felix run and get help – Mr Clarke next door is home, run Felix quick, quick!'

The child ran faster than he'd ever run. His face scarlet as he tore through the gate and pounded on Mr Clarke's door. 'Help! Help!' he yelled as loud as a small boy can. The neighbour, retired and none too sprightly, rushed to the door.

'What's the matter, Felix?'

'Man – man got Meadow, help!'

Mr Clarke grabbed his walking stick and an umbrella from the front stand and followed the boy, both running, but Mr Clarke not very quickly.

At the shed, the neighbour shouted, 'Let her go now or I'll call the police.'

The man inside let go of Meadow's arm and stood quietly, his head down.

He looked elderly but it was hard to tell his age exactly. He was a mess, his hair wispy – grey and stringy, his eyes glazed and blood-shot. His mouth quivered, his hands shook. *What a wreck!* He was stick-thin. His dirty clothes smelled of alcohol and urine.

Felix stared at the now calm man who shuffled from foot to foot. The child pulled up an old wooden box from the shed and climbed up. He looked into the man's eyes.

'You look sad. You stink. What's your name?'

'Jimmy.'

The man reached out a shaky hand to touch Felix. Meadow sprang to his defence and pushed the man's hand away from the child.

'Don't touch him!'

The derelict man shrank back into the garden shed.

Mr Clarke spoke to him.

'You'll have to come out and leave this property immediately. You are trespassing and scaring these children. Go now or I will definitely have to call the police.'

'Sarah said I could stay in the shed if I was desperate.'

'What? You know our mum?'

The man, still wobbly on his feet, came out and walked towards the path that led to the front garden.

Felix ran after him, not frightened now at all. 'Come back tomowwow man.'

Jimmy turned his head back to look at the child with dull and yet puzzled eyes. He averted them, looked back to the path and left through the front gate.

'Why on earth did you tell him to come back Felix? Stupid boy.'

'Thanks a lot Mr Clarke.'

'That's nothing Meadow. Call me anytime, but if you see him again call the police. He's a vagrant and has occasionally been spotted walking along our street over the last few months. Other neighbours have reported seeing him.'

Nathan, when he heard all about it, decided to lock the garage and garden shed. He felt they needed to get away from the house for a while, so he rang Sarah's mum and she invited them to tea. She always wanted to see the children, they were like a tonic to her.

At Gran's house, Felix looked at the faded framed photographs hanging in her hallway; Gran and Grandfather's wedding, Sarah as a baby, her brother as a baby, the siblings as children, then a picture with Gran and the two children. The recent ones were Mummy and Daddy's wedding, Meadow's baby shot and Felix snapped when he'd started walking.

The child dragged a chair, scraping and bumping over to the wall. He stood up so his eyes were level with the faded black and white wedding photo of Gran and Grandfather. The children had never met him. He had left a long time before Sarah was married.

Felix gazed at the man in the picture.

'Same man, same man, same man, look Med.'

She came over to him and looked really hard at the man's face – he did look a bit like the homeless guy.

'I can't say it *is* the same person Felix – the eyes and mouth do look a bit like that man's.'

But the man was destroyed, a ruin. How could he be the same person?

'What was grandfather's name?'

'James. A nice name for a useless man.' She rolled her eyes.

'Well that means he could be called Jim or Jimmy, doesn't it?'

The next day at work Nathan told Jess about the man in the shed and how Felix had asked the man to come back again.

'But Nathan, that's dangerous. The children should have been stopped. Felix could have been badly hurt. Those types of people – alcoholics or whatever, are often foul-tempered and violent. I would have kept a closer eye on them. That sort of thing wouldn't happen if I were their mother.'

After school the next day Meadow decided to do some detective work on her own. She went next door to ask Mr Clarke how best to track down Jimmy.

'Why would you want to do that?'

'We think it's someone we know, Mr Clarke, and we might be able to help him.'

Dad would never allow that. He thinks he's dangerous, because I was terrified by the hand grabbing me as I opened the shed door. But we know now the man is harmless.

'Please don't tell Dad, Mr Clarke, he'll only get anxious.'

'Well, Jimmy has been caught stealing, only food, but also begging on the streets. I don't think you should go too close, he could be unpredictable.'

Before Nathan got home from work, sister and therefore little brother, decided to go for a walk into the town, only about ten minutes away. It wasn't long before they found Stinky Jimmy, as he was known to the Welfare Department, in front of a shop in the main street. They had taken a bottle of juice from home, some French Brie cheese and a bag of oranges. They gave him five pounds from their pocket money. 'Here Grandfaver,' said Felix.

Meadow had told the child that's who Jimmy probably was. The man, almost unconscious, slumped down on his old coat and buried his head in his nicotine-stained hands, an empty wine bottle beside him.

'We just want to ask you some questions, Jimmy. When did you see Mum, I mean, Sarah?'

The vagrant spoke slowly, his speech slurred. 'A long time ago. I can't remember but she seemed shocked when I told her I was her father. She asked me lots of questions – she said she didn't believe me. But she told me I could stay in her garden shed if I had nowhere to sleep when it was very cold.' He dribbled as he spoke.

Felix patted Jimmy on the shoulder. 'Sanx Jimmy.'

The siblings went back home. 'That didn't tell us anything new about Mum, Felix, but we helped him didn't we?'

Jimmy sold the oranges and cheese to a homeless friend and with the five-Pound note bought a flagon of cheap wine.

In the morning, Nathan went to take out the rubbish and found Jimmy lying on the pavement outside their house. There was blood under his head and his eyes were open but he looked dead.

Nathan ran in and told Meadow to dial 999 for an ambulance. 'Why Dad?'

'Jimmy's had an accident. He's out by the gate.'

Felix tore down the path and threw himself onto the vomit stained chest. 'Grandfaver. Oh no.'

He lifted one arm but it fell with a thud to the ground. He looked into the tramp's unseeing yellowed eyes that stared upwards at the heavens.

'Med, Jimmy sick.'

He's killed himself or the alcohol has. His liver must be almost eaten through.

'Couldn't we have loved him back to life Dad?'

'I'm sure the social services and missions did all they could. He was an alcoholic, an addict. It's like a disease, but it's a disease of the mind first. He needed to stop drinking 20 years ago.'

'I wish we'd found him then. He told us that he really was Mum's father.' Felix planted a little kiss on the dead man's cheek.

'Come on Felix, he's dirty and he's gone now. Come on, get away from him.'

The police knew Jimmy very well even though he'd only been in their district a few months.

'We expect he came to scrounge when he found out he had family here, sir. He's left a trail of petty thefts and had numerous alcoholic collapses and attempts at drying out.'

'I'm glad we took him food and were kind to him before he died, Dad.'

'That was sweet of you two.'

'That was a good idea of yours, Felix.' Meadow kissed the boy's cold cheek.

Nathan imagined that Sarah would have been deeply ashamed of her father. *Maybe that was another reason for her vanishing.*

CHAPTER 29
Early 1941

Louis spent his 21st birthday in the Cherche-Midi under the sentence of death by firing squad.

But the German major, who had given his word over the amnesty, risked his own career to keep his promise. He interceded on behalf of the Guernsey prisoners.

'When one gives his word, one keeps his word,' he said. His actions toward British subjects during wartime were surely full of chivalry and honour. He was demoted a short while later and his family put under surveillance.

So the case was dismissed against the assistants of the two young commandos. The two boys were sent to a POW camp just as the original deal had stated. But before they were sent away, they had been allowed to see their parents, just before their flight to the coast, in Emile's case just his mother of course. They didn't know how long it would be or if ever they would see one another again.

Louis' Letter

February 26th

Dear Mum and Dad,
I hope very much you are both well and settled back into island life.

We are in the far northeast of the country. It's still the middle of winter of course, absolutely freezing. Emile and I have a few moth-eaten covers but we have to put our coats on over our uniforms to sleep. The cells are small and poorly ventilated. They are revoltingly filthy too. Most of the prisoners have been here a long time. The Jewish prisoners are the only ones leaving. The rest of us have to stay until the end of the war, let's hope it's soon.

I was in a cell on my own. I nearly went nuts with boredom so I counted the number of A's on each page of the only book I had, then the number of B's and so on. Then they came and took the book away.

On January the 29th, almost a month ago, Emile and I were put in a double cell. At last someone to talk to and thump on the back! Actually we had a short boxing match – we just had to do something physical.

When the person in the next cell told me he was leaving, as we were emptying our buckets, I asked him for his soap. When we got back to our cells, I used a piece of string I had in my army jacket and tied a spoon to it. I hung it out of the window and swung it along the wall like a pendulum until he caught it. He tied the soap to the string and after a nervous few minutes, when I thought the soap would fall off, voilà, we are cleaner now!

Although we are locked in our cells day and night, we are allowed to send and receive mail – as you can see.

Please send my best regards to Alice. I have not written to her directly.

Last news before I sign off. We are being transferred to Stalag XX tomorrow. Please don't worry about us. We are fine.

Louis, with deepest love.

CHAPTER 30

Alice's Diary

1941. I've returned to my beloved island and life is near normal, although the Germans are in charge. I go about my daily routine as before that episode of terrors. It feels like it was just a dream, a nightmare but a dream all the same. Now at home, it's as if we never left. Dad is back at work. I am dancing again with my friends. Did all that really happen? I only have to see the Jerries driving through the town to know it did.

I'm almost twenty-one. My latest dancing partner is Henry. We met at a party on New Year's Eve two years ago and I haven't given him another thought since then, but now with Louis away, I think I need to find a new boyfriend. Who knows if Lou and I will ever see each other again? Henry is actually Italian and ten years older than me. We dance together cabaret style; he is a superb dancer with flair and rhythm in his every move. We've just won the Channel Islands Ballroom competition for the Tango, Slow Foxtrot and Latin American dance and received a huge silver trophy.

With Lou out of my vision, I've fallen madly in love with Henry. Honestly, I love him with all my heart, he's so romantic, dashing and attentive, what more could I possibly need? Of course he hasn't a profession in the Victorian sense of the word, and Catholics are still inferior in Mum's eyes.

Last week he asked me to marry him in the typical way, down on one knee and holding out a little red box.

He gave me a beautiful engagement ring, very simple, gold with pearls and one diamond set high. He'd managed to get it somehow during occupation conditions.

Mother heard it first of course when I swirled into her room laughing and showed her the ring on my finger. She didn't say a word. She didn't even smile. 'Mum, aren't you going to say anything?'

'Yes, I'll talk to your father about it when he gets home.' They whispered about it for half an hour behind the closed kitchen door. She's put a stop to our plans and roped Daddy into it too!

Daddy's not as strong as he was before the Great War. He escaped unharmed physically, but the tragic scenes, the blown up bodies, the memory of the dead crying out has scarred his soul. He's become more resigned and less able to combat Mother's strong opinions. He gives in to her wishes so he doesn't cause her stress or the heart attack she fears, and Daddy seems to have weakened mental stamina.

Henry is thirty-one and a chef; he runs the Café Central. 'Not good enough!' After a horrible, loud, spiteful fight I packed my suitcase, sobbing wildly, and was leaving home to marry him. My father stopped me on the downstairs landing and held me firmly to stop my hysterical crying.

'Alice, think about this. It will break our hearts. He's not the man for you. You are so young; there is plenty of time to find someone more suitable.'

'But I love him Daddy; we are engaged.'

'Well he didn't do the right thing and come and ask us if it was all right to marry you did he? Admit it. Don't leave, it will be the death of your mother. I will explain everything to him, don't worry, he'll understand.'

With a grief-stricken heart, that felt like an axe had sliced it into two pieces, I climbed back up the stairs and threw myself on my bed. 'Mother, why do you always control my life? And ruin it, yes ruin it. I have to give him up. I have no other choice. If marrying Henry would kill my mother, I'm trapped.'

Yesterday I received his note. I read it in my room curled up on my bed. 'I am a broken man and will never ever get over you.' Oh to be loved but then to lose that love.

Outside the window I can hear the sound of marching. Germans are always marching through our roads. And they are singing! It seems they all have lovely voices. I think it's beautiful. I feel a little bit cheered up. I remember the Christmas carols in the Paris jail and I'm grateful to have been freed and not shot for assisting a spy.

Next door the house has been taken over by the German Field Post Office. Curt came into our garden, knocked on the door and asked for baking powder. He returned later with a German Army loaf, dark rye bread, delicious. So different from the tasteless rationed bread. The officers next door have given Dad permission to dig a vegetable patch in their back garden.

These crops make dinner times much more varied for all of us. Our family has become good friends with the nice, friendly enemy.

Some people's neighbours act as informants, telling the occupiers of any illegal trade, but not ours.

I have become very bitter against my mother and everything else. I've grown moody, sullen and aloof. Even Amy says so. I can't bear to look at my parents. I won't let them forget the misery they are causing me.

The only thing that is still a joy is my dancing.

October 1941. Sixteen of us, under the direction of Simon Marchant have decided to produce shows for the entertainment-starved population.

The Lyric Theatre has been born. We create costumes out of scraps of fabric and remodel clothes. There are singers, tap dancers, ballroom and Latin American dancers. I choreograph many of the items; coming up with ideas is an exciting challenge. I love every minute of it. No ration books can limit our exhilaration. This is a diversion from the occupation. Now this occupation hasn't brought only bad things. Sometimes we totally forget there is a war. These are becoming some of the happiest days of my life, so far. We are bringing that happiness to the locals. Well, a few hours pleasure I believe.

With Victor, a flirtation of mine, a tall, exceptionally angelic-looking young man, loved by all the girls, I dance a duet called the Blue Danube. I wear a full-length circular chiffon frock. The bodice is a blue heart and the skirt many shades of blue. He wears white tails. Every time we perform this dance we have many 'encores'.

Germans are permitted to attend the shows, of course, as they rule the island. Two German naval officers have been in the front row for several nights.

Two nights ago after the show, a huge bouquet was delivered to me. A note was attached. It said, 'From your admirer in the front row.'

After last night's performance I found Fritz and his friend — the two German officers, waiting outside to meet me. Because of the curfew, Dad had come to accompany me home. They asked him if it was OK to speak to me.

'You'll have to come home if you want to do that.'

They followed us home and came inside, met my mother and brother and Fritz became an instant friend. I can't understand why. Is it because of his good manners, his charm or his rank?

At odd times Fritz Ehrling now brings us a lobster or some other edible treat. After a week or two, he's started to call almost every day, bringing German sausage, oh it's divine, and pumpernickel bread. We've begun to be quite a bit better off than our neighbours.

Some parents cry when they see Oswald. He reminds them of their children who they haven't seen for years and don't know when they ever will.

Good night Diary.

During the German Occupation and all over Europe, it was a struggle for existence. Morality was discarded by some, forgotten. It seemed cheating, lying and betrayal was normal. Closing eyes to evil the most common degradation.

As the war progressed hundreds of slave labourers were brought to the Sunshine Island to build defence installations around the coast. Only a few people did anything for these mistreated and disregarded people. Many of the slaves died right there in the Sunshine Island. Unknown French, Polish, Russian people suffering right in front of everyone's eyes. Dragging their wasted bodies around in thin rags, their eyes sunken and blank. Alice's family, like many others, ignored them. Couldn't they have done something?

Marie, a Salvation Army major, complained to the German commandant about the appalling treatment of the foreign workers.

She had heard their screams half a mile away. Marie was jailed. She died soon after she was released, an almost unknown heroine.

One runaway Russian slave sought refuge in a church bell tower, but he was discovered and frogmarched out of the church by the SS. He escaped into the cemetery but was eventually caught and shot. These and similar unheard of dramas occurred in all areas of occupied territory during those harrowing years. Thousands upon thousands of small personal tragedies.

Over the last two years of the war, life became difficult for many of the islanders too – with their hunt for food and food-scraps. Many thefts were reported: bread, potatoes and tea. People were taking their ration books to bed with them to keep them safe. Grown men weighed only eight or nine stone.

Many of the people had to make desperately needed objects out of almost nothing. The children used hosepipe for tyres on their bicycles, joined by thick string. It made a very bumpy but exhilarating ride. There was a thrill in overcoming hardships by ingenuity, and repairing worn out objects with odd pieces of metal and wire, sometimes taking two things apart and making one good one, like an old clock or a forbidden crystal set.

Alice and other young people thrived on the challenges.

Alice's Diary
November 1944. German provisions have been cut off from France for quite some time.

The Germans have begun eating the cats. Horrible. Their bread has apparently got maggots in it.

A bowl of plucked and cooked sparrows is a delicacy.
December.

The Christmas season has arrived, the sparsest in living memory, certainly on this island where abundance was the expected state — the world-renowned cows, glorious yellow butter, clotted cream, beef, tomatoes and fruit. Some people are so thin they look like skeletons jerking around.

Mother has kept four lumps of sugar for the special day. Carefully dipped in cochineal, wrapped in wisps of paper from Christmas past, they will sit one on each breakfast plate. Over the last few months, people have survived on seaweed, grated parsnip cakes, peelings, acorns and lupin seeds roasted and ground into coffee. Camellia and blackberry leaves are made into tea. The islanders have started praying for food.

December 26th. A large ship steamed up the harbour, unexpected, as if in answer. She calmly moved into our docks. It appeared like a metal angel of Christmas joy. Inside it were parcels, from the Swedish Red Cross — one for each family, tins of meat, blocks of sugar and lard, biscuits and even chocolate. How could any Christmas to come be as thrilling as this one?

CHAPTER 31
February 22nd

Nothing arrived from her mother. She had to be dead or cruel beyond imagining. Gran and Nan had sent her parcels. They were waiting for her on the doorstep when she got home from school. She ripped them open and sighed when she saw two different cosmetic bags and travel shampoo and conditioner sets.

'They must think alike those grans. But they will be useful for our trip.' She rang them to say thanks and of course Felix had to say hello too.

Four friends from school were coming for her birthday tea. They brought her little gifts: sweets, a make your own bracelet kit, pretty hair slides, and best of all, a lockable diary. Now she could start to write out her own detective thoughts and notes, plans too. And they would be secret.

Felix gave her little things of his own: a drawing from kindergarten and his favourite coloured stone, grey with streaks of pink running through. Nathan hadn't had time to take him shopping.

'Oh Felix, thank you. I know this is your very loved stone.'

She gave him a big sloppy kiss. He wiped it away with the back of his hand. Meadow crouched down in front of the little person.

'I love you Felix.' His smile showed all his little teeth. Dad had bought his girl a new detective novel and some soft muslin hankies. Goodness knows she needed more of those. Felix tried to be very helpful. He picked up the gift-wrap and stacked her presents in a precarious pile.

'I don't think you are a real boy today, but a little angel.' Tears welled up then rolled like dripping taps when they sang Happy Birthday and blew out the candles. Most of her friends knew why she was upset, but Felix just cuddled her.

'All wite Med. All wite. New hankie?'

She loved looking after her little brother so much, she changed her ambition from being a vet to being a primary school teacher.

'Fight for your dreams, Meadow!' Dad said when she told him. *It may be too late for her mother's dreams, but I won't make the same mistake twice.*

The child was always busy. Felix never sat around thinking, moping, dwelling on the past or the future. He had to be doing. Pretending to be a policeman or a fireman with his little plastic figures. Fighting imaginary enemies, knocking down block-built barricades then rebuilding them in a different spot. He was never inward looking or contemplative. Action was the answer.

So Nathan and Meadow followed the little one's lead. They set themselves tasks: dinners to make, cakes to try baking.

The results were variable but a very successful Victoria sponge was a triumph they all enjoyed. Papa and Felix clapped Meadow when they had eaten their first piece. The child's hands covered with jam.

Nathan sanded and repainted little spots on the woodwork that had been long-neglected by dint of long business hours. He began to feel the satisfaction of achieving small tasks, physical tasks. Dad and Meadow talked it over. Even sadness-filled activity, sad because Mum wasn't there, can help take away the sadness they decided.

There had not been any news about Sarah for so long, almost four months. It seemed hopeless. There was nothing, no proof she was alive. There was not even a letter, a phone call or a postcard. The trail had gone cold. No money had been withdrawn from her bank account since the week she'd left. 'Dad, how can Mamma live, if she is alive, without taking out any more money?'

'Well, two thousand pounds is a lot of money. If she lived carefully it's still possible to stretch it out for quite a while. But to be honest, Honey, I think she would have run out by now if she were alive.'

'She has to be dead.' Meadow was able to say it now, without crying, just like it was a fact. It would maybe stop hurting completely if they could only find out the truth. They continued to refine their plans to visit Madrid together at Easter time and tried to make it a fun activity by looking up tourist sites and famous buildings to visit. Madrid looked amazing in the brochures Meadow collected during the half term.

OK, so we will be asking everyone we see if they have seen this woman in the photo, just like they do on detective programs on TV, but we can make it a happy time too. It will be a lot warmer than England. That can't be bad.

They went shopping for Chorizo, chickpeas and Churros. 'So we can get used to the food.' They tried to cook a few Spanish foods at home for fun to try to lighten the gloomy atmosphere that hung in the air like a haze. 'Torrijas', the dessert eaten during holy week, was quite easy to make, similar to French Toast. Of course Felix loved it because it was covered in icing sugar and cut into strips like soldiers. Nathan, with Meadow's help and Felix's constant interruptions, constructed Paella. Well it looked a little similar. Dad and his girl ate it, imagining themselves in a Spanish café. Felix spat it out.

They looked up Flamenco dancing on YouTube and watched

in silence at the fierceness of the dance and loud rhythmic guitar sounds. The male dancers were deeply passionate and serious. They held their arms in the air, their hands expressively twisting with feeling. Their high pants accentuating their waists and bottoms and their arched backs like insects on hind legs.

But the stamping of the feet was thrilling. Meadow tried it herself but the rhythm and clapping were difficult to copy. The women dancers emotional in their red dresses, black veils and stompy tap shoes twirling and turning. Were they angry or sad? She couldn't decide. Maybe both.

Well, that's how I feel anyway, both.

The loud stamping was very therapeutic. She did it again.

When Felix had watched the Flamenco dancers he held his head very erect and waved his arms like a duck flapping.

'Ha-ha Felix, you're too short and stubby!'

But his footwork wasn't too bad. He found the timing instinctively. 'We'll have to take him to a live show in Madrid, Dad.'

Sarah appeared to Nathan as he slept. He felt her kiss his cheek. He woke immediately and looked around, his eyes searching the room. The kiss lingered. He touched the spot on his face, closed his moistened eyes and fell asleep again.

CHAPTER 32
9th May 1945

Alice's Diary

*Liberation Day. Such joy down at the harbour! Our turn to sing;
Sarnia Cherie rose spontaneously from the people and drifted
out over the sea to mingle with the gulls' cries in a triumph of
freedom.*

*I had never valued freedom because it seemed to me I always
had it. (Apart from my mother of course.) But now when we see
the British liberators and the relief on the once tense faces of my
fellow islanders and feel the liberty of no longer being punished
for anything, going wherever we choose at any time of the day or
night with no fears of arrest, I feel the value to the human soul of
true freedom. Those poor boys who died to preserve ours, fighting
in the air, sea and on land, some of them only eighteen years old.
Thank you to each one of you.*

I won't waste that freedom you bought, I promise.

Emile and Louis were welcomed back to the Sunshine Island with
great honour. They received their military crosses in a ceremony
in front of a local crowd. The two heroes had already been for-
mally presented with the honours in their regiment before they
were demobilised.

Although Lou was back, there was something intangible missing
between him and Alice.

Alice's Diary

September 1946. The excitement has all gone now everything is normal and we are all safe again. I feel no romantic spark flash when I meet up with Lou. I've started to find fault with him. He is so correct and unspontaneous. I think I've become used to always having stimulating activity. He is a great loving friend of course. Actually his dad has told him about my flings with Henry and Vic. He's told him to keep away from me, that I'm unsteady. What a cheek!

Dad managed to buy our house a few years before the war with his earnings from the business, but Dad and Mum have decided to sell up our lovely home and move to England – really soon, in only a few weeks. I'm puzzled. Why are they doing this? Does everyone know we have been good friends with the Germans? Do they think we have been collaborators? Surely not when we were sent to the Paris prison for sheltering Lou. But Mum seems afraid to show her face and hardly goes into town anymore. Dad did trade with the Germans. We did have an easier time than a lot of our acquaintances – at least with food quantities. Many people were near to starvation. Maybe that's what people are thinking – collaborators – a dirty word. What right did we have to befriend the enemy while Allied Forces were being slaughtered and Jews unmercifully tortured, dying like animals, men, women and too horrifying to even whisper, babies. We didn't know of these things, we really didn't know.

I've started to write to Fritz. Actually I've written to quite a few of the German military who were on Guernsey during the occupation. Not all romantically of course. My parents have encouraged me to write to Fritz. They say he is a young gentle-man, a doctor and not a Catholic. We've begun a correspondence relationship. Letters have been arriving and leaving almost every other day, at least three times a week. Quite exciting!

He needs help. There is so little work in Germany after the war. He thinks if he came to Britain he might have a better chance. So I have begun the huge effort, on my part, of writing to legal advisers, the diplomatic service and the Home Office. I went up to London to the High Commission last week to intercede on his behalf to try and get him a British visa. The Brits are very good about it, seeing we have really only just begun to recover from the war.

I've sent Fritz a series of little sepia photos; proofs really, of myself, some serious, some laughing. My hair is in two different styles; swept up off my forehead and parted on the side with lovely waves, like Lauren Bacall, in her latest film. The images show my many moods from mischievous to solemn but there isn't one sad face!

A large photo has arrived from Fritz in return. He is standing upright but turned slightly, his head cocked on one side, a sly smile on his lips looking a bit like an arrogant film star himself.

Fritz is striking – a strong face, even devilish and seductive. Uniforms have sucked in, swayed many women. It's the manliness of them – sexiness really.

I choose to believe he has been an innocent of the war too. He was never a Nazi, he made that very clear, and we knew him quite well during the occupation of the Channel Islands didn't we?

We have all found out the true and secret terrors of the war years; the atrocities, the utter inhumanity, but we still don't want to believe it. Germany's own people seem completely unwilling to accept the crimes that have been committed and every unspeakable act that has occurred.

Hitler's madness, his preposterous ideas, could only get a foothold in an amoral society. One with a black hole of lost-ness out of which climbed disguised monsters; the philosophies that led to the destruction of Jews, of Christians, of gypsies, even of children.

CHAPTER 33

Cologne, 6th July 1946.

Dear Mr and Mrs Beauvoir,
Some long and cruel years have passed and now I want to write to tell you I am still living and also all my family are safe and well too.

How are you, Mrs Beauvoir? I remember that you had oppression of the heart. Is it any better now?

Did the two sirs, Mr Robilliard and Mr Courbet return home?

All the members of my family suffered greatly, because they were persuaded. My mother and brother in law had to live in concentration camps in the end.

I myself was removed from office.

I will write all the details later if you would like the correspondence.

Please excuse my poor English.

Please remember me to Miss Alice and Miss Amy.

With kind regards
Werner Wulf.

The letter never reached the Beauvoirs. They had already moved to England.

CHAPTER 34
The Beach

February 24th. The family were doing a lot more together now they were more focussed on each other and wanting to keep the child's life happy – More outings and activities than they had done when there were four of them. Nathan once again regretted his previous obsession with keeping up a good solid life and sound investments, working to get to the top of his career – but mostly just being over-responsible and having little time to really live.

'Let's let go a bit and have more fun together. This is my new mission statement.' Meadow stared at him.

Nathan would have given mental assent to that philosophy before but would never have been able to break the habits of a life-time. It took the loss of Sarah to break him apart enough to receive the new.

On the next fine weekend in February they decided together to make a beach trip. True, it was still icy in the wind, but an adventure was better than sitting at home.

'Me want cwabs.'

They remembered, and bent double hooting with laughter, the last time they had gone crabbing. Felix had been obsessed. He wanted more and more of them in his bucket. The estuary they had gone to was very muddy and the tiny crabs were squirming around in the murky, shallow water. Felix had been desperate and refused to stop hunting until the bucket was half full of the revolting little creatures.

'Stop now you have enough, Felix, we're sick of it.'

'Go away,' he mouthed, no sound coming out. It had ended quite suddenly when Felix fell flat in the mud. They helped him up out of the slime but they got covered in the grey clay themselves. Everything was filthy, smelly and damp. The inside of the car was a mess that took a few days to clean up. Their clothes all streaked and stained. Felix couldn't have cared less. The bucket was full of his captives. They all died over the next couple of days and were buried in the garden when he wasn't looking.

Nathan suggested asking Jess to come with them to the coast.

'It'll be more fun with four.'

Meadow's face was enough to put a stop to that idea.

Felix ran after seagulls and pursued foam bubbles. They had to chase him to forget about the bleak dunes and the wind-tossed water. It helped to keep that chilling wind from creeping inside their jackets and their thoughts.

Felix took off running down the long stretch of sand.

'Come back!' He wouldn't stop.

'Felix, you naughty boy, come back!'

'What is he doing?'

They had no choice but to run after him, he wasn't hard to catch. Short chubby legs are no match for long, lean ones. Meadow had inherited Sarah's shape and Felix his dad's. *Lucky it wasn't the other way round.*

Way in the distance the child was running towards a group of figures walking together along the edge of the grey tide. Two of them were holding hands. The tall lady had dark hair, a slim build, and wore a black coat.

Felix ran for a full two minutes. They had almost caught up to him, they couldn't let him just run off – *little children are so unpredictable.*

Nathan could see the bucket and spade left behind in the distance as he looked back. Felix came to a sudden stop when he was near the lady. He stared at her then turned around, ran and jumped into his dad's arms. He put his head down to rest it on Nathan's shoulder. He stayed very still and clingy. Dad and daughter thought they knew what the boy had been thinking. *When your heart is full of someone, you see them everywhere.*

Standing on the edge of the foam line staring over the Channel, Nathan gazed at that wretched grey ocean that separated them, deep, murky and cold. England and France. Nathan and Spain. The Three and Sarah. *It's like I'm in the shadows and the light is over in Europe.* The clouds parted briefly; the warmth of hope glimmered inside him. Then the sun shone for a short moment and its beams like searchlights found spots to turn into diamonds. He gathered himself and strengthened his resolve. *I will follow the trail wherever it leads. She is the piece of the puzzle that has to be, has to be, put back into our family portrait.*

He was glad he hadn't invited the other woman now. He wouldn't have been able to realise how passionately he missed Sarah. He'd felt his love rekindling – a little fire but still a flame, and finally now a love that would pursue her. *What a fool! Such a coward! Why didn't I go to Madrid straight away when the police told me the tracking stopped there? The trail wouldn't have gone cold. It would have been easy to find her, probably still alive and willing to come home.*

Nothing else mattered to him anymore. He began to dream about her at night and during the day. It seemed trifling to be concerned with work and mundane matters.

He recalled the passion he felt for Sarah before they were married. She was a wild, intelligent and fascinating person, so interested in everything and so hopeful about the future. What had their life done to that girl? He felt again the softness of heart he had had and the joyous happiness they had shared on their wedding day. On his return home he swiped through his albums, trying to capture the feeling of love and hope. You could see it in those photographs, the tender eyes and gentle smiles.

The intimacy of the innocent pair had produced Meadow nine months after the honeymoon. Even at that unspeakable time another being had come to them.

Those months were difficult with little sleep and stresses from baby uncertainties but their love for each other and amazement at the little one brought weeks of great closeness.

It had turned to custard sometime since then, yet seasons of intimacy of heart had peppered the years until he had buried himself in work. Sarah had grown listless. *What should we have done to prevent the loss of so deep a relationship?* He hadn't even noticed it slipping away like the end of summer.

Sarah was wonderful, she never hounded me for more love – perhaps she should have – rather than sink inwards. She may have tried, I can't recall.

If only I had stopped and thought about all this before Sarah left – we could have rebuilt the ruins and restored the fairy tale. I really think we could have.

Over the weeks before she went missing, Sarah had been very quiet. She seemed lethargic, hardly wanting to get out of bed. Meadow had seen her crying soft tears. They were just slowly coming out of the ends of her eyes like squeezed lemon drops; there was no sound of crying. Sarah had lost interest in making the house tidy or cooking interesting food. Nathan could see the signs, but it was easier to ignore them and think it was just a temporary mood.

Maybe Sarah has left with the idea of renewal in her head, of swapping her depressing thoughts for a new way of thinking – to clear her head, literally. But something tragic had happened, she couldn't do it, so she gave up, made an end of it all. I have been such a coward. I can't be one for a moment longer. I have only one chance to get it right for Felix, Meadow and me.

'Right then,' he said aloud.

Now Nathan had reaffirmed his sense of direction. *We will find out what happened to her. It's imperative for all of us, or we'll be stuck in this deadly quagmire, unable to move on.*

I owe it to her memory, as my wife, the mother of the children and Sarah's own being.

CHAPTER 35
1947

Alice continued to dance, this time to entertain troops stationed, post-war, in various parts of England. It helped to fill in the time while she waited for letters from Fritz.

> **Alice's Diary**
>
> *October 28th. No news from Fritz for five days. Worried.*
>
> *I've sent him a parcel. Germany is now in dire need of food and other goods. The parcel, wrapped in brown paper, was tinned pears, pudding, milk, cocoa, cigarettes, a crunchie bar and some butter.*
>
> *'It is Fritz for me forever. Letter arrived!'*

The letters continued coming every two days.

After Fritz finally got the clearance to come to England, he wrote and told Alice the day and time the ferry was to arrive at Dover. She rushed down, having to change trains twice, and waited there at the docks. She walked about all evening. He didn't come. She went to the pictures at the Odeon to take her mind off worrying. There was no way to contact him so she stayed the night in a cheap guest-house and repeated the vigil all the next day and evening. *Is that him?* Her eyes were sore from scanning the incoming passengers.

'Fritz, Fritz here.' She waved and smiled.

'Alice, how good to see you.' His English near perfect but with a strong German accent.

'Come on, it's cold.' He gave her a hug and they went off to the train station arm in arm. She'd been hoping for a warmer welcome after all the effort she had put in to get him accepted into Britain. More than that she wanted him to at least kiss her and say something about how pretty she looked. She was used to that from the years of the Lyric Theatre. He had paid her more attention then than he was doing now. His clothes were shabby – it was hard to buy anything in Germany now. His hat jauntily cocked to the side, he looked handsome still, even without the uniform, and the accent added to the romantic picture Alice had already formed in her mind.

They were greeted warmly by Rose and Albert and welcomed inside the seaside house.

Fritz was tired and went upstairs to bed. Alice couldn't sleep; she lay on top of her bed on her stomach, her chin on her folded hands. She thought about her freedom and yet the firm security of marriage while she looked up dreamily and swung her legs like a contented child reading. At breakfast, not too early in the morning, Fritz, tousle-haired and sleepy-eyed, asked if they had any coffee.

'Yes we do have some. Wait a minute, I'll make a pot.'

With coffee in hand Fritz said, 'Come with me into the garden Alice.'

'But it's very cold.'

'Then get your coat.'

Outside Fritz turned to her and held her hand. 'Will you marry me, Alice?' He asked this in quite a business-like way. No bended knee; no little red box.

'Yes, Fritz, I will.' They hugged and kissed. It was not the romantic kiss Alice had seen so many times in the films she loved to watch, but her eyes shone and she made a little pirouette. He laughed at her. 'Funny English girl.'

Arm in arm they knocked on Mr and Mrs Beauvoir's closed sitting room door.

'You'll have to ask my dad first, even though I'm twenty-seven. It's what they expect.'

After much discussion the pair decided on a date for a wedding, and once again Alice did all the preparation and running around: finding the venue, getting the licence and inviting guests. She got a permit for the wedding cake – food was still rationed, and paid the one-Pound deposit. The date was set to be in only fourteen days time.

On the day of the wedding Alice was calm and steady. It didn't feel like mad passionate love; instead it was the wise thing to do. Her parents, her brother, her friends were all for it: the prospects, the intelligence, the good family, a very polite young man, and a doctor.

Alice wore a white dress with a sweetheart neckline. It was overlaid with primrose tulle taken from an old dancing gown. Her hair adorned with white carnations to give her height and covered by a light lemon veil which hung delicately over her high forehead and down below her chin. At the back it was almost floor length. The bride and bridesmaid – Oswald's girlfriend – carried posies of violet and mauve papery windflowers. Bert walked her in on his arm. A white carnation in his hired immaculate fitted grey morning coat. The trees already bare from the November winds stood behind the churchyard moving and filtering the watery sun. The couple looked flushed and eager. They honeymooned in Devon as Rose and Albert had done. The black and white photographs of the wedding day portrayed a happy smiling group. The Guernsey newspaper reported: 'Well-known dancer weds German doctor.'

Alice's Diary

We are staying with Mother and Daddy for a few weeks, but Fritz is at a loose end. He is a cultured and professional man. He misses his friends and fellow students and seems bored with my parents' conversations. I've begun to wonder if I've made a mistake marrying him.

Fritz hasn't been able to find any work in England and has to return to Germany to finish the last semester of his medical degree anyway.

I have married a foreigner so I can't travel on my British passport. I'll have to apply for a pass, a certificate of identity and permission to join my husband.

It's arrived. The little blue cardboard pass is hand written in delicate handwriting with red ink. But there are more forms to fill out. It's taking much longer than I ever imagined. There is a lot of red tape to unwind for a British citizen to enter the late enemy's land. Fritz has gone on ahead.

I had got a job at a clothing wholesalers owned by Jewish brothers. When I told them yesterday that my husband was German, they asked me to leave!

I am so wide-eyed, I haven't given much thought to English attitudes to Germans. Or to how a British Jew might feel.

Alice set off from Dover and arrived in Ostend. From there she went by Nord-Express train. It rushed through Belgium and at the first frontier crossing, Alice had to get off while the train was searched. They looked for wanted men; war crimes criminals, escapees from punishment, contraband, people without the necessary documents. At passport control, German, Belgian and British inspectors worked side by side.

Alice's Diary

The train's destination was Dusseldorf then I had to change for Munster. Travelling over the Rhine across the bridge, many young exuberant passengers waved and cheered. You would think they had won the war. Yet Germany has suffered a monstrous punishment in death and destruction. Far far more of their young men died than ours.

It was dark when I arrived. Munster City was in ruins: bombed out like a film set.

Fritz met me and we had to scramble over piles of rubble, stones, bricks, the broken walls of homes, carrying heavy suitcases. Fritz knew his way easily over the debris that led to his flat in Prinz Eugen Strasse.

A new life has begun in a bedsitter. The mattress filled with straw, the language only slightly familiar. Food has become a problem again. Mother sends parcels and always packets of cigarettes from Daddy. We exchange them for anything edible or for coffee. I had to join food queues. I stood for two hours to get four lemons and then went back to our flat triumphant to make a batch of lemon curd. I've tasted celery at last. Delicious. But I've felt a little strange over the past few weeks. My body seems out of kilter with its usual routines.

'Fritz, I have some exciting news.' Alice looked into her young husband's eyes, her expressive face shining – her own eyes sparkling. 'I'm expecting our baby.'

'Oh, at this time. Well we'll have to cope with it.'

'You don't seem very pleased about it.'

Alice looked at the floor. *Maybe that's the German way.* In private she shed tears of bitter disappointment. The sadness was buried by the university holidays, they planned to see as much of the country as possible. That Christmas was her second in Germany. There were no luxuries; they ate roll mops – soused herrings. It was far more spartan than it had ever been for Alice in occupied Guernsey during the war. Still they managed to enjoy themselves for two months touring scenic, snow-covered mountain resorts, meeting all Fritz's family and friends. His parents now lived in Krefeld; their hometown had been completely flattened in 1944.

When Alice was heavily pregnant the couple returned to England so that Alice could have their child there. Elizabeth was born in Hampshire in the hospital where Fritz had been offered temporary work as an intern. The position only lasted eighteen months, no other work was found in Great Britain. The authorities wouldn't accept the German qualification. Fritz could only find work back in Germany. He returned. Alice went through the same rigours of applying for a visa again. They were apart for four months. This time she had to take many baby items needed for Elizabeth so was laden down with luggage and the child.

Fritz met them at the Munster station like the first time she'd arrived there. After the hug and the kiss and the cuddle of Elizabeth, Fritz said, 'I have something I must tell you, Alice, before anyone else does.'

'Oh, what?' Alice was half in fear, half hope.

He stammered out, 'I have become extremely close to a nurse called Hanne. Everyone knows about it.'

Sickness hit Alice's stomach and almost made her vomit.

Tears ran down onto her grey winter coat. Some fell on Elizabeth's light blond hair.

'Why? How could you do this to me? How could you treat me like I'm nothing at all – we've only been married three years. You rotten dog!' But her voice was weak and shaky. She wanted to shout at him, but her utter humiliation had taken the power from her expressions of rage.

She pummelled his chest with her fists as the tears fell.

I'm not wanted. What is so wrong with me? She turned away from him. 'But you want me, my love, my darling daughter. I have you.' Alice looked into the eyes of her small fair blue-eyed child and hugged her closer to her chest. 'All my days and thoughts will be devoted to you.'

That painful feeling of failure that had dogged her childhood was back. She gave up her right to be loved – her shoulders slumped. She raised her free hand as she gazed toward heaven. *Why does this happen to me?*

Then her mouth tightened. Her eyes became flint-hard. She straightened up and the tears stopped falling.

OK. The Germans are not going to win. They will lose again.

Fritz's unfaithfulness felt like a dull ache in Alice's chest. The ache remained there, a dull deadness inside. It felt like something was growing; a rotten seed had taken root in already fertile soil. Out of it would grow a yearning, a compulsion for affirmation, affection, romance even – with a careless approach to the consequences. It transformed into a physical need that bypassed her reasoning.

The two adults, Alice carrying the baby, continued walking over the uneven streets until they arrived at Fritz's digs.

Alice decided to pretend to the landlady that she was carefree, untroubled. Fritz was puzzled about Alice's reaction but relieved.

That wasn't so bad.

It seemed Alice had forgotten the betrayal because she soon had a part-time job as a secretary to a stationed British Army Captain and was enjoying the social contact, back into the occasional party and theatre visit, when they could get the landlady to babysit.

There was still very little food about and nothing to buy in the near-empty shops.

Alice again wrote to her mother to ask for a few things to be sent from England. Soon the first of many packages arrived.

'At last – Bovril! And pea and ham soup in a tin.'

Fritz was often out late and had started to drink quite heavily. Rarely the pair would go together to the British army headquarters in the city and sit and chat to the personnel. They made a few friends. Sometimes they even danced. Their dancing was much admired. When Fritz wasn't home, Alice went alone to the club. She left Elizabeth with the nanny that the hospital had now provided for her. Many men, lonely for their wives, looked at her admiringly. She struck up a friendship with a young olive-skinned man who knew Fritz very well; he worked with him in the hospital.

'Fritz is on duty tonight. Come on home to our flat and have a nightcap. I have a 20-month-old child asleep there but she won't wake up, she sleeps blissfully.'

'Really? Are you sure?'

'Yes, sure! The war is over, we've survived. We need to enjoy every minute.'

Ray showed her all the attention she didn't get from her husband. He told her how lovely she looked, what a great dancer she was and how he enjoyed her company. He comforted her when she told him about Fritz's unfaithfulness. He put his arms around Alice and drew her close.

'Let's not worry about him.' He kissed her gently on the mouth. Feelings of desire quickly overtook Alice's mental objections. *After all, he's done the dirty on me. I need this love and affection to stay alive in this desolate country.*

CHAPTER 36
Felix Talks

Felix had a new pair of navy-blue jeans. His other ones were too short – he was growing at a great rate of knots. That morning he refused to wear the new pair. He threw himself onto the sofa, kicked and screamed. They ignored him but had to cover their ears, it was such a piercing wail. They exited the room fast and left him to yell himself out.

He loved his old jeans, the rips, stains, the softness and the pockets that housed favourite stones and snail shells. Mamma had bought the old pair one fun day when he had had an ice cream treat for patiently trying on various pairs until they found the perfect fit.

But they were way too short now. His ankles and the bottom parts of his chubby legs stuck out of the ends. Really he looked like a mini Huckleberry Finn.

Meadow teased him: 'Felix Finn!' He had no idea what that was but he jumped about and imitated her mockery when she rolled up the bottoms of her jeans nearly to her knees and danced around.

'They are actually quite fashionable, Dad – the roll-ups.'

The only solution to the new pair problem was to throw the old jeans into the washing machine and turn it on. But the screams returned.

'He'll get over it Daddy.'

In the evening when Nathan arrived home after work, he was relieved he didn't have to think about what to have for dinner.

'Dad, I got the steak out of the freezer when I got home.'

'Cool, Med. Thanks.' Soon the kitchen was filled with the savoury smell of frying oil.

Felix helped to mash spuds and carrot with butter, pushing down hard forcing long thin orange lumps to spray all over his shirt. The three clung to each other laughing. Meadow assembled a winter salad from a recipe book. They sat down to dinner telling each other about their busy days. Felix's tales were hard to understand but hilarious. Bliss.

At night a small voice could be heard coming from the child's room. It sounded like chatting. Meadow heard the word 'Mamma.'

Why would Felix start talking to Mamma out loud at night now, when she isn't even here? At first Meadow ran into his room thinking Mum had suddenly returned, ever hopeful. She expected to see her standing there. She'd done this a dozen times now and was no longer really surprised when it was another false alarm. It disturbed her to hear her little brother talking to a Mamma that wasn't there. She crept in and listened to the one-way conversation.

'Mamma, today I play wiv my pwaymobile and we had fight. I ate my dinner, not my sawad, sowwy. Med and Felix had a barf. Daddy read me a storwee. I got new jeans; I hate them. I cwied. Mamma, what are you doing?'

He waited silently, but of course no answer came. Then he sang a little song and closed his eyes. He was asleep.

His sister moved quietly over to his bed and looked at him. His bed was so big and he looked so small. There were a few drying tears on his cheeks. His lips were apart, he was breathing through his mouth. On his bed lay toys and books. His slippers, so cute, miniature dad's slippers, grey and emerald tartan, lay on the carpet beside the wooden bed. On the avocado green walls were taped up paintings he'd done at kindergarten; lollipop people, suns, houses, flowers and bumble bees. *That about sums up his whole life, all except bicycles and food!*

The talks to Mamma continued on and off for a few weeks then stopped. *Does that mean anything?*

CHAPTER 37
1953

When Alice found she was pregnant she was not horrified. At first she thought she could pretend it was Fritz's child. *That will never work – he's a doctor. We weren't even intimate during that time.* She had been cold to her husband when he was at home. It was impossible to carry on the pretence in private.

'You only married me so you could get a British Visa.'

'Not true Alice. I thought it would work out with you.'

'You didn't give the marriage any chance to survive but snuffed it out before it had time to grow into a decent thing.'

'I'm willing to give it another chance.'

Her eyes glinted as she said to him in a calm voice, 'Too late, I'm expecting another baby.'

'You can't be. We haven't slept together since you arrived here.'

'Well I am.'

Fritz threw his arms up and then thumped them on the table. Cups and plates crashed to the floor. He saw their framed wedding photo on the bureau – he grabbed it and hurled it down onto the linoleum. It smashed into fragments. He tore the photo in two pieces down the middle.

Alice ran into the only other room and slammed the door. She fell onto the bed and gave vent to the emotional turmoil with screams that the landlord would most definitely hear. The door to the flat slammed shut. The room shook with the violence of it.

'I should have married Henry. I should have, I should have.'

She curled herself into a little ball and let the weeping and the sobs run their course. An hour later she had decided on her plan.

'I will return to Mum and Dad when the time comes nearer to the birth.'

When Alice was six months pregnant, she arrived on Bert and Rose's front door step, Elizabeth on her hip and a heavy brown suitcase in her hand. Alice fell onto her father's chest.

'Oh Alice, what now?'

'Come inside you two, come on.'

'Why didn't you tell us?'

'Too difficult to write about Mum.' Elizabeth ran happily up and down the stairs, while sorrowing and ashamed Alice told them the whole truth. She spared nothing. This was not Victorian England. Now it was 1953.

The child's grandparents were very kind to her; paid her a lot of attention. Rose had very swollen ankles from her deteriorating heart condition so she couldn't do much chasing or lifting, but Grandad played games with Elizabeth and sat her on his knee and gently brushed her hair. This became her first memory – that tingly feeling of contentment and relaxation that crept down her spine.

The baby was born, a healthy little boy, dark haired – no similarity to Elizabeth at all. Alice's parents helped with the adoption process that they had insisted on. But the few weeks of nursing the boy, then giving him up, tore another piece off Alice's soul; it left a wound she covered by denying it and just pretending the whole episode had never happened.

'What a fool I am – an absolute fool.'

CHAPTER 38
1957

Alice craved excitement; she pined for times past. The remembrance of the years of the adrenalin rush during the occupation had begun to gnaw at her emotions. She huffed and panted as she did her household tasks. After all, she had been famous in her own way – on a small island – a big fish in a small pond – she had been adored by the crowds that came to the dance shows.

'It ruined me for a normal existence. How can a return to average be possible? I always was a glutton for the sweet things of life,' she said aloud to her image in the bathroom mirror.

After Alice's divorce came through, she began to feel more unsettled and hungered for a new relationship – someone who would really love her like Henry had. She also yearned for a more adventurous existence. Life had become dull after the challenges during wartime with the rationing, the hiding of Louis and the threat of death. She didn't rationalise it, but just felt the need for something real to fight against, an obstacle to overcome. She might have become an adrenalin junkie. But she called it wanderlust.

For several years she worked as a housekeeper to widows or divorced men, usually moving on after a while when the situations didn't work out. Elizabeth was still a child, so happily uprooted with each move without a murmur.

Several years went by in this way, constant moving and resettling. Elizabeth could remember a few men, but not those that had come before she was about nine years old. At that time, mother and girl had spent some time, just the two of them, living in a little caravan at a residential park. Alice was pleased. It was the first time she had owned a dwelling that was all her own, though it wasn't a house exactly.

It didn't last – the contentment, but Alice and Elizabeth were close during those months.

'Gibby' – Alice's nickname when her daughter was preteen – 'I do love you so much. Can't we go out to the little villages in the New Forest today and look in those quaint old shops and then meander around on the heath to see the wild creatures, the pretty ponies, and then go for a walk in the woods and watch the squirrels?'

'Of course we can, Sarnia, and tell me everything that you would like to do when you're older, on the way.' Sarnia was one old name for Guernsey. 'You know I would have named you Sarnia if your father hadn't insisted it be a German name.'

'I'm awfully glad you didn't. How is Elizabeth a German name?'

'Well it's pronounced differently, but it's still a common name there.'

They went by bus to Burley and everywhere else. The pair had no car or anything much. Lizzie got most of her clothes from Charity shops and hated them.

The New Forest was full of quivering trees and small streams. 'Mum, I love nature study – it's the only thing I get good marks for. I will be a naturalist I think.' It was the drawing really that gave her the success.

When Elizabeth was nearing teen-age the loneliness crept back into Alice and threatened to overwhelm her. *My girl will leave one day and then what will I have?*

Alice poured through newspapers and answered a few adverts in the lonely heart's column. She found a sweet advert for a friendship with a view to marriage. It was from a Welsh farmer, a widower.

They went to meet him. His house was cold and its out-dated décor depressed Elizabeth. 'There's no light in here. The windows are so small.'

'But it'll be cosy when the fire is going and you can draw all those amazing landscapes and wildflowers and birds.'

Alun was very interested in Alice's life story and they wrote and phoned and managed to meet up a few more times. He travelled a long way to pursue the friendship.

He took Alice for a tour of his beloved Wales. In the north were heavily glaciated mountains and the Welsh countryside further south was rugged and strikingly beautiful. It was blue hills and purple moor grass, but in other parts wooded, with many waterfalls running through them banked by spray splashed boulders luxuriant with moss. Ferns and wood anemone dotted the shady spots. The red kite birds circled the mountain slopes overhead. Standing on the heights, Alice saw the valleys spotted with lakes, shiny gemstones among the shale rock.

She sat down by a gushing stream, her head in her hands. *This wonderful landscape is absolutely nothing like my own Channel Island. Could I live here?* The sound of the tinkling water calmed her and brought peace. The wind swept her hair back and Alun held out his hand to lift her to her feet.

After a three month courtship, Alun asked Alice to marry him. She accepted, quite thrilled with her new prospects.

I don't remember being consulted, Elizabeth thought.

Lizzie found it unbearable living in isolation. She hated the cold stone house. The farm was a long way from anywhere. The local hamlet only a few houses, the school a long distance by bus. She had been dragged away from her friends, her pets and the beautiful Hampshire towns and villages that she had grown up in.

She was only thirteen. She had a new stepfather, she didn't want to be adopted by him as he'd hoped, she hardly knew the man. He obviously loved her in a way – but she was concerned about what way. His fascination for nude figurines and the movie *Lolita* was a red flag.

During the hot summer holidays, she lay on a long low deck-chair in the field behind the house in her bikini, tanning herself. Alice had seen Alun watching her. Lizzie was spooked, but knew little at her tender age of what some men are made of. Possibilities of attack or rape were unreal fleeting thoughts – even when the neighbouring farmer was sent to prison for abusing his partner's daughter.

I'm sure Mum will protect me. She always has.

Her life had been a sheltered one in that area. It was 1968. There was no easily available adult news as has become commonplace today. No YouTube with its gory and disgusting images to assault her half-innocent mind.

Elizabeth's Notebook

2015. You know I must have been around when all sorts of things were going on. In those years before Mum married Alun, there are a few men's faces I can still remember clearly.

It's a bad decision to marry a man you barely know, let alone when the woman has a young daughter – it's asking for trouble. I was quite innocent as a child. My passions were birds, wild-flowers and sketching. I think those things protected my mind for that time.

When I was sixteen, I gained entrance to an Art College. By this time I couldn't wait to get away. The farm life didn't suit a teenager who'd metamorphosed from a child to a bleached haired– boy-hungry rebel. Typical I guess – but what a shame.

So I left home to live in Winchester and never lived under that roof again. Naturally I went back for birthdays, Christmas and some holidays, but Mum and I never were bonded close again after that. She said I'd left home too early, but if she'd wanted it to be just the two of us, she shouldn't have married Alun or moved into the Welsh hills, should she?

Living in a city five hours away was only difficult occasionally. Liz found that irritation with her mother and then remorse followed each other in a repeated round, only seconds apart.

Living quite a distance was mostly for me a blessed deliverance – from fights and total misunderstandings like 'Brocklewood – how is Steven Brocklewood? He must come from Hampshire, you know. Brockenhurst is a town there.'
  'Mum!' I'd yell, 'His name is Brookbanks.'
  'Yes, dear.'
  She didn't listen to me. Her life was only in her head. Later she would talk about the Brocklewood boy again. How could there be any real meeting of minds or emotions when we were never on the same wavelength? Still, the ties weren't in the mind but in the heart. I've been my mother's friend, helper, and enemy for sixty years.

Alice's Diary
1970. Cried bitter salty tears as Elizabeth's bus left the station.
  On my drive home to the cottage, I thought, Have I done it again? Made another mistake? The dearest one I have has gone because I needed a man to love me. I've chosen him. I do love Alun; I've grown attached to him.
  It's painful loosening the ties, such strong blood ties, but if I'm honest they have been unravelling for several years. She's too young to go at sixteen, but she has her own path to choose. I hope and pray she never has to live such painful years as I've endured – at least wartime is over. I'll never stand in her way like my mother did – I've made a promise to myself.

She drove into her driveway; the dogs barked – the door opened.

'I've just made a cuppa.'

Yes, I need this settled home now and a husband to love me.

But she couldn't get Elizabeth off her mind. *What will her life be?* She finished her tea and then looked around at the many tasks that needed doing. The busyness relieved her of her train of thought.

Alun whistled the dogs and walked down the valley for his final evening check. He was 'a stick and a dog shepherd'. Old school, but he loved it.

Later that evening Alice wrote to her daughter. The letters leaving and arriving continued the pattern of wartime contact Alice was used to.

Can I stick at this life without Elizabeth being here?

As she cleared away the dishes she visualised her home in the Channel Islands, her childhood home, the walk down to the town and the cycling along the cliff paths, the sea in its moodiness – roaring or lapping. The wild white spray; the sea lashed, sea crashed coast. Sand glinting in the sunshine and the happiness that had filled her heart and mind, but then she glanced around at her shabby walls. Two worlds in opposition – the old one she yearned after.

Can you long for a place like you long for a lover? She believed so. What is it about a place you love, a country, a scene, a district that evokes such desire that you groan and tears instantly fill your eyes with desire to be there. It's so deep in the psyche that it's an actual part of you, inseparable – an organ of your being that controls your belly and causes it to tighten in successive aches.

She felt a poem stirring in her mind and jotted down a few poignant lines.

Half to forget the wandering and pain
Half to remember days that have gone

And dream
Just dream I was home again.

Alice's Diary

December 1970. Zero degrees tonight, fine weather – full moon – an absolute beauty of a sky. Glad to sit down at 5.30 pm.

But it's New Year's Eve tonight! No celebration. What a contrast to the years on my island. I have to be content with their newspapers and my memories. I'm saving every penny so I can have a holiday before my dear Guernsey friends fade away and me with them. Went to find my photos of a New Year's Eve when I danced in the cabaret. Looked through them all slowly and relived every moment.

January 13th. Dear Henry's birthday. I thought of him all day – sentimental fool that I am.

It's foggy, dark and dismal. My chest aches from carrying wood into the kitchen. Alun is cruel with his words and things he does. Seems I've been doomed to repeat the same mistakes again. I might see a marriage counsellor. I should have known that home, my island, would be where I'd find love. I should have known.

1998. Got some devastating news.

Bunty wrote, Louis died today of septicaemia after an operation on his leg.

Every day spent in my youth came into my head like a series of scenes. How I wept. Oh what could have been.

Poem for Lou

The sun's hot rays
Never seared our friendship
Instead the pastures

Child

Remain green
From my falling tears

I love this quote by Helen Keller: 'The best and most beautiful things in this world cannot be seen or even heard, but must be felt with the heart.'

CHAPTER 39

Nathan picked up Lizzie's notebook and read some notes his mother had written over the last few days:

They were married for 42 years. But how can a person born on an island ever be content inland? Mum stuck it out finally and even joined the local Farmers' Wives group. She loved the farm and the garden, and living in the wild, but her regret was the hours-long drive to the beach. No harbour, no sea.

'Oh she didn't like everything about her years on the farm then?'

'No, it rained a lot and was often biting cold too. The people from the north of Wales come from tough Welsh peasant stock. Alun Williams was independent and needed no company. He liked only staying around home. An old saying applied to him perfectly, "A Welshman loves his brother best when he is dead."'

'That could be true of a lot of us really though,' she winked at Nathan.

'On my visits home I gained a new compassion for old Alun. He could barely read or write and Mum harassed him about his lack of education, thinking hers had been marvellous, quite forgetting she had left school early too. He was doing all right until he was eighty then he developed severe angina and other symptoms of his heart trouble.'

'Yes, I can remember clearly seeing him growing thinner and staggering to walk with only the help of a farmyard stick. It was worse I think in a man who had been only physical all his life.'

Liz picked up an old diary of Alice's from 2005:

I find Alun today failing – his legs are so weak he can barely walk. He has great difficulty going up and down our three steps. His sight is nil. He can't read anything at all and his hearing nearly as bad. He has a lot of pain. I think he feels the light is going out and he is in deep depression. I really believe that now I am the nurse that I was always meant to be. He wouldn't be able to do anything without my help – It's just like nursing a child.

Elizabeth put the diary down. 'He got sicker and sicker each year, as we all realised when we got together on the farm every Christmas. Alun fought going to hospital. He hated the doctor's appointments. He felt like a refugee in a foreign camp. He had no confidence at all in his ability to talk to townies. I remember when the call came that Alun had died. I ran all the way home from the village where I had gone for a walk. Tears unstoppable. I pitied the old man, once a strong shepherd, fading and weakening until there was no life left. It had been a stormy marriage, tempers and yelling, yet Mum missed him right to the end of her life. Forty-two years can't be wiped away with a funeral.'

'They'll have to carry me out of this house. I'm not moving,' he'd said.

'They did. I was there,' said Lizzie, when the undertakers lifted his grey and wasted body out of his beloved farmhouse and into the vehicle. He had died in one second in the end. Just fell back on the bed. Gone.'

'Come and look at him,' Alice had said.

'Truly, that was the first dead body I'd seen at close range. He had gone. It certainly wasn't Alun. Yes, his body, but nothing in it. I mean no him. Come and read this bit, Nat.'

Alice's Diary
He has been coughing for weeks with water building up in his lungs and around his heart. Night after night I get up to him, prop him up on the pillow, bring him a bottle.

'She was dead tired of it all. I don't know how she did it at 84. On the night before he died she wrote in her diary:'

Shall I move into the other bedroom so I can get some sleep? It wouldn't hurt for one night.

But she hadn't left him alone. Elizabeth flipped over the page. Her diary entry for the next day,

Spent the night with Alun. Glad I stayed in the same bed. It was our last night together.

There were ravens in the old oak and birch woods and plenty of otters in the larger rivers. She would miss the mountains too. But an old person can't live in the hills alone.

Alice was now stuck out on the farm. At eighty-four with no family near. She could stay but she'd only grow older – she would need the hospital herself one day. Reluctantly she decided to sell up and move back to Hampshire to be nearer Elizabeth.

Not too near I hope, thought Liz, *she drives me crackers with her repetition and never listening to anything I say. Just talking about herself all the time. She asks me how I'm doing, I begin to tell her, but then she interrupts me to continue the story of her own day's non-events. I*

suppose hoards of people are like that. But her love for the kids is strong. That's the truth.

Alice was complaining again of missing Wales. 'Oh I did love the farm and the views, the wildness of the nature and the peace.'

'Well you could have stayed.' Behind Alice's back, Liz grimaced. She grew hot and impatient.

How can she complain now? She's never content. It's a lovely little home, in a nice neighbourhood handy to shops, just a short walk. And the doctor is only five minutes away and her church too.

Elizabeth let out a long sigh. Alice had become impulsive, constantly changing her mind. *But has she actually always been this way?*

How can someone who grew up turning serious issues, like war and death, into cabaret find comfort in reality? Victor Hugo exiled on Guernsey wrote his most brilliant book there. That's been turned into a popular musical. Would he have approved of that? How can singers sing like that amidst tragedy? It takes the reality away doesn't it?

Human nature in its tragedy binds us together in families by birth, blood and DNA, but separates us by differences in our minds. Longing is arrayed against revulsion, our heart-ties stuck fast to people who irritate us with every thought, word and action.

Lizzie loved Alice but she couldn't stand her; a seemingly insurmountable problem in many relationships and families in every generation. Alice's lifelong voiced need of Lizzie drained her. Although she loved and pitied her mother, she was always desperate to get away from her.

Liz stopped her reverie and turned back to her son.

'She has made friends with Ted, the old man of ninety next door.'

'Is he her new boyfriend?'

'Ha, every night they have tea together and they always phone each other once or twice during the day.

He has promised to look after her. What a strange thing. Well some men are kind, and they must have a job to do.

It suits me fine.

I still go to work. I can't be watching Mum all the time. Being part of the sandwich generation is difficult. We are torn between aged parents and our beautiful grandchildren.' Thinking of Felix and Meadow, 'No contest really.'

When she wasn't missing Wales, Alice was pleased with her little bungalow. It looked very much like everyone else's, but she didn't see that.

'It's all mine. Finally a house that's all my own.' She was eighty-five, an act of bravery to sell up, pack up and move house.

CHAPTER 40
Decision – February 26th

Meadow edged closer to her brother to analyse his thoughtful face. *Is anything going on in that little brain? It can't be much – he doesn't have enough words to think deep thoughts.* The child's eyebrows were just pale tufts. The irises of his eyes were ringed in a darker green shade. The sunshine filtering through the window highlighted the downy hair on his arms. He rested his elbow on the bed, one hand touched his forehead, three fingers on his skin and one in the air. He gazed unfocussed eyes into near space. Looking at the little boy, and what Meadow thought he must be suffering, brought on a trickle of teardrops.

Meadow and Felix often sat on Mum and Dad's bed and cried together. The child didn't understand why he was crying but he was easily affected by his sister's grief. She had been utterly abandoned by the person she had loved and trusted. *It feels like I have been kicked in the stomach. There's just an empty hole there that hurts like a bruise.*

One minute she would be happy, then a cruel interruption, like a hallucination, coloured and vivid would invade with an image or a feeling. Thank God, they only lasted moments. And thank God, Felix demanded a lot of attention, not deliberately always, but just because of his age. It shook her back to a relieved return to the material world.

Nathan sat deep in thought too, his brow furrowed, his eyes staring, his chin propped up by his hands.

If I had been alone I would have sunk beneath this separation, but we are busy because of the child.

'Time is a great healer.' *What a load of rot! As time stretches on, instead of feeling less, I feel more. It's torment not knowing where she is or even* if *she is.*

Nathan's body ached to hold Sarah and he craved the sound of her voice. He couldn't recall the tone – he had no video records or answer phone message to listen to over and over. He searched again on his mobile for any voice messages, but he'd deleted them obviously.

This has been five months. How do people survive when it is a year or a lifetime of not knowing? Imagination is worse than reality – it throws up so many possible frightful scenarios – multiplying the gulf. When in reality, there is only one true answer.

The anger, the grieving couldn't reach their fullness because of the unsolved mystery of Sarah's whereabouts. The question of her death or life tore at them all and wouldn't let them go, instead of fury or deep grief – just interminable ups and downs. Alive? Dead? How? Why? Maybes.

We cannot rest. It all hinges on Easter. But what if we can't find any solution then?

Nathan determined for the sake of the three of them he would file for divorce after the Easter holiday so they could put the emotional swinging behind them. A mark, a final full stop. He visited a friend of his to discuss the legal side and found it was costly but straightforward. He made the mistake of telling Jess.

'Nathan, that's good to hear. I'm sure that's the right decision. You've been very patient. I'm sure she doesn't deserve all this consideration after what she's done.'

He wasn't listening.

Six months will be long enough to ascertain she won't come back, if she is alive by any chance. Oh, but if she does return I could marry her again. She won't come back.

What crazy stuff am I thinking? No, six months it is. Not because I don't love her – now I realise how much I do – always have. It was blurred under a sea of mundane responsibilities and neglect. I forgot to love her. Neglected her, oh my God, that word neglect. Aren't neglected children cared for by the state? Isn't it a punishable offence? Why should neglected wives be able to cope any better than children?

Nah, it wasn't that bad surely. He shifted his position, walked twice around the room then turned his neck right and left to stretch it.

For the sake of the children I will put a big black marker dot at the end of six months. No more hunting, hurting, wondering torture. That's it!

Then when we've all come to terms with it – the children accept it – and have grieved properly – we'll start again. But people who think there's a time limit for grief have never lost a chunk of their heart. It will be half a year, but only a tiny fraction of our lives will be whole by then. I may never find another love like Sarah – of course I'll never find anyone like Sarah. That's a stupid thought. It is because of her, Med and Felix are so adorable – and why I got side tracked by responsibility. The motive was right to provide and protect – it just wasn't her need.

He stopped his meditating about his plans and walked to the window to stare at the sodden, grey and brown garden. It didn't inspire hope in him, so he turned back toward the kitchen to make some coffee. But the thoughts returned.

What she needed was life – love, excitement, plans, joys and hope and cherishing. Well, she had the kids, didn't she? Ah, but then she may have inherited a psychological disorder. Who knows what made her father into a troubled alcoholic and her mum is nuts – or would be if she stopped taking all those pills.

All this time Jess had sat watching Nathan as he pondered, his eyes moving in various directions and his lips pressing together or making small shapes.

'Nathan, you have that silly dreamy look again. Wake up!'

Jess had come over to keep Nathan company and was wanting to have a long talk to him. Med and Felix went for a walk to get the paper for Dad and came home with liquorice straps which hung out of their mouths like long dogs' tongues. Jess looked unamused. She was alone in the house at that moment.

'If I'd known you were going to the shop I would have got you to buy me a paper too. It wouldn't have been extra work and it would have saved me time. I've had to clean up all the breakfast dishes with no one to help me.'

Felix looked at Meadow who was trying not to laugh and almost choking on her liquorice. They ran away into the garage and gave Dad his paper.

She is never horrible in front of him. I don't think he'd believe me if I told him about her. I know he thinks I'm jealous of her — I know he does because she's told him that — I bet she has.

Jess hinted to Nat that Meadow had left the dishes for her to clean up. 'But I asked her to do them.'

'Then I think she is a very obstinate and ungrateful girl if she doesn't do what her Daddy wants her to do.' *Extremely ungrateful — after all he is doing for them. And considering how she is left without a mother and her father is so desperately alone. It's good that at least he has me for a friend.*

She walked into the kitchen, softly closing the door and speaking in a low tone.

'Let me advise you, Meadow, not to put yourself above the needs of your father. Remember his needs must come first — yours and Felix's are second in importance. He has to work each day to take care of you both. Dear Nathan.'

Tears welled in Meadow's eyes, her heart pounded, her fists clenched beside her little frame. She left the room.

That afternoon the girl stayed in her bedroom. Felix came in looking for her. 'Good, Felix, come here, now we can play some games.'

'I spy wiv my little eye somefing beginning with P.'

'Pillow.'

'No'

'Poster.'

'No.'

'Pink jumper.'

'No.'

'Give up.'

'Bed.'

Meadow fell about chortling – all his letters were wrong.

'Let's do the speaking game.'

For two minutes a person has to talk on a given topic without being interrupted. Then the other people can ask one question. Then it's the other person's turn.

With Felix it had to be a topic that he knew about. He couldn't talk on abstract ideas or places or things he'd never experienced.

'Gardens.'

'In the garden we have peas. We have a shed. Jimmy was there. We have birds.'

'Think, Felix, think!'

'We love it.'

'Good boy. Now give me a topic.'

'Mamma.'

'No, not that one. Another one.'

'Daddy.'

That was easy for the girl. Two minutes whizzed by while Felix listened with a serious expression and fiddled with the fringe on her cream bedspread.

'Good, Med.'

'Ha ha! Felix, you funny little man.'

Nathan came upstairs to get the children to come down to eat their tea at the table with him and Jess.

Meadow came down the stairs scowling. Felix looked at her and tried to copy the face. They ate in silence. When the woman stared horrified at the way Felix was holding his fork, Meadow gave Jess evil black looks.

'Cheer up you two!'

After dinner Nathan said he still had a bit of work to do in the garage. He was sorting his tools, sharpening them and hanging them with perfect precision on a tool board he'd been making as one of their experiments at doing practical activities to overcome their negative daydreaming. He was fastidious in the process of hanging them all at exactly the right distance from one another. He stood back and admired the completed project. He wanted to show Felix his handiwork so went inside to fetch him.

Jess was cheesed that she'd been left alone so long. The kids were no companionship for her. It was Nathan she wanted.

When Nathan came looking for the boy, Jess said, 'My dear Nathan – Meadow and Felix should go to bed.'

'Go to bed? It's only 8 o'clock. Certainly it's past Felix's bedtime, but my girl can stay up for at least another hour.'

The girl, with her back to the woman, made a 'haha' face and poked out her tongue. 'Thanks Dad.' She dashed upstairs with Felix following. *Oh hurry up Easter!*

CHAPTER 41
Fear

It was almost time for Alice to go to bed, only 8.30 pm, really early she knew, but tiredness was coming on earlier in the evening lately. She switched off the kitchen light, checked again that the doors were locked and then Alice's eyes were captivated as she looked through the fuzzy glass panel in her back door. She jumped at the huge shape of a man standing right outside. He moved slowly, standing on one foot and then on the other. *He must be trying to see how to open the door. Did I lock it? I don't remember if I did.* She ducked down and hid behind the room divider. Her knee was really painful as it usually was when she bent or stooped. She slid gradually over to the side of the servery to see if the man was still there. He was – this time waving and swaying. *He must be drunk. There have been a lot of break-ins and vicious attacks on elderly people, some have even been bashed or worse.* Her heartbeat was loud in her ears. Fear rose in her mind and body, a horrible nightmare. She saw herself lying lifeless in a pool of blood on her kitchen floor. *I can't call Ted – the man will hear me and break through the glass and roar in. I can't call Ted, what can I do?' Oh I'm so scared. I'll have to do something. What? What? God, oh help me. He's much bigger than me, huge. Why won't he go away and leave me alone?* She was nearly frozen to the spot, hardly able to think or breathe. She shook in the cold, dressed only in her pyjamas. An icy sweat formed on her forehead. *I'll creep to the bedroom phone and call 999.*

The police dog was heard only a few minutes later barking and running around the little house, padding and panting and then a knock on the door.

'It's the police, Madam. It's all OK.'

Alice went to the door, opened it, and grabbed the young officer, dressed in his uniform, by the hand.

'Thank you. Oh thank you so much. Did you catch him?'

'Well, actually Madam, the dog found no scent to follow. There was no man. I think if I may come in for a minute, I'll show you what happened.'

'Of course.' She was feeling so relieved even a smile appeared on her ashen face.

'You see Madam, that tree, the cypress tree, is waving and bending in the wind. There is moonlight and it's making a huge shadow on your door. Look do you see what I mean?'

'Oh goodness, yes.' She reddened. 'I feel such a fool.'

'It's understandable to be afraid when you are alone and elderly, especially when the TV and papers print such sensational stories about break-ins. They make people very frightened. Don't worry about it, we are glad to help you.'

'Thank you again, Officer.'

She wrote a letter the next day to the police department to thank them for their excellent service.

The cypress tree was cut down with a chainsaw that week.

She had been terrified, she told Liz.

'Why didn't Alice appear to have had much fear in the Paris prison when she could quite easily have been shot, Nathan?'

'It could be she hasn't admitted being afraid to herself.'

'Or she may have been still the child that lived in costumes acting parts of other characters on the stage, believing the prison scenes to be theatre. They say maturity begins when drama is over. In that case…' she smiled at her son.

'Yet surely this terror must be a hang over from those few weeks in the Cherche-Midi.'

CHAPTER 42
The End – February 28th

Jess has been manipulating Dad for a long time, Meadow thought.

'You know Nathan, it's been a full five months since your wife left, she couldn't come back now even if she was alive. You wouldn't be as weak as that to just let her walk back in, would you?'

Nathan didn't like her talking to him about Sarah. Now she was subtly criticising him again.

'Daddy can do whatever he likes.'

'I know that Meadow, but I'm sure he's not that stupid.'

'Meadow knows me Jess. She knows the way my mind works.'

He always took the children's side in little disputes.

Jess decided it was hopeless trying to get Nathan to be her partner. She resolved to let him go. *This little family are unhealthily attached to one another. It isn't right – children should be children not running the family. That girl is a little dictator.*

'I can't take any more of this ingratitude from your children, Nathan. I won't be coming around anymore.'

Jess kissed him on the cheek, shook his hand and started to go. Nathan got up to open the door for her but didn't try to stop her leaving. She dared not look at the children. Not one glance or smile even to the boy. He made a gleeful face because his sister was secretly punching fists in the air. Watching Felix's face, 'You're as funny as a nana. Whoops!' she whispered. She watched her dad, contented.

I know people can survive well with only one parent if they really love you.

Meadow looked down and then reached out for Felix's fingers. They sat silently.

Nathan felt deliciously free. A weight fell from his mind. If Jess hadn't decided to leave, he would have had to tell her to go. He was grateful for all her help and concern, but it was too much strain on the family. He didn't say she was getting on his nerves and was relieved to see the back of her. *How will we get on at work now?*

On Monday he found she had requested a transfer to another branch.

'Well, your daughter got her way at last.' She was resentful.

I'm not going to carry on this conversation.

'Sorry you're leaving.' But he wasn't. *There are more important things than efficiency.*

With Jess out of the picture, Nathan was free to pursue Sarah. Now he had the blinkers torn off, he made the pursuit his consuming passion.

Now he could devote all his spare time to following the track that would lead to Sarah's whereabouts. No more wasted Saturday hours or tense evening outings. The discovery of her whereabouts was imperative.

Methodically he went trawling through his list of possibilities. He crossed them off in his diary when they proved useless. He spent hours on the Internet, tracking Spanish Police Departments, train timetables, public transport routes, taxi companies and private detective links. He had a lost costly pearl to find and went after it like a hawk after prey.

He emailed Sarah's photograph to tourist information kiosks and hotels in every major city in Spain. He made preparations for the Easter holiday so it would really be taking them as close to

Sarah's mystery location as possible. *It will be a much more fruitful trip now. What else can I do? I'm not going to quit. The mystery must have an answer.*

Nat had also made some progress in the books he was now dipping into to help him relax. Stuff that he thought might help him understand women better. He highlighted passages that were important to him in Fluoro yellow so he could re-read them over and over until they made sense. He dwelled on the thought that women long to be sought after with the whole heart of the pursuer. *Is that true? The whole world does seem designed for romance – the mountains, rivers, the sea, flowers, music, weddings, the coming of spring after a frozen winter is all more than just practical. It must have another purpose because these things are all beautiful – like women. I forget all this stuff when I get wrapped up in work and duty.*

Nathan took a sheet of A4 paper from the printer and absent-mindedly started drawing on it. He took a blue pen and made a huge heart on the page, then decorated around the edge with little hearts and crosses and circles. He let his mind drift and wrote words in the centre in a big scratchy hand. He used a red pen to shade in some of the mini hearts. He pushed his chair back to have a better look. *What has come over me?* He tucked the sketch under his diary.

Nathan was now making other plans in his head. He planned all the things he would say to her if she returned. It was stupid to think of it. *Where there's life, there's hope* – another silly cliché. *How do I know there's life? If by some miracle she is still alive, I'm going to apologise to her for the dull life I've given her, a girl who had so much potential.*

'I will say:' and he practised aloud, 'I'll help you in every way I can. You can go to university and study anything that brings you fulfilment. You can have your plans and make the most of yourself so that you will have something to look forward to and goals to reach.' He wiped his brow with his hand.

Nathan tidied his desk, putting all his papers, bills, receipts, brochures in order, and filed them. Then his reflections popped back into his head.

I've been so scared that she would not need me if she became independent. And now I know about my dad, I can see that my other fears were partly a reaction to his irresponsibility. But to be honest I think I was really just too insecure. Worried about money. A song his mother used to play when he was a child appeared in his memory: 'You don't know what you've got till it's gone'. *I hope beyond hope it's not too late. I shall continue to dream until we know whether she is alive or not.* He didn't want to say 'dead'. It was not all over yet.

I will tell her she's beautiful no matter what she's done. She was my first and only love. I'll tell her that her thoughts are valuable.

'I won't stand in your way, Sarah. Sarah,' he said it aloud, 'Sarah.' *Oh give me another chance. I want to know you more than I have – heart and soul. What is a soul?* He pondered and had wondered before. Felix, Meadow and silence had resurfaced a knowing he'd had as a small boy. *Ah, it's the you that lasts forever.*

His thoughts returned to the now. *My poor mother was in constant stress because of poverty. I hated that feeling. I guess I just reacted to that by wanting security at all costs. But what you hang onto you lose. Well I've probably almost lost everything now. I have the children, but mustn't make the same mistakes with them. If I hold onto them too tightly, I may lose them too.* Nathan made his way back into the kitchen – what to do right now? One could always have another coffee.

Meadow wandered into the bedroom and over to the desk where her dad kept his papers and diary. She picked it up and looked around to make sure she wasn't being watched.

She opened the diary, looking for secrets her dad might be holding back from her – nothing interesting she hadn't already seen. Her eyes were riveted on the heart sketch that had been underneath. She looked and listened. No one was close by. She read the words to herself:

Beloved Mercedes,

I adore you my beautiful princess – rule and reign with me over Ovington and Arlesford, Itchen Abbas, Itchen Stoke and Kings Worthy and beyond and far. And be crowned with me in Winchester Cathedral and we will make love on the royal barge on the Itchen in high summer with larks ascending.

Love Forever,
Dantes xxxxxxx

Meadow returned everything carefully to its place.

She glided down the stairs, her eyes moving as she thought.

'Dad, who is Dantes?'

'Oh, he's the hero in your mamma's favourite movie, *The Count of Monte Cristo.* Why?'

'Nothing.' The girl turned her head away, rolled in her lips to hide the smirk and held her hands in a tight clasp.

CHAPTER 43
Great Alice

Alice had rung Nathan a couple of times during the last few months, just for a chat. She never minded not talking to Sarah or even asked where she was. She was not a blood relative and therefore not a real one. At Christmas, Nathan and the children got twice as many gifts as Sarah. He and Meadow were sorry for Mamma but she didn't care. She understood Great Alice's ways and forgave her anyway.

Lizzie hadn't told her mother about Sarah's disappearance. She knew the fuss she'd make about it and couldn't handle what she knew would be the constant pestering. Felix, of course – how can a child keep a secret – had let it slip when they'd all gone to visit Great Alice last month.

'Mamma in Spain – we go too,' he'd said eager-eyed, before any-one could shush him up. Alice latched onto it instantly, pouncing like a cat.

'What do you mean?'

'Oh Gran, Sarah's gone to Spain for a while.'

'For how long?'

'Well Sweet Alice, we're not sure.'

That evening she made a phone call to Elizabeth.

'I knew she was no good. Nathan, that wonderful boy, has always worked hard – provided for them in every way – like a faithful dog. He's always been good to me, sent me cards, rung me on birthdays.

Oh the poor boy. When those two boys used to love coming to stay on the farm, he was always the thoughtful one.'

Alice rang the family the next day. Meadow answered the phone. She made a face, her mouth down, her eyes squinted – she mouthed, 'It's Great Alice' and held the phone out to Nathan.

Felix ran over. 'Hello Gweat Gwan, me eating apple.'

Then silence.

His sister lurched forward to catch the phone before it was thrust back in its stand.

'Here, I'll take it.' Then, just as Lizzie knew would happen, streams of questions.

'Why did she go? How could she? Are you all right?

Do you need any money or anything? Have the police been told? How are the kids coping?'

She asked too many questions. They were impossible. He didn't know the answers.

Nathan sat stiffly, defending Sarah. He spoke in short sentences and couldn't wait to hang up.

'What did she want to know?'

'The obvious.'

Lizzie had asked Alice to promise not to ring Nathan.

'Mum, I asked you not to and you promised.'

'I know that girl has run off with another man and she's probably pregnant.'

'Mum, you should know.'

'What do you mean?'

She must have a selective memory. She appears to have completely forgotten any mistakes she's ever made. It is always justifiable if she has made the error or otherwise it's someone else's fault.

'It's natural to react badly to ill-treatment. But that Sarah has no excuses. Nathan is the sweetest thing alive. She's a wilful little hussy. She was never good enough for him.'

Funny how we always judge people for what we ourselves are. Liz kept her mouth shut to avoid another argument. She'd only just learned how to do that since Alice had become so frail, in body – but not yet in soul.

It took Elizabeth years; nearly a lifetime to realise her mother was not *her mother* but a person with a name – Alice Rose. A personality and soul totally separate from hers – they may have nothing in common at all – well they didn't. But she now knew her mother was a human being and so deserved respect – even honour like any stranger she might meet in the street – to be greeted civilly and shown kindness. *Strange how seeing people as one thing, like a mother for example, blinds you to the reality of their actuality.* Lizzie still longed for sensible parents who she could talk to even in her sixties.

Three days later Alice was taken to hospital and it was looking very serious this time. They suggested moving her to a hospice. Liz rang her son. Who else would care?

'I had no idea it was that dire. She has cried wolf for years, mostly in panic, but I'd stopped believing she would ever really die. She said she was waiting for the telegram from the queen, the doctor had told her she'd be sure to get one. But now the team at the hospice are saying it will only be a little while.'

Nathan and the children drove to Nan's. She grabbed him and gave him a bear hug.

'Reality's hit. I feel so nauseous. The sour taste in my mouth won't go away – I can't eat anything. It's like morning sickness but with no baby at the end of it.'

Alice had kept writing her diaries for years. Mostly filled with boring everyday stuff about how hot it was, how tired she felt, how much bottling she did on the farm. It was revealing to Liz, here were clues that helped her understand who this Alice Rose really was, but also what her needs had been. Every page was filled with unceasing doing. Phone calls, many of them daily. Pop-ins, trips to friends' houses, She helped in the charity shop, weeded, baked, bought things – all listed with their prices, with a note 'Shouldn't have overspent like that.' Then another visit to the doctor recorded and so on. This meant she had had to do a lot of driving; she had lived so far away on the farm. One entry was poignant but over-dramatic Lizzie thought:

The loves of my life have all gone. Lou – my very dearest Lou – a school romance, a fine young brave officer who risked his life, after five years of being a POW, he returned and I sadly turned him down. He died in 1998. Henry, my dashing Italian. I'll never forget the love, we could have been so happy. Alun, where are you?

Meadow once again took Felix away to find something to amuse him, so they didn't have to listen to all that G.A. stuff. In the lounge she found the button box. *This will do.* She invented stories about where each button had come from and who had worn them on their clothes. Felix held each one in his hand and listened enraptured. 'Well, that used up about ten minutes,' she said.

Liz continued her chatter to Nathan. It helped her to talk about her dying mother who had so unexpectedly become dear to her.

'At the back of the diaries was an itemised account of the year's purchases – all together this time. Vest 3 pounds. Hair 24 pounds – Present for Tony 12 Pounds 50p – Screeds of itemised goods and figures. She had plenty of money in her savings accounts. Must have been a habit clinging from the war years and the ration cards.'

Elizabeth looked at her son. 'Do you mind if I rave on a bit more?' He shook his head and smiled at her.

'"You're all I have," she often said to me. That made me so angry, what a burden to have put on you. "You're all I have," she repeated. No Mum, you have your friends, your neighbour, your grandsons, your… She ignored me completely. When she phoned me she said it again. "You're all I have, Love." By now I was seething. You don't have me! I snapped. But it was true in a way. Looking at the photos of the two of us when I was three, four, five and so on. It was just she and I. I didn't know what a family was.'

The children returned; the button box had reached its limit.

'My beloved mother. Why could I never call her that when she was conscious? Of course I know the answer. I felt if I gave her any indication of affection that she would take advantage of it to control me or suffocate me with emotion.'

'Did you ever feel like that, Meadow?

'No, never.'

Sarah had never demanded Meadow's love so she had been free to give it. That had made it harder for the girl. True love makes you so vulnerable and uncovered.

Nathan was spending quite a bit of time with Liz at the moment. He knew she had no one else. His brother made regular phone calls, but it wasn't the same as the actual presence of the person. Meadow and Felix made pleasant background noise that made the house feel full.

Nathan and Liz, carrying a pile of diaries, moved off into the kitchen to put the kettle on.

'You know reading these journals of Mum's, she was busy from 8 am to 5 pm, even at eighty-eight.'

Her constant comment, 'Glad to sit down at last.'

'What makes a person so hungry for activity and company? I don't feel that need and I don't think you do.'

'It must have started very young, Nan.' Meadow had just joined them in the kitchen looking for a snack. 'Maybe being pushed to practise and practise in order to compete in dance competitions set it in motion.'

'I think before that really, when she obviously failed to feel loved.' The desire to feel satisfied, to earn her right to be someone.

'The same driven-ness answered a thank-you letter with a thank-you letter.'

'Ha. That was a funny quirk.'

'A gift of apples from an overloaded tree reciprocated in a cake, a lift somewhere with a petrol voucher. She never accepted help or a present without the instant reaction.

What can I give them in return?

It was as if she wasn't worthy to be given anything or to receive help.

Poor Mum. She was never relaxed enough to shut down her anxieties – still she's lived to ninety-three almost ninety-four.

Last night, when I went to visit her, she said. 'You are so beautiful Elizabeth.' Not in the usual flattery-type of way. It seemed real so it demanded no rebuffing. No arguing. I just let it go. *Why have I always fought back?*

Elizabeth had started to go through Alice's multitudes of belongings, much of it memorabilia dating back to her childhood. She'd kept it all. Her brother's drawings, her school photographs, every card and note she'd ever received, the last letter her mother wrote to her before she'd died, her mother's cutlery and Royal Doulton china and boxes and boxes of papers. It was overwhelming. Then there were all the other diaries, literally about fifty of them.

She opened one at random and read:

Dad's birthday today – he'd have been one hundred and seven.

Now that's totally mad, and Elizabeth laughed aloud.

Then she tenderly washed a cup and saucer she remembered giving her mother as a child – fine bone china with a delicate floral design and a plate they used in the little caravan they'd shared. She put the valuable things into a big trunk. The special cup saucer and plate she put separately. A loud cracking noise made her jump as the bundles of papers tipped and fell, pushing the precious china onto the floor. It shattered into little bits. Liz stood there staring at the pieces of the pretty flower cup and the sailing ship plate. She almost cried, but it seemed daft after the importance of that compared to a human being who was shattered and broken. *Mum has kept all that china for over fifty years. I've broken it in one minute.* They were pieces of Elizabeth's childhood. Well and truly over now her mother was dying. Any remaining immaturity in her forced to depart forever.

Great Alice's house was a burden to the family now she was in the hospice. They were spending hours there every other weekend. It took ninety minutes to get there because of road congestion.

'With all that activity she did, I thought clearing out her home might be easy. But the inside of her cupboards must be what the inside of her busy mind was like. Look at this, Nathan.' Liz picked up a little orange card and opened it. 'It's Mum's wartime Guernsey certificate of identification, covered with stamps and signatures, isn't it a lovely photo? There are boxes and files; hundreds of things, memories, and souvenirs saved, all the grandchildren's little notes and ones I gave her when I was four, five, six and so on, all the funeral brochures of friends who've already died, there are heaps of those. She is the only one left of her Guernsey friends and most of the Welsh ones too, batteries by the dozen, just in case, eight containers of baking soda. The shelves are deep and the interiors invisible, crowded by triple packets of everything. Well, her memory failed I mustn't forget that.'

Liz held in her hand a tiny navy blue leather diary dated 1940 and an even smaller maroon Letts Diary from 1947. Here were direct thoughts transposed from those dates to today – like time capsules. 'I'd never save any of my old notebooks or letters.' But these were absorbing now that Alice was fading, soon to be gone. *Why did I never ask to see them when she was capable of showing them to me? I think nearly all mourning children and partners have regrets. We are not what we could have been. I was not all I should have been.*

'The trouble with memorabilia is it keeps you rooted in the past. Every thought is a backward glance, a memory of a previous time nostalgically viewed as a happier era. Mum was in love with a dream,' said Liz.

Meadow looked at her Nan and nodded.

'Now is when we are actually alive and can change things.

The future is our dreams and they are dreamed now too, aren't they?'

'Felix is right again, Meadow. He never thinks about the past.'

'Schmelix, hey. Try this! Walk forward but look behind you. Watch me.' Meadow modelled it for him. 'You see you can do it but you stumble into things.'

Felix copied, walking quickly with his eyes turned over his shoulder. The child walked into the kitchen doorframe and fell with a thud. He looked up puzzled and ready to yell. A wail escaped. His sister had to laugh at him a little.

'Sorry Felix, sorry.' Meadow picked him up and cuddled him quickly. He snuggled into her neck, wiping his streaming eyes and nose on the front of her jumper. 'Hey!' But it was her fault he'd got hurt and it had been a perfect illustration to look ahead not at what's behind you.

Nathan picked through the cupboards.

'Still another hangover from the war, the hoarding?'

'They did have a tough time on the Channel Islands, much harder than most of the mainland.'

'Ah, but not unendurable like the continual bombings in Coventry, Bristol, Birmingham or London.'

'True, but they were almost starving towards the end. A Red Cross boat saved them – bringing everyone parcels of what must have seemed like Manna from heaven. But there was no system in Mum's buying, just thoughts, feelings then reactions. Any idea that flew into her mind started a resulting action.'

'Oh, so wearisome.'

'I'm exhausted already,' said Meadow, 'just hearing about a brain that's so busy. I must catch these compulsions before they become my habits – after all, she is my great grandma. I may have inherited some of that.'

'No, Sweetheart, you are secure in who you are, strong.'

'Oh I was until Mamma left us or died.' She could not voice or acknowledge for a moment that Mamma may have committed suicide, as that would be the one outcome she could never recover from. Well, none of them would.

'Now I find horrible habits appearing.'

'Ah, but you can see them. You will not be overcome by them, little angel.'

CHAPTER 44
Moments

Felix had continued his little habit of staring out of his upstairs bedroom window. While it was still daylight, before supper, just for a few minutes each day he stood on tiptoe quietly looking out. From the window he looked down on the front garden, the path to the gate, the hedge along the front, he even saw part of the footpath and the road before it turned the corner.

A few people walked past and one or two cars drove that way, nothing eventful – sometimes a person walking a dog. Then Felix would call out, 'Look, look, doggy.' And Meadow would jump up and join him. She wondered if he was looking for Mum but didn't want to say anything in case he had actually quite forgotten her.

'Come on silly, we have to go and help Dad get the table ready. It's time for tea. You can put the knives, forks and spoons at our places please. And, we're having chicken.'

'Nug– nug– nuggets on heaven's door,' Felix sang.

Meadow beamed – *loopy lad.*

They charged downstairs to the kitchen. Felix loved helping but never did it correctly. Meadow just laughed and fixed it for him every time.

In the evening Nathan popped into Meadow's room to kiss her good night.

'What is it Daddy? You look like you have something to tell me.'

'No. Well, but I have been thinking. Do you mind if I talk to you for a bit? Of course it's about Mamma.'

'Sure.'

'Well, I've realised there are a few things I should have done but failed to do. I know that now.' He hesitated; it was quite a painful confession. 'I should have treasured your mamma like one is supposed to treasure a child. Looked for her uniqueness and the bits that needed to be loved to life. No one had cherished her in that way. The way that someone picks up a jewel and holds it to the light adoringly, lovingly, then grabs it to one's chest.' Nathan crossed his arms over his heart then clasped his hands tightly.

'People need treasuring, that's what I've discovered,' he continued. 'Each one has as much value as the finest cut diamond, ruby or emerald. When they are children especially, someone must value them like precious stones. Love from the heart, without this – this is where it all starts to go horribly wrong.' He shook his head. 'An unvalued soul fights for worth like a drowning person desperate for air, gasping as they pop their head above water.' Nathan flailed his arms in the air then made fists to emphasise his points. '"Give me love! Celebrate me!" and runs this way and the other grabbing at people, "Value me please." But the ones they grab are repulsed, revolted, suffocated and pulled under.' He paused for breath.

'I've learned this from the Great Grandma saga my mum's been telling me about. You can't dote on someone who asks you to – you must choose to do it. It's free will. I should have prized Sarah more. Her unique views, her faith in God, her desire to do what was right, her stories from the past, the things that meant a lot to her, that I wasn't interested in. To value someone you need to do that. We do it for Felix.' He looked at his daughter with his eyes wide and his eyebrows raised.

'We aren't really interested in toy dinosaurs or little towns, but we love him so we show interest in those things. If we saw older people as children too, got photos of them at three, six, twelve, and so forth, and remembered that that was the true person, it would help us to cherish them. You can't wait until they are dead. Oh. Drop everything. Value them now! We should have funerals before the person dies so we can tell them all the great things they do and have done. What we love about them. Listen to their favourite music, and cry about how much you'll miss them one day. Kiss them and hold them.'

Meadow's face broke up into a crumpled image, tears tearing down the broken surfaces into her mouth and dripping from her chin. Sobs shook her shoulders and caught away her breath.

'Oh, Mummy, Mummy.'

Nathan was cut open, exposed and raw. 'Darling Sarah,' he said. 'Sorry to burden you with this, Med.' He held her close. 'Would you remind me if I forget this?'

'Yes,' she sniffed and inhaled, 'but a star shines for thousands of years after it's dead. How do we know moments don't continue to exist? The precious ones I mean. Really?'

CHAPTER 45
Email – March 1st

Re Sarah Barclay

Nathan was loath to open it. He'd had a few replies from his research before – always saying 'Sorry I can't help you.'

He had a bit of a sick feeling about this one though. He clicked on it and it read:

Dear Mr Barclay,
We think that we have positively identified your wife as you can see in the enclosed attachment.
Please reply if we can be of any further assistance.

He sat stiff and unmoving. *I don't want to see it.*

Three minutes passed while he thought of all the things it could contain. A dead body, an injured beyond recognition hospital patient, a marriage certificate to someone else – that wouldn't have been legal, it was ridiculous, an image of her in jail with her hands through the bars pleading. *I've seen far too many movies.* When he had breathed steadily and calmed down he opened the file. It was a photograph of a Sarah-like woman and a man who looked Spanish, taken from CCTV footage in a hotel foyer. The image was blurry, the face unclear and turned three-quarters on.

It was from Seville not Madrid. That was a double hit.

He sat a moment and looked at his shaking hands.

Waves of sickness filled his stomach. He couldn't cry. He just sat and stared into space – shell-shocked, punch drunk. Another one of his headaches started throbbing in his temple.

Bravery wasn't a natural attribute, but this was sink or swim – breathe or die stuff.

It's possibly her. I'm not replying. It could be a scam for money.

A fleeting worry crossed his mind. *How am I going to pay for the accommodation if we have to stay longer? Alice's money won't be available for at least six months. I refuse to put it on the credit card.*

After several moments his intuition kicked in. *Well I'm not changing our plans. And I'm not sharing this with Meadow either. It might not be her. It only looks somewhat like her. This will be my secret. The man might not be a lover. He could be a friend – but a hotel foyer?*

Stop kidding yourself. Well I'm just going to pretend it didn't arrive. I'm good at hiding things. When we get to Madrid, if there's no trace we'll get the train to Seville, extend our holiday by three days or so if necessary. What if she doesn't want to be found? Too bad! If I can find her there I will present her with her children. There is absolutely no way she will be able to resist them.

Here it is. He raised his eyes, now brimming with unexpected hope – *it's been given to me – a possible second chance to be the lover and husband of my priceless girl – If it is her.*

He didn't feel like visiting his mother in the evening like he'd arranged. But he did. She needed him.

The three sat in the car silently on the way to Nan's. Meadow leaned toward Nathan. 'What's wrong with Felix?'

'I'm quiet 'cause I'm not allowed to say fart anymore,' said Felix.

Her lips pressed tight to suppress her laugh. She and Nathan just stared straight ahead.

Nathan kissed Liz on the cheek when he walked in and waited for her to spill all again, as he knew she would want to. Alice was the only topic on her mind.

'When I visited her yesterday afternoon she was lying in the hospital bed, no previous hairstyle visible, her hair swept over to the side by my caresses – it became the same forehead and hairstyle as the fourteen-year-old girl in the 1935 sepia school photo on her wall. I know what she must have been like then. I wish I could have been her school friend, I think I would have loved her. I don't believe her mind ever changed from fourteen to ninety-three – apart from memory loss.

'She lived through horrible disappointments, betrayal, imprisonment, the consequences of foolish decisions, parents dying young, giving up a baby for adoption, a war, leaving friends behind, but amazingly – no grudges – like a child – an easy forgiveness and forgetting. Fears, however, hung around her like a noose. Children are plagued with them too aren't they?'

Liz sat down at the tea table, set with mugs, plates and biscuits.

'The child Alice was the ninety-three-year-old Alice. The fourteen year old face looking out of the ninety-three-year-old dying woman's body in the hospital bed unaware of the dazzling spring stirring outside, the grass vivid green, birds frenziedly darting, trees bursting into leaf and flower, blue skies with racing white clouds. While inside that room, a body shutting down like an old steam engine, slowly putting on its breaks – steam hissing, water leaking, crunching and a standstill, liquids in the body drying up and the room already smelling like a grave. Hearing is apparently the last sense to leave. Should people have said all the words they did in front of her?

'It took me until I was sixty-three and seeing my mother dying in front of me to realise two things. My pride and defensiveness were ugly and that I loved her for who she was; not for who I wanted her to be. This was what she'd needed all her life. I missed it. Oh my goodness, that Nazi gene was embedded in me. An inner Nazi, well it must lurk in everyone looking for an opportunity to express itself. Humans are wicked in situations of power, even domestic ones.'

Liz leaned over and grabbed Nathan's arm. She looked him full in the face.

'Mum told me a month or so ago that she'd had a wonderful life. It sure wasn't my idea of wonderful. Broken heart, exiled from her true home, only one child who lived a long distance away. She must have been thinking of her childhood, her sporty good health, the dance and performances, then the five years of German rule in which she thrived, then the farm, the animals and birds she loved feeding, seeing me married, her lovely Nathan and the two adorables – Med and Felix. Well what a positive attitude even during real death threats – a Pollyanna. What an interesting person I could have had for a friend if we hadn't misunderstood one another every time we spoke. I'd tried hundreds of times. This time I'm just going to let her talk and be patient. It lasted five minutes maximum.

'How many times have we broken each other's hearts?'

There was silence for a minute, then Liz's voice stuttered with emotion, '"My girl is 18 today. She is all my life, all I live for." That's what I read in another of her diaries last night.'

Nan bent over and clutched her stomach; she could barely speak. For several minutes she moaned like a mourning dove while the water escaped from her screwed up eyes. Nathan let her sorrow subside. He waited patiently, not having any words of comfort.

'Why did those words do that terrible thing to me? They were sitting in the book waiting to ambush me with tenderness, pity, regret and other unproductive emotions. Imagine me at 18 not caring a hoot for my mother miles away in another county and her writing with love and longing for her baby.' The weeping began again. She dabbed her eyes with a fresh tissue.

'I didn't mind her being far away and only talking on the phone, but now when she's leaving this planet… *Sorrow not as those who have no hope,* Mum's visiting pastor said to me.' *Oh remember that, Lizzie, remember, remember!* she said over and over in her mind.

Meadow had listened but was becoming bored with the repetition. She twisted and looked around the room then back at her grandmother.

'Nan, I don't think those emotions are unproductive. They work in you, I think for the sake of other people – like us for example. Now you know what I'm living through.'

Nan nodded at Meadow and made a kiss in her direction but Liz needed to unburden herself further. 'Outwardly I fought with her and contended over every little thing, but strangely dread was present inwardly. I just couldn't handle her emotionalism. I lived from my head but she from her heart. Now my heart is rising, I'm learning to feel but it hurts like a new born baby suddenly breathing in the earth's atmosphere as it cries out – to step into the world of feelings is a shock – yet you have to – to be alive. Only the unborn feel nothing.'

'Are you sure they feel nothing, Nan?'

'One day,' said Nathan, 'we will all look back on this as a time of value.'

Meadow snorted.

'Family support – it's so important – at least I've learnt that. I won't be so glib with my sayings to those who are really suffering: "It will all come right in the end, you live and learn." That's not very helpful is it?'

'Daddy want a cuddle?' A small voice behind him said, then a thin arm crept around his leg and a little warm hand felt for his. Nathan lifted the child up and looked into his guileless eyes.

Nan had recovered herself and was holding onto Meadow's fingers.

'You poor sweethearts, you must feel like this often at the most unexpected moments.'

'True, but anyway, Mum, we're not going to sit here like trapped squirrels anymore. We have plans. First we'll search for her in Madrid, other cities in Spain or wherever the trail leads in every way that's possible, then when we know – we'll plan a new life and start from there.'

Thank God it won't be with Jess.

'But what if you never know what happened?'

'We can't think like that Nan. We'll hunt until we find an answer.'

Felix still sat cuddling Papa. He reached out for a homemade biscuit, looked at Nan, she winked. He bit into it, crumbs dropping on the floor.

'Good old Felix. That's the way.'

Then he squirmed out of Nathan's arms and ran off to play with a stripy cat he'd just seen sneak through the slightly ajar back door. 'Meadow, you'd better keep an eye on him.'

'Mum, one good thing has happened in this time of darkness. Sarah has done me a big favour.'

'I can't see what.'

'I've become a father.'

'What? You always were.'

'No a real one – a father to and with my children. We are together now. I've been reading how crucial fathers are to daughters especially. Their influence is huge, even more than mothers.'

Liz looked down at her feet. 'I'm sorry you had such a bad example.'

Nathan put his hand on her shoulder. 'Yes Mum, but listen, anyway I was a boy. A father sets a course for his daughter's life. There's been lots of research done on this. Just listen please.' He wanted her full attention. She had begun to fiddle with the dishes on the table. 'That was one of the things that affected Sarah and even Gran Alice. Her father never stood up for her against her well-meaning but domineering mother. Alice I mean not Sarah.

'Meadow has been saved really from fatherlessness. I could have continued to be just another absent father. Daughters need the attention of a father or they look for it elsewhere – among males usually. The research says a girl gains her confidence from her dad's guidance. She gives him authority that she gives to no other man. If it's not there well…

'I know I'm spouting off what I've just read, but I believe it. It makes total sense. A dad can save his girl, if he does his job well, from promiscuity, alcohol abuse, illegal drugs, predatory boys and on and on.'

Liz looked uncomfortable. She was thinking about her own childhood and her missing father.

'It's all been analysed and graphed.' He sat up straight in the chair and brushed his hair away from his temple.

'The daughter watches everything a father does apparently, even in mundane simple everyday things. Her papa can be the most important man in her life – always.

'The book I'm reading says the influence that pop culture, fashion, movies and music comes nowhere close to the influence of a father. Strong fathers, strong daughters.

'I think it's happened just in the nick of time. Thank God I have a chance with Meadow.'

'I suppose having a bad father might be worse than having none – well it is none – it's minus none,' Liz said. Then she thought about Alice again and her unfortunate marriages.

Meadow came back from watching her little brother. *Daddy has red eyes wet with unfallen tears. He must be upset about Great-Grandma.* She went over to him and gave him a quick hug. He drew her back toward him, held her tightly and kissed the top of her forehead.

'I might have lost you, Meadow, and the little one. I might have lost you.'

There was a long pause. Meadow didn't get it but she didn't think it was a good time for explanations.

CHAPTER 46
Very early March

It was going to be another rare stunning day. One of those sunny, still, blue-skied but freezing days. Myriad meringue clouds hung in the sky. Already the mistle thrush was sending magnificent songs into the air. Early flowering bulbs were breaking through the soil. The white magnolia was still in flower. It could have been paradise. Except for the feeling of emptiness that persisted in the household. The questions, the lack of answers, nothing resolved, like a half-made cake or a tune stopped mid-way.

It wasn't time to pack the suitcases, but Meadow had packed and unpacked them twenty times. The trip was the bright spot on the horizon – the plan – the hope.

Meadow asked a friend home after school. It was easy for her classmate to call her parent and tell her she'd be home later. On the way home after Med picked up Felix, they walked on back to the house, interrupted by a skipping boy darting here and there raving about drops of rain and an empty snail shell. She passed the tree that she had seen in midwinter at the time of her deepest grief. The black bare trunk had filled her with images of abandonment, even of the end of everything. She stopped to stare at it again.

Was it the same tree? It looked transformed. The filtered sunlight shone on the delicate chartreuse leaf-buds. She could see new baby branches sticking out awkwardly at odd places along the boughs.

'What on earth are you staring at Meadow? You look as if you've had a vision.'

'Oh just noticed the old dead-looking tree has new stuff growing out of it.'

'Daft girl, that happens every year. It's called spring!'

She put out her tongue and wiggled her head.

Felix had run on ahead loping like a hyena.

'Wait, you nutter.'

Meadow had been much brighter since the trip was finalised, Nathan thought.

Ah, I see how important it is to have little things to look forward to. Poor Sarah, she had nothing much to dream about.

Still, she could have made her own plans, saved up money, oh right – she did.

There was a passive pause in Nathan's thoughts while the humiliation flooded over him. He felt hot and was sure he had gone red. Meadow would notice and endlessly interrogate him, but she was busy doing homework with her friend.

By nature Nathan wasn't a poetic man, but he found these evenings alone were times of discovery. He discovered 'longing' and yearning atypical of his regular character.

He found Sarah was always on his mind, often in picture form. His only desire – to be with her – nothing else. She was so real to him now that he talked to her. 'I miss you terribly. I am so sorry.' He had spoken to her off and on over the last five months but this was becoming a continual part of his new night-time ritual.

Demoted as he now was, he was still preoccupied during work hours even with his new mundane job. He quite forgot about Sarah during the day, but walking in the door at 5.15 he was blasted with images and sensations, secretly still hoping that by some miraculous event she might be waiting inside for him.

Nathan closed his eyes as he laid his head on the pillow that night. He fell in love with the way he remembered Sarah, body, soul, everything about her – even the dreams she'd spoken about – and he'd dismissed. They rushed back like a flood of water and as he slept they became his own.

While driving home the following day, he realised he'd felt dead inside for a few years. He couldn't put it down to an occasion or a time when it had happened – perhaps he had always been that way.

How many people a day do I NOT see? Inside their heads and

hearts are oceans of moving scenes, emotional dramas, dreams lived and unlived, hopes and longings, achievements appreciated and unappreciated all swilling around in a multi-coloured soup.

Life was gently waking up in him. Much like the peas they'd planted. The seed or bulb had to die first.

Why must it take tragedy?

There was no Sarah waiting at the door. *Why do I keep torturing myself?*

But Meadow and Felix ran to him as he stepped through the front door. They both jumped up like puppies to kiss his face.

To have someone to love and to love them – that's it – that's all there is. I'll take it. Let me keep it.

How truly dreadful to have no family during times of stress and sorrow – To be alone. He couldn't dwell on it too long – because Sarah was alone, cut off from the ones who truly loved her. *I can say it now, I love her. It was just a thing I used to say as I dashed out the door to work. But living or dead or even with some other man, I know because I can hear my heart tell me, I love her.*

There was a soft knock on Meadow's half-open bedroom door.

'Med, I need another chat, can you bear it?'

Nathan was using her really, for the intimate companionship that he should have had in his relationship with Sarah. He'd let that opportunity slip through his fingers, he hadn't even recognised it was in his hands.

'It's just that I've been thinking about forgiveness.'

'I'm glad you've been thinking about something, Daddy. I've been worried about you for a while, so silent and looking unconcerned.'

'Ha, well you're wrong there. We don't all show our emotions on the outside, lots of people have depths we never see. Anyway, forgiveness is an accounting term. We use it at work. It means to cancel someone's debts.'

'You mean if someone owes the bank one thousand pounds the bank can forgive that person?'

'Well they could – but of course they scarcely ever do. But let's think about people now. If I owed you kindness, but I gave you nastiness and you forgave me, it would cost you a lot. You'd have to give up the expectation – let go of it – all the kindness I owed you.'

'I don't get it.'

'OK then, when a man and a woman get married, they promise to do certain things like look after the other person if they get sick for instance. If they don't keep that promise, it's a real debt – as real as if it were one thousand pounds. If you forgive them for breaking that promise – then you let go of it – you lose the thousand pounds. It should have been yours, the care. Letting go of it is a painful sacrifice, but it's a good pain – it leads to freedom.'

'Good pain? No Daddy, no pain can ever be good.'

'Well otherwise that person is in control of you, always in your thoughts, making you angry, upset or full of hate.'

Meadow began to undo her navy school cardigan and then do it up again. She fiddled with the little blue buttons, putting them in the wrong buttonholes so had to start all over.

'But it's not fair.'

'That's true. It's unjust. But love is greater than justice, I'm beginning to see.'

'I have an ex-friend at school, Bella. She said such rotten things about Mamma leaving me – gossiped it and suggested rude reasons. I told her to shut up and that I hated her.'

'Have you been able to forget about it?'

'No. I think about it during interval and at lunch times and try to avoid even seeing her all day. She drives me crazy.' Meadow once more started to undo her cardigan.

'Let's try to forgive her – after all, what are we if not forgiven?'

'But I don't want to – I like hating that horrible bitch.'

Nathan stared at his sweet innocent girl. The little fair-haired cutie he used to carry on his shoulders while she held onto his head, her hands plastered over his forehead so he could hardly see.

Why do kids have to grow up? If only we all stayed small.

'Well Med, it looks like she is controlling you.'

'Yup, I'll have to think about this a bit more Daddy, it's not easy is it?'

She pulled off her uniform and rammed her head through her pyjama top then grabbed her pants, fiercely tugging them up, then she pushed herself down into the sheets.

Nathan kissed her good night and tucked her in, like she was five years old again.

CHAPTER 47
Secret

Elizabeth rang Nathan in the morning. He no longer ran for his phone. It was the call he expected this time.

'I got a text this morning at 3.30 am: "So sorry for your loss. Your mother died at 2.30 am."'

'Oh Mum, we are so sorry too. I'll just call work and then we'll be right over.' They bought some pink and maroon peonies on the way over. The three all put their arms around Lizzie when they went inside. They let her cry. They didn't know what to say to her. Felix jumped away and grabbed the flowers and pushed them into Liz's arms. He had heard Meadow say something in the car so he repeated it loudly.

'Now she is Gweat Alice in Wonderland.'

That broke the tension as they poked him and laughed.

Meadow went to the kitchen to put the kettle on, as tea was the answer to nearly everything she'd learnt.

Everyone keeps their secrets until they are ready to share them – it's self-preservation. But Alice wasn't ready to share hers. It forced it's way into their lives like an unwelcome intruder.

'You know, Nathan, I've never told you what I discovered last year. I swore to Mum that I wouldn't tell anyone. She was so ashamed of it. But she's gone now so I'm sure she won't mind.

'What?'

'Well, first I'll tell you how her secret was discovered. I kept on getting little messages on my social media sites: "Do you know you have a half sister?"'

'What, really Nan?'

'Yes, I didn't believe them so I replied, "No I haven't." But then there came more details; a date, a place, a birth certificate with Mum's name, her married family name and her maiden name. So I couldn't doubt it any longer. I asked her about it all.'

'So this person is your half sister?'

'She sure is.'

'No, really?'

'Yes, my new sister told me the whole story by email. I asked Mum about it. She started crying. "Oh why does this have to come out now I'm 93 years old? You won't respect me anymore. You'll judge me harshly." "No Mum, of course not – I love you. Everyone has accidents." But I thought, what? Was there no birth control in 1955? How could you be so stupid getting pregnant again after having had the boy only two years earlier? But she was like that you see, overcome with emotion and the fun of the moment and thoughtless of consequences. She'd never made very sound choices. Oh I did feel so deeply sorry for her, not angry or critical at all. She had been able to tell no one. Mum had gone down to Cornwall for a supposed temporary job, taking me with her, had the baby in a little home for unmarried mothers, all alone. Then handed her over within the hour.'

'Oh my God, that's so sad.'

'My half sister wanted to know if I could tell her what her father's name was. On the birth certificate it said: Father unknown. And that's the truth. Well, I think so but now we'll never know. Mum said: "Oh I can't remember his name. He was a well-built good-looking fellow. He took off when I told him I was pregnant. I never saw him again." She tried really hard to recall the name. Even looked in her old diaries, but she didn't have one for 1955 or any of the years from 53 to 60. She'd said: "I threw them away I wasn't happy about the contents." I never thought to ask why. Three children with three different fathers! Uncle Oswald had once said his sister had laughed that she couldn't tie her shoelaces up, she was getting too fat, just before her trek to Cornwall. They had their suspicions that she was a "good time girl".'

'No, surely not.'

'Are you going to meet your half sister?'

'Absolutely. I plan to travel down to see her in the summer – it should be nice in Cornwall then. I can make it a holiday too.'

'What does she look like Nan? From the photos you've seen.'

'Well, a bit like Great Alice actually.'

'Ha, of course.'

'Well, it's never too late for the truth to come out is it?' Nan asked with her finger over her lips and with questioning eyes.

'I think the truth always sets people free from something and opens new entryways into the heart.'

The others nodded, even Felix.

'You little rascal!'

Nathan turned his eyes upward looking at no one. The news of Alice's out-of-marriage births and adoptions added a new horrific possibility to Nathan's already bulging list of what ifs. He chilled all over as he thought over the likelihood of Sarah being pregnant and running away in a copy of his grandmother's younger years. *Could this be the real answer? Might the listlessness be pregnancy depression? She had been depressed with the news of their second baby coming so long after the first because she had already neatly mapped out her plans and ambitions for the next few years, and then Felix arrived and put a stop to all that.* 'But what a blessing he'd been.' He spoke silently.

But what if this was his own baby, but she couldn't face having it? What if it was someone else's? She had been having an affair. That would have made her unmotivated. What if she'd had an abortion and it had gone terribly wrong? No, Sarah didn't believe in terminating life, she was hot on that topic.

These thoughts were like bullets that fired rapidly through his brain, but they didn't exit. They lodged.

He had settled it with the lawyer, to file for separation and then divorce when he returned from Spain. He would at least have done his utmost. He hadn't done that yet because he'd left it so late to go after her, it took life minus Sarah to wake him from his stupor. *I will keep hunting.* He had turned up nothing on his online searches, apart from that dubious image, but he'd laid a good foundation and eliminated a lot of dead ends. It was essential for the children to know their family story, exactly what had happened to their mother. It helped him to know his place in the world when he finally knew his own family's secrets. *It is ugly but it's better to know the truth.*

The final preparation before they could get the tickets to fly to Spain was getting the passports in order. Meadow still had one that was valid, though she looked like a little girl in it. But Felix hadn't ever been abroad. Nathan hadn't believed in wasting money on unnecessaries. Their holidays had been inexpensive package deals within Great Britain. He recalled they had had fun times with the little kids anyway. Well he had. Maybe Sarah hadn't, he thought. Felix's passport photo was required quickly so they could send off the application. Nathan had kept postponing it as he was hoping it wouldn't be needed. Now there was no choice.

At the chemist Felix had to stand in front of a screen. He wore his green shirt, which toned in with his eyes – Meadow's idea.

'Don't smile Felix! It's not allowed.'

So the child frowned emphatically and hunched his shoulders. His eyes narrowed as he put on a mean face.

'Ha, now you look like a tiny gangster.'
'No Felix, put your shoulders down.'
He stared blankly into the camera.
'At last. Woo hoo!'
The child looked crossly at the finished photo.
'All passport photos make people look like idiots, eh Dad?'

CHAPTER 48
Demise

As Alice was coming in and out of consciousness during that final week of her life – a morphine pump attached to her body delivering doses every hour to keep her semi-comatose or at least very sleepy and pain-free, smiles of recognition and sweetness would steal across her face and be seen in her glassy eyes. Words sometimes popped out unexpectedly.

Nathan sat beside Liz at the table. He remained quiet as she leaned on her elbows to tell him more about her final hours with her newly dear mother. He listened with his head on one side like a dog listening for some special sound.

'"You're here!" Mum said. I'd been there for ten days but the short-term memory had failed a year or two earlier. Every time my face appeared it was like the first time again. "You're here!" I felt annoyed for a fraction of a second. She always made such a song and dance about any little thing. But this couldn't be that. It was raw, true honest emotion from her sub-conscious heart and soul. She even recognised Brett and said, "Ah the last one." Then smiled softly.'

Liz stopped for breath, inhaled, sighed, and began again.

'I'd never seen Mum as a sweet person – but truly I think I never really knew her, like she never knew me. Two people bound so closely by blood, birth, experience, dependence and yes, love, but so diametrically different.

'But now, oh I knew what had changed, hah – she was quiet.' Liz sighed; a relieved smile flickered across her face. 'Never stopped talking before – never at rest.

'The Filipino nurse asked me in the morning if Alice knew anyone called Lloyd. She had kept calling that name.

'I was puzzled then a flash of realisation. "Oh yes it's 'Lord'; you know, 'Lord Jesus'." That was a wonderful moment. She will be safe forever; I knew for sure then.'

A peaceful expression stole across Lizzie's face and her eyes blinked slowly.

'When you have felt, since you were sixteen, much older than your mother and then over a whole lifetime – the childlike mother becoming more and more dependent, well, not deliberately – but I felt increasingly responsible for her – after Alun died and the older and sicker she got, a mother to my mother. In fact I read that she said I was her mother in one of her diaries!'

Elizabeth reached into her pocket and pulled out a sodden hanky.

'Oh, and what Mum said to me the night before she died nearly broke my heart. "I don't want you to see me die." First, now she knew this was it, Nathan – curtains, secondly she wanted to spare me the awful moment and the picture of it that would ever remain in my mind. Me, I was the only one. She was so brave.

'We had been together through everything. As a little child I'd been there with her but unaware when she had the first baby – the boy she had to adopt out. And then the second one – the little girl, I must have been almost five. You would think I would have noticed something funny about Mum's stomach. She named her after her best friend at school, Mary-Kate. Handed her over and had to recover alone. Of course she couldn't tell her parents she was pregnant again, less than two years after the last catastrophe. Why couldn't she have used her brain not her emotions or her passion, or

bodily instincts? Birth control was possible in the 1950s, wasn't it?'
Liz threw her hands in the air, still puzzled by such a big mistake.

'My now-discovered half sister, she's a nurse you know, like my
mother always wanted to be, tells me people who are dying want to
go. When they are with a loved one it's harder for them, they want
to stay on earth to be with them but it's exhausting. She thinks that
was why she told me she didn't want me to see her die. I was the
loved one, the kept one. It was easier to let go without me being
there.'

Nathan twitched with discomfort, his thoughts always flying to
Sarah and her demise. He held a big white handkerchief to his eyes,
not to stop the flood caused by Alice's death but the grief of Sarah's.

'Just a bit more Nathan, I'll stop soon I promise.'

'No, go on Mum, I don't mind, really.'

'Well then, over the last three days I sat and watched the life
ebbing out, the spirit separating, the body losing control of all its
functions. Her tongue hung out like an animal with thirst. I remembered the cat I had found under our house. It turned and turned,
its bones slowing, its muscles stiffening, miaowing and deep groaning as it half-consciously looked for comfort. Your father's death
was instant – almost, one minute living, the next a corpse. So I saw
no dying with him just like I saw no dying with Alun – only the
end result. That's why watching my mother depart was so shocking
– more shocking than finding someone gone.

'Instant death was what I'd hoped for my mother. None of this
dying business, this slow process – the machine running down like
a battery-run toy rabbit.

'From time to time she spoke. "I'm dancing," she said, her eyes
still closed.'

'How wonderful.'

'Yes, the light in her eyes still shone out at intervals from the glazed and unfocused look. She opened them for a moment only and another word of sweetness popped out. "Love you, love you, love you." I'd never heard her say that before. Maybe it was something she'd said to someone else – a lover in her past? How many had she had? I've found out about seven so far.

'Her ordinariness blinded me – those habits and the effects of time obscured the truth. I hadn't been able to see it until those last three days, but by then she was in such a state of peace I couldn't disturb her. My lips wouldn't move except to add to something she'd said. How could I bring up all the awful things when she was seeing angels?'

Meadow came in at that moment.

'Oh, I need Sarah right now. I have no daughter of my own.' Meadow hugged Nan for a full five minutes as the woman wept. She understood. They had both lost their precious mothers.

The funeral was touching and honoured great Alice for her bravery during her wartime imprisonment, her boldness in starting the ballet school, her stage performances, her solo mother episode, her courage moving to the farm, her loyalty and membership of the Women's Institute, her giggling, her hospitality and her many friendships and her faith, which she had come to quite late in her life. Nothing was said about the secret acts of bravery or passion.

Nathan was having a short battle of images in his head. Was it Great Alice in that long wooden box or his wife? He struggled and fought off the picture of a waxen Sarah, her hands folded over her chest, her brown eyes closed.

The flowers on the shiny oak coffin were lilacs, imported from goodness knows where, sprays of greenery and silver and also flowers in Alice's favourite colour – orange. A giant bouquet she would have loved.

Felix sat very still during the service. He was dressed in a new shirt and his new jeans. Meadow held his hand. He sang the hymns or pretended to and walked very slowly behind the coffin as it left the church. Meadow had had to be a pallbearer as they were one short. She felt honoured to do it. Great Alice had become so tiny over the last year that the coffin wasn't heavy anyway.

Felix walked alone trailing the adults. He looked like a miniature man. Looking back at him made Meadow smile.

'He's being so good Dad, I can't believe it.'

At the cemetery Felix became himself again. He tore around the grassy areas and then begged to turn the handle that let the coffin, covered with the huge bouquet, down into the deep muddy hole. He stared down as he turned the winch. Felix called down to the coffin, 'See you 'gen, Great Alice.'

Yes I can't wait to see your restored and happy smile again, thought Liz. *My goodness, this is the only time I can remember longing to see Mum.*

When the shiny box reached the bottom and was steady, the whole family sang together from song-sheets. It was the most gorgeous sunny weather and birdsong was everywhere. The mistle thrush crescendoed his music to fill the air with joy. Not a gloomy picture at all. Everyone laughed at the funny things Alice had said and done. Then to end the interment they threw her favourite red roses, Dublin Bay, down onto the top of the lid. Nathan took some photos for Liz to keep.

He asked Felix where Great Alice was – just to see what he thought.

'She's gone to the flowers,' he said and smiled.

CHAPTER 49
Early March

Miles away on a comfortable sun-lounger, she sat, staring at hills shimmering in sunlight. Distant towns, golden and chalky topped by terracotta roofs – so harmonious, mellow, melded into surrounding trees and low mountains. The air smelled of oranges.

Without warning, a bolt of terror ran through her as tangible as a knife blade. It lasted only a moment, then dulled and disappeared. The woman, her face pale, yet pretty, framed by her wispy chestnut hair, knew instinctively that the time of happiness she'd been enjoying had reached its fullness. It was not going to continue undisturbed.

The second searing stab followed just as unexpectedly, quite quickly after the first. The following days interrupted by many aches that Sarah identified as pangs of regret. Sometimes they were shocks of guilt and other times a great crushing desire to hold her children. To hear their voices, just to be near them. Even Nathan appeared in her thoughts as a person she needed to touch.

Never had she given these pains and aches a possibility of striking, when she'd left them. They came unbidden, unforeseen.

She didn't have a smartphone and had thrown her old mobile away at the airport – did she have any photos?

Desperately looking through her tan bag, she searched for pictures of Meadow and Felix. Now, suddenly she could hardly say their names without weeping. She found photos of the children deep in her wallet, tucked behind bankcards and old coffee receipts, but none of Nathan. She held them to her heart and stifled the sobs. He mustn't hear her crying. She hadn't looked for the children's images before because she had dreamed that if she never thought of them or saw them, she could pretend her old life had never existed. *What complete denial.* She hadn't planned to stay away this long either.

When she left, Sarah had been at a point of discontent so deep nothing of her life had seemed worth hanging onto. Now these new unwanted thoughts began to appear regularly at inappropriate moments, disturbing the new life she had promised herself. The life she used to dream of while she was doing some thankless task in a home lacking in dreams; the elegant room, the new exciting partner, the gorgeous towns, villages, the music and the small tapas bars, walking by rivers followed by exotic fiery suppers and delicious evenings. Who was she kidding? These thrills had already begun to lose their charm. She knew none of this was the answer to what she had really needed, but in a weak and foolish mood had succumbed.

Very gradually, little thought bites of a new form of discontent crept back into her heart and settled there like puppies, their tales between their legs – sneaking under the table.

Her new sense of loss cut so deep she felt it in her body as a groan, a grief like the death of a loved one.

Once those thoughts had taken possession they returned with frightening rapidity and a train of others followed.

I have to go back.

The guilt, regret and cutting self-knowledge of her utter selfishness spoke to her like real voices. 'You left them, when they needed you. You deserted your own children. You did everything you don't believe in. You betrayed your husband. You are no better than your father who walked out.'

She turned her eyes to heaven then closed them, whispering in gushes, 'Jesus, when I ran away I buried You along with my husband and children. Please forgive me, help me get back to them Lord.'

She felt the darkness inwardly like a fresh slash. Shame covered her like a heavy woollen blanket. She fought off the smothering. She moved her shoulders back violently and pulled with her arms, her fists taut. 'No, you will not have me. I'm going to do the right thing. There will be mercy. I will learn to forgive myself too.'

There had been no intention on her part to get involved with another man. Living with intention would be her new promise to herself. *I will make it up to them.*

When you run in the wrong direction, wrong things attach themselves to you.

If the Spaniard affair comes out later, as I know all secrets will, then OK, but enough to handle one thing at a time. She knew it was wrong in her conscience, though it is accepted today as freedom of choice, a legitimate part of a contemporary lifestyle.

Nothing that damages other people can be good. She was amazed at her mind arguing blindly with her heart, giving her dozens of reasons why what she'd done was natural, only fair, did no one any harm, she'd needed it. Nathan deserved it and more.

He wasn't a bad husband, just a dead one. My life was going nowhere. I'm still young, the future ahead appeared to me to be sheer boredom and heading towards a desperate end. But he was faithful, steady and kind; when he tried to be! I should never have married him, but I did. He never gets really angry, never is unfaithful, never is anything. But surprisingly, she felt she missed him, his gentleness, his love for the children, his strong moral code. *That gave me such security but it was also so predictable, and he has such an annoying habit of using clichés instead of speaking from the heart. What heart?* 'Now that is harsh,' she told herself aloud.

Nathan's romance with Sarah had been dropped into a file

labelled – *To Do Later.* Every woman wants to be pursued, first place in her lover's life. Her husband was her lover, but she was sure he'd forgotten her. The adventures they could have together had been shelved – *To Save Up For.* Her beauty wasn't noticed anymore – there was no file for that in Nat's life.

Sarah had thought, when she made the snap decision to leave, that Nathan was totally reliable and responsible and that at last he would take some time off that dreaded job he loved so much. He would be forced to spend more time with the children and get to know them intimately, hopefully – unless he palmed it off to his mother.

Meadow would be fine with her dad – she was his pet anyway. Felix would be fine with Meadow – he adored her. It wasn't as if they would be orphans. They'd have each other. She might be away only for a couple of weeks – just enough time to teach Nathan a lesson – that she existed and her feelings were real. He hadn't seemed to take seriously her depression symptoms. He would come home and she had hardly done anything. She couldn't be bothered keeping the house clean or tidy. What was the point? But he didn't seem to care.

Besides, since she'd been reading up on psychology, the subject that he had said was 'useless because it would bring in no income', Sarah had found out that a depressed parent badly affects the children's chances at school and in life. Goodness, didn't she already know that from her own past. She didn't want to do to them what had been done to her. She wanted to get away to protect them from herself so she wouldn't contaminate them with her negativity.

Despite all this reasoning, she knew without a moment of actual doubt, she must return.

CHAPTER 50
Burial

Nathan drove alone to Elizabeth's house after the interment. The children had gone in Liz's car and were already inside. Meadow knew that Nan would want to talk to Dad again and was dreading it. She couldn't think of any way of escape. She sat with Felix on her knees hugging him.

'What an excellent young man you were today.'

'You too, Med.'

'Ha, silly.'

Nan couldn't wait for Nathan to be ready, so began her unburdening to Meadow.

'You know, Meadow. People say, "Sorry for your loss." It's on many of the sympathy cards people have sent me, a meaningless phrase to me up till now. Oh but I feel it. It's like after a theft, something valuable has been taken, it's just missing, definitely loss, a whole person gone – part of your own life has been stolen. "Tu me manques," the French say – "You are missing from me." That's better said.'

'But imagine, Nan, if you hadn't seen her die, she'd just vanished. Wouldn't you be looking everywhere, thinking you saw her in every shop? People in the street or on a bus of similar height and age – you may be watching for them.'

'Yes, I think I would be Tuppence. I haven't realised how bad it's been for you all. I only thought of how unfair it all was. And of course, my mother's gradual deterioration blocked it out. Forgive me?'

Now with a smile at Nathan as he walked in, Meadow nodded, 'Sure.'

Now Liz directed her eyes to her son,

'You know I'm ashamed and so regret the lack of sympathy I had for Great Alice during the last few years. I couldn't believe she was actually going to die. She had had so many so-called catastrophes before.' Nathan and Liz made eye rolls and nodded, both remembering the false alarms. 'Then I realised during the actual dying process, which only took about three weeks, that she really was going this time. I felt nauseous for days, I've lost three kilos.' She patted her smaller stomach.

'In the weeks leading up to this final crisis when I was so frustrated, irritated and angry, I wanted to yell at the pathetic old woman, I'd recall the photos of her at eight, fifteen then twenty-four and realise that outer hag-like woman wasn't the person within. When she was as helpless as a baby towards the end, unable to turn herself over or feed herself and she wore nappies and kept her eyes closed most of the time like a newborn – then, oh then, she became a darling. I hadn't been able to see it before.'

This theme had been thoroughly examined before but Meadow came closer and sat on the edge of her dad's chair.

'I believe we are under a spell. Do you remember that scene in the movie we watched last time I babysat about the old king who in one minute was restored to youth, all his wrinkles smoothing out and his eyes enlarging his hair growing back when the curse on him was broken? Well the spell on us says, "Die before you reach one hundred. This is your limit." And a buzzer goes off – time over. You know, Nathan, your dad's death didn't affect me, but this – I was totally attached heart and soul, I didn't even know it. Compassion and pity appeared in my heart in quantities I couldn't contain. Yet I was completely diminished.'

'The spell, Nan – what about people who live in war zones or in the midst of epidemics?'

'Ah that. Can't give you the answer, Pet. But death itself is the enemy that's for sure. If you've ever seen it or felt it, it's no friend, even when someone wants to go. You know somehow I don't think your mamma is dead. It just doesn't seem real to me.'

'Then you and Felix are the only people who think that way Nan, and well, if she's run away why didn't she take me like Great Alice took you Nan? No. She's dead, a corpse, an empty shell, her soul lost to me when I needed her most. My age is such a vulnerable time, my counsellor at school told me. Just becoming a woman. It's now I need a mother. But you will help me, won't you Nan?'

Meadow stood up. They wrapped their arms around each other while silent tears fell on each other's shoulders. Then the girl felt the need for her mamma more and leant her whole weight on Elizabeth. She gave vent to pain with a groan coming from her inside, her chest almost to her stomach tightened in agony. It lasted a minute or more.

Lizzie's heart had expanded wide for her little family – to make a place for their sorrows in her affections. They would remain there now for every day she had left on the Earth.

Nan said, 'To be loved by someone when you are born and loved when you die, oh my goodness that's the zenith of human experience – the blessing of all blessings.'

On the way home in the car, Felix fell asleep in his booster seat, his head flopping from side to side.

'Dad, that's three losses we've had in five months.' Nathan nodded. He wasn't even tempted to tell his secret. 'I'm glad I wasn't really close to Jimmy and Great Alice.'

'Yes but my mum was close to her – she feels it painfully. Alice was her mother like your mamma, Sarah, was to you.'

CHAPTER 51
Escape

New schemes of how to return were dropping into her mind even as she was walking hand in hand through the frenetic peopled streets in the strong sunshine.

'I'm scared of leaving. He might become dangerously angry.' He was as volatile as Nathan was calm. She'd heard so many stories of women being killed or beaten by partners who felt slighted and humiliated by being deserted or rejected. Most suicides too, she'd read, involved these same feelings. No. There was absolutely zero per cent of that happening. He would find someone else in a few days – hours maybe.

Pondering on the get-away thoughts that assaulted her brain, she gaily agreed to go to the authentic and noisy little bar again before they left the town for a new one tomorrow. A thump of panic began to rise in her chest.

How can I get back home?

How can I get away without him knowing? He hardly ever leaves me alone. Longing to be alone again, she pictured the peace she had had when it was just she and her little boy in the house together.

As Sarah and the Spaniard swung their arms and smiled at strangers, she thought of a hundred ways of escape. *Flying is impossible. I could get a taxi to the airport but there's no guarantee a flight would be leaving right away, and who knows if I could get a seat? He would head straight for the airport, find me and persuade me to stay. I've never had courage to speak my mind. I must be more like Nathan than I thought. If I ring to book something, the man will hear me. Even though this is the second time I've been through all this must-get-away stuff, it isn't any easier. It should be. Calm down, don't panic, breathe slowly.*

I'll have to walk out taking nothing as I did before. Somehow I'll walk down to the station on the way down to the restaurant. It was out of the way but she would say she needed more exercise. *He will suggest dancing at that crazy, touristy club after dinner. But for once I will have to have my own way.*

I will leave very early, the first train, with only my passport and bag. Nothing else. I'll ditch my cell phone, the second one! Oh it will be cold when I get back home, I'll take my coat too. Just as well it's black, not too easy to spot.

The earliest suburban train was at 5 am, too early. There was one every thirty minutes after that. The 6 am would be better, not so dark then. She'd never find her way to the station in blackness. She'd made mental note of the timetable as they walked slowly past the station. Later, at about 9 pm while picking from small plates of olives with saffron and cheese and poking the patatas bravas, making pleasant talk about travelling, her mind was in two very different places. Perspiration dripped down her sides as her thoughts wandered to the reality of tomorrow. She folded her slippery hands together and rubbed the sweat away.

How will I get away in the morning? He can be really frightening when he gets angry.

Her heart began to move irregularly and even skip a few beats. She looked down at her heart. It seemed to be visible through her thin summery blouse. Her breath was coming a bit too fast and her temperature swung between feverish and chill. *I must not have a panic attack now. Brain, listen to me, it's going to be OK.*

I'll leave a note. 'Gone for an early morning walk.' Hopefully it won't be raining. He always sleeps late. No work to go to – goodness knows where he gets his income from.

It rained nine days in the month of March according to her tourist info. *Please not today – I can't take an umbrella, that would look strange. Who would go for a walk in the rain anyway?*

Early morning in Seville at the beginning of March was still cool. During the winter, the pair had moved further and further south to get away from the cold weather. *But it shouldn't be too bad.*

They got back to the small apartment late; she fussed around in the shower and made pretence of tidying up. Sarah was a little dizzy from the Rioja and it had made her head ache. She had the perfect excuse to go straight to sleep.

She awoke instinctively from only a half-sleep before 5 am, got out of bed carefully and went to the bathroom. It was already growing lighter – he might wake any minute, she knew, and reach out for her. She wrote her little note and left it on the toilet seat, no time to use the toilet now, grabbed her bag with her passport in it and her coat which she'd put together the night before and tried the outside door.

It was locked.

Her heart was thumping fast and her breathing coming in short pants. She felt along the window ledge and found the key. As she put it in the lock she could hear him turning over in bed. *No, is he getting up?* Should she lock the door and take the key with her? *No that would be suspicious.* So she very gently closed the door behind her.

Thank goodness the Spanish aren't larks by nature.

She would have to go a different route to the station in case he came looking for her. She had fifteen minutes to kill before arriving. *It's no good waiting for the train, he might see me. I'll have to arrive a moment before it leaves. I'll buy the ticket on the train. 'Only the bullfights start on time in Spain.' It's got to be on time, oh please.* Her thoughts and heart raced.

The sun was already up. She circled the streets leading to the suburban station trying to appear normal but stopping behind parked cars, bending down to adjust her sandals so she could make furtive backward glances.

The train, she could hear it. *Run now!*

She arrived at the station and burst through the entrance, ran to the first carriage, took a jump into it almost slipping, ran to the toilet, slammed the door shut and locked it. Waiting for the train to leave, she looked down at her trembling hands, her weakened shaky legs. Sarah sat on the toilet. She listened to her pounding heart thumping in her ears. Someone knocked on the door several times. She was so scared she nearly vomited in the filthy basin; the smell of the enclosed room was increasing her nausea.

She relieved herself on the horrible unsteady loo, and felt a little better.

The train began to move. *Thank you God.* It picked up speed. When it was going quite fast, she opened the toilet door, came out looking around her cautiously and found a seat. It was a relief to be moving, to be out of that tiny musty room, to have acted on her plan. She felt exhausted, absolutely spent. She would have to change trains at the central station. She wouldn't be able to jump on this time. She must pre-purchase her ticket. *I'm not in the clear yet. I'll have to buy the tickets and wait in the toilets again. No man can come in there.*

Her black coat proved helpful, she thought, with the collar turned up and her hair tucked inside it. She would be hard to spot on the journey from the toilets to the train. The station was thronging with people. *Great!*

She bought tickets from the machine. There was a bit of a fluster here as she was stressed and too quickly pushed the buttons. Twice she got it wrong and had to cancel and restart. *Calm down, Sarah. At least there are English instructions.* She hadn't bothered learning much Spanish. The man spoke English well.

When on the long distance train she would have plenty of time to recover; it was going to be a long trip, changing trains many times to make it back to the coast of France. *I think catching a ferry would be a good way to go. It might help to lose my scent.*

There was no trouble buying the tickets on the zig-zag routes she took. She would crisscross the country to be on the safe side like a criminal would. She looked out of the window at the wonderful cities in the distance and the majestic architecture from the many different time periods in Spanish history: a mixture of Gothic, Moorish and Italian and then, of course, Gaudi. From close up she only saw the backs of buildings and rather scruffy gardens at the sides of the tracks from the railway.

The Spaniard had given her lots of money, *how unlike Nathan,* so she wasn't bothered by the cost of anything.

Probably the man wouldn't come chasing after her. It wasn't love.

Easy come easy go — that reminds me of Nat again. Suddenly she was calling him by his familiar name.

Sarah had hoped, unvoiced, undeclared to herself, that Nathan might race after her when he found out she was in Spain. But he hadn't come; it proved he didn't care.

Will he even speak to me? I know he doesn't understand impulsive and emotional actions. Why would he understand what I did? I don't have any logic for it myself — just that impelling urge to run. But if he'd come searching for me in Madrid, I would never have gone to my Spanish friend. Still, it was my choice. No one compelled me to.

When I was sinking slowly, I needed Nathan to show his strength, to have him speak up on my behalf. When he was silent I almost drowned, he abandoned me like the other — like my father.

She had had to throw her second mobile phone in the rubbish. It was only a cheap pre-plan so she could find maps and locations and keep in touch with her companion. It was a new sim so there was no info from home. She never checked her email or logged into any of her sites because hiding is hiding. And denial is denial.

She had left the old life behind her and pretended it never existed. Finding her father was stinky Jimmy was the last straw. She couldn't face the huge gut-wrenching inward changes she would be forced to make — facing the marriage disappointments, the counselling, her mother, the fear of boredom and of wasting her life, but worse knuckling down to face her part in their life situation. It stung to know she was no longer able to blame her past, her husband or her circumstances or have any other excuse for her choices.

Although her mother had struggled to bring her up well, she didn't get on well with her. Sarah had blamed her for being the reason her father had left. It may not have been true. In fact her mother knew well why he had left and didn't want to tell Sarah all the details. Gran suffered from hopelessness, as her daughter seemed to in the weeks before she'd left. Sarah's mother had let many black thoughts take up residence in her mind. They stayed there squatting. The diagnosis was depression, and the doctor's answers were pills. For years she had been on strong antidepressants because she had suffered panic attacks that had increased to the level of a psychotic disorder. In those years only shock therapy and heavy medication were the treatment. Her mother was calm now — so calm she never felt happy or sad, excited or energetic. A 'zombie', Sarah called her behind her back.

Now she might have more patience and understanding with her. *When I'm free, I might be able to take Mum on a similar journey to freedom to the one I'm just beginning to take. She might be too old, but I hope not.*

Many thoughts swirled in Sarah's mind, in no particular order.

Sarah had worked after Meadow went to school, but the job was unsatisfying, she knew she had way more inside her. She hadn't reached her potential in her mind or her abilities. *I know I messed about at school, lots of people do.* When she was in her early thirties she had really wanted to have another chance at study. When Felix went to kindergarten would be the right time. She would need to study for a long time because she could only do it part-time for the first few years.

She and Nathan had had a biting argument, Sarah doing most of the arguing – Nathan was reasonably calm and unemotional as usual. He couldn't understand her needs. They didn't seem real to him. She needed to feel significant and to be a whole person, to reach her full capabilities. He provided enough money for them to live well. She didn't even need to study, especially something which didn't seem useful to Nathan. Being a practical man, he saw no point in something that wouldn't benefit them financially and he was afraid it would pull her away from him and the children. He refused to pay for Sarah's university fees. That was a blow that almost knocked her down.

CHAPTER 52
Mementos

'Come on, let's throw this out.'

Brett had come to help Liz to sort out more of Alice's belongings. 'Let's sell this, I'll do it for you online. I never liked this old chair.'

'No stop! I can't get rid of all these things yet. They're the last pieces of her that I can actually touch. She loved these things and besides, I suddenly quite like them. Some of her things are lovely. The blue antique Wedgewood with the silver trim, that was precious to Mum because it belonged to her mother and maybe to her mother's mother. Let me hang onto them a bit longer. It's like she hasn't quite left and is still here with me.' *These things conjure up her presence – not her old decrepit presence – but the presence when she was full of laughter and wild enthusiasm – totally unrealistic but carefree. The mother I had when I was in those intermediate years before she married Alun and I had her all to myself.*

'But you'll have to sell them or dump them sometime.' He held in his clumsy quick hands those things that had lived with Alice through births, a war and the numerous deaths of all her family and friends.

'I know, Brett, but they are mine now and I'm hanging onto them for a while. So put them down carefully please.'

Secretly Lizzie had kept one of Alice's lipsticks. When she slowly applied it to her own lips she was a close as she could get now, almost skin to skin.

'I heard a report on the radio about a mother who lost a child. She kept his jumper by her bed, she smelled it and cuddled into it for comfort.'

'Gross.'

'No it's not Brett. I thought it was needless pain but I was wrong. The clothing or favourite possessions truly seem to bring the presence of the person back. Funny isn't it.'

Looking back into Alice's boxes of collected nostalgia, Liz said, 'What a waste – imagine if I'd listened to her story and asked to see all the old wartime visas, photos and reports. There are dozens of first places in dance competitions.' *The silver cups were badly tarnished. I'll shine them for her. I never knew she was that good. Families are like that – they don't recognise what's among them because they are too familiar with the everyday life, the faults and foibles. Not seeing who they really are is like walking to work every day and not stopping to gasp at the sycamore seeds as they helicopter down.*

'These photographs, now so badly faded, capture what I think the times must have felt like. I didn't really think Mum was that well known as a dancer. I didn't even listen or show any interest in her past. Oh, imagine if I had sat down and looked at an album with her and just let her talk. She was a recognisable celebrity on that island. Miss Personality. Loved by all accounts. Must have been hard to become a nobody after that.'

Liz peeked inside a large metallic envelope filled full to bursting with newspaper clippings and sighed.

'She would have loved it if we'd had a memorial day once a year where she could pick out one of her folders and show and tell like kids do at school. Why must that stop when you grow up? No one ever regrets kindness or gentle words and time spent laughing together, but every moment of impatience and harsh words stand out like dark threatening fists in your face. Why was I so hard, blind and yes, heartless?'

Brett rolled his eyes. 'I think we all are aren't we?'

Liz started to cry with remorse. She'd been in tears whenever she was alone. Every time she had a shower, the tears mingled with the spraying water. *I'm not really crying all the time for my dear mother but about the unbearable pain and suffering on this Earth — I know it's common to all places and people. It's just that she's personified it. Oh it's so unnatural, alien — that dying cat from years ago stayed with me for weeks — a person almost one with you must take years. Oh, the poor children and Sarah.*

Nathan and the kids drove up. Liz blew her nose and waved from the window.

'We've come to give Brett a hand.' Nathan bent to give his mother a kiss on her cheek.

'We were still sorting through Great Alice's endless boxes.

Come and see all this old jewellery, Meadow.' The girl held her elbows and pulled her arms tight to her body to quell the excitement.

'She has left everything to me, but you'll get the nice stuff when I'm gone.'

'Oh Nan, don't say that!' She clutched Liz's wrist and looked up at her with pathetic eyes, like a stray kitten.

'Come on. I know you're busting to have a look.'

'Is there anything valuable or really old?'

'Yes, amongst a lot of yucky old beads — it all needs sorting out, can you help?' Nan had a peculiar smile on her still teary face. Meadow gazed at the dirty old containers but fingered each piece as she lifted them out.

Jewellery so intricate, engraved, filigree broaches, an exquisite cameo with tiny winged cherubs. Badges from World War Two. A marcasite bow, a little gold balalaika — Great Alice adored Greece — and a medal from the Sunshine Dance competitions — second in all England. 'Oh my goodness, she was a star.' *A silver cross from*

Great-Great-Grandfather's time in WW1, the gold and sapphire ring from Alun – She'd been so proud of it. Oh I'm holding tangible proof of a departed soul's existence. Nothing from her German husband, not one thing.

Alice had become boxes full of loved papers and pictures and old items, some to keep – some to throw away.

Meadow picked up one of the diaries from the toppling pile. 'Hey listen to this Nan…'

Alice's Diary

My wandering around the world in search of happiness is over. I'm going to stay where I am and make the best of it. My love for the sea was my strongest natural pull, of course born on an island. My dream was to live within the sound of the sea – but now it's too late I think.

'How sad.'

'Keep reading.'

The years on the farm haven't been wasted. I've learnt a lot, but to marry for security is not the path to happiness. Again I found I'd chosen unwisely.

Meadow scanned the pages for another interesting paragraph, hopefully more positive.

You were so young, Lizzie, when you left. I understand why but I was left severed – the distance and the infrequent times we met were not enough to bind us together.

'What a cheek! Actually it was 'cause she married and lived miles away in Wales. We were bound together when it was just she and I in Hampshire. See what I mean about her?'

'OK, one last bit Nan.'

Spring has arrived once more — the air is full of it. Anemones, crocus, snowdrops, hyacinths, violets, cyclamen, jonquils…

'Cor she could have opened a florist's.'

'Let me continue…'

…are all pushing through — The fluttering and twittering of birds… would that my life would end just so, with the birds singing under my window and the sky bright with light.

'Nan! Dad! It *was* that sort of day with just *those* flowers and *those* bird notes.'

CHAPTER 53
March 14th

And now Sarah's heart felt penitent – she pondered for a long time about her mistakes.

I never intended to pair up with the man; I just needed to get away, completely away to think and heal. I haven't healed yet, but at least I'm not without hope anymore. She knew that the panic attacks she'd started having at home were not a hereditary condition because they had stopped occurring the moment she left the airport and boarded the plane. *So it's just negative ways of thinking about my life, feeling like I'm snared, a pattern of thoughts that have been uncontrollable. I must learn to stem them at the source. I will have to have help.*

She felt quite happy with herself that her plan of escape from the Spaniard had come off. It appeared to have been successful.

Why must I escape from difficult stuff? Why can't I just face it? Well I'm trapped now, but in a different way. It's my longing to hold my babies and maybe, a smattering of love for Nathan – he's as faithful as an old dog – that's trapping me. Well, It's more like a pang than a trap. If they have me back, I will have chosen to be there from free will.

Now she was on the train going back, she could hardly wait to get there. *Why didn't I leave weeks or even months ago?* With trepidation she thought, *how on earth are those children doing without their mamma?* She wept softly with grief for the pain she must have caused them all.

I will make it up to them. But will they be able to heal? They will always have scars, but hopefully not ruinous ones, disfiguring ones.

'Father in Heaven, I need you very much. Please help us all to recover, even though I don't deserve it.' She looked up as she spoke.

Sarah, by her decision to return, realised she'd broken a pattern, turned off a gene switch that had been passed along her family line with the rest of her DNA. Her father had left her and her mother when she was only a young child. She would be able to break the habit of hers of running from difficult situations and stand up to them instead. Although she actually felt like the shrinking man rather than a fighter, it was a brave decision to return, to take the first step on the path to the defeat of the fear of being beaten by depression like her mother had been.

If they'll have me back I'll promise to go and get help. Doing the C B Therapy and confessing all to a counsellor won't seem so long and confronting after this ordeal, surely it'll seem much easier than this.

'But will they take me back?'

Looking into the cold English Channel waters was bleak. They were green-grey, like Felix's eyes if she remembered correctly, but unwelcoming. How different from the brilliant blue waters of the coastal seas around Spain. She recalled the day trip to the white city – Cadiz, and the sea that was sapphire.

When the ferry arrived back, she was recognised by the immigration officer in charge from the photo of the missing person on his computer screen, when the passport went through. He called her into a little office for questioning. 'It's humiliating to tell you the truth,' she said. *But it's the best way I think.*

I know this is the first of loads of humiliating times I'm going to face. But it'll be worth it to see those kids. Oh why, oh why did I do such a dreadfully dumb thing? And then she remembered why she had left and how she had felt like she was sinking down, down, and how driven she had felt and desperate as if her life was going to be over and how it was like being stifled in a box with the lid pressed down and she had been almost unable to breathe.

She got the bus from the terminal, but it was nearly dark, cold too. *I'm so incredibly glad I brought my coat.*

She got off at the town close to her home and knocked on the red door of a B and B. 'Just one night, please. Continental breakfast at 8 am.'

I certainly couldn't stomach a full English.

Now, how was she expected to sleep? Sarah was in hope, in dread, both at once. *Would they even want her back? What if they say they don't want to see me again, I kind of don't blame them. But Felix won't think like that, my darling, sweetheart little boy.* She took the scruffy photos out of her bag to look at one last time.

He might look different now. It's nearly six months; oh my God.

After breakfast she walked quickly around her local town to do some shopping. *I can't go home without gifts, rats, I should have brought them stuff from Spain. No! That would have been totally the wrong thing to do. I'll get some groceries and a little something for the kids.* She chose a book for Felix, 'He must have grown quite a bit, *what a fool, what have I missed.* She felt hot all over with shame. It was hard to think of a trinket for Meadow. *Ah, yes, exactly a trinket – an elegant silver bracelet, delicate and tinkly.* Sarah glanced at her antique ruby ring, she knew how much her daughter adored jewellery.

Nathan – I can't get him anything. It would be an insult, just some English cheese and sourdough, so we can have a snack. Oh, I'm already thinking like the mother again. This time I'm going to make it fun. If they let me back that is. Oh God, maybe Nathan has found someone else.

Her thoughts flipping rapidly from one idea to the next, she bought things without looking at prices or receipts. Now she had supermarket bags to carry.

Sarah walked from the town slowly, forcing one foot in front of the other, putting off the emotional scene that would be inevitable. As she approached the familiar streets that surrounded her home, her typical fast-beating heart and short breaths reappeared. Sweat was forming on her palms though it was really cold in the spring winds. She noticed the greening of the oaks and the hedges in their bright lime first leaves. There were still primroses here and there, under the hedges and on the patches of wild in between streets. It looked very ordinary and domestic, nothing like the dramatic ambience of the towns she'd been travelling through.

The questions knocking on her brain were unstoppable.

But where will I go if they tell me to get lost? How will I bear to see my children and then have to say goodbye to them? Will they yell at me and hate me? Will Felix remember me? Oh God, please help me. Tears were forcing themselves out of her eyes and running relentlessly down onto her coat. She put down the bags and felt in her pocket for a tissue, wiped her eyes and blew her nose. It was useless. No sooner had she done that but the next lot of tears were coming. Everything looked blurry through her clouded water-filled eyes. She could just see their street now, and the two storey 1940's house with the front hedge and even the gate.

The thumping of her heart filled her head and drowned out every other sound. Sarah began to tremble; now it was more than emotion, more like a panic attack. It felt like she was facing a death penalty, a firing squad. But she couldn't stop; she would have to go through with the whole horrific business.

She looked up at the children's bedroom window. *Is that little head Felix?* He was looking down and seemed to see her. She was sure that her heart had stopped completely, waiting to faint or have a heart attack; afraid to move she stood still a few moments.

She moved towards the gate, she struggled with opening it, her hands full of bags. She was already sobbing wildly, almost collapsing. She could see the front door inching open.

Upstairs, looking out of the window had been the little face of the child.

'Meadow, Meadow!' He screamed and jumped and stamped his feet. She came hurtling into the room.

'What now, Felix, a dog?'

'Mummy, Mummy, Mummy,' he pointed, yelled, shouted and jumped around again.

'Oh, my God, it is.' Meadow felt her heart close up like a flower at night. Her emotions grew hard and cold. She clenched her teeth together and gripped Felix. Holding him tightly, she said: 'Quick, let's find Daddy.'

They raced together across the landing, both yelling, 'Dad, Dad.'

'She's back, she's here. Mum, she's really here, right now. What shall we do?' Meadow, trembling, looked imploringly into Nathan's face hoping for clues. But his heart hardly dared to believe her. It thumped inside him like a drum. In this morning light his sandy hair, translucent skin and pale eyes made his soul appear to exude out of his face. To Meadow he seemed more spirit than body. It was from there these words came, not from his brain.

'Remember Meadow, Sweetheart, our promise. We look to Felix and act like he does.'

'But I'm so angry; who does she think she is – coming back – just like that?'

Nathan held Meadow as she shook, then she hugged him desperately.

'Nothing will come between us now, Dad – you, Felix and me. We're family – not her.'

'We've discussed this many times, Tuppence, remember. Hold

my hand and we'll face this together. If she asks for forgiveness we'll have to give it to her.'

Felix had run barefoot into his room, pulled off his new jeans, stepped into his old ones, dragged them up and raced downstairs.

The child had already gone to the front door – stood on a chair and unbolted it, turned the handle and opened it a little bit. He wasn't completely sure it was his mummy. She looked different. Her face was a mess, twisted with emotion, her make-up ruined, her eyes swollen.

She was coming down the path towards him, something about her hair and her ears Felix recognised, he realised in a moment it was she.

He screamed out, 'Mummy come home.'

She fell on her knees on the lawn by the path to the front door.

'I'm so sorry, so sorry, Felix, forgive me. I love you.'

He was by her side in a moment.

Jesus, thank you thank you thank you thank you. Sarah moaned.

'Oh, Mummy get up,' and pulling her arm, 'come on.'

Then Sarah dropped her shopping and her bag and sitting on the grass held out her arms and he jumped into them. That moment was terrifying and so beautiful – safe – safe.

Felix didn't know or care what his mamma had done. In one moment he had forgiven her, forgotten that they were ever apart. They were together now, covering each other with kisses and tears.

Father and daughter, holding hands, watched from the doorway. When Meadow saw them hugging, her heart was torn, divided. She could feel her muscles tighten, her eyes narrow. Her heart with its shell-like topping cracked with each kiss. Each kiss was a hammer blow on the nut-hard shell around her soul. A soft kernel lay in there protected by its cover. It chipped, cracked, fractured then broke away. *Why should I forgive her for what she's done to us?* She struggled between bitterness and forgiveness, almost an agony, then the kernel turned to mush, her heart melted, her resolve collapsed. *Oh my mummy – I need my mother.* She rushed out too, falling, just falling into her mamma's embrace.

'I never forgot you, Meadow. I love you. Please forgive me.' She looked into Meadow's eyes – the eyes that revealed her injured heart – and she saw her own reflection. *I've done that to her.* Grief circled around her, like a bird of prey waiting for her to break down.

But the children pulled her to her feet and dragged her nearer to the open front door. Daddy stepped out.

Nathan was the hardest to face. She had caused him pain and been disloyal, she knew, he didn't know it all, thank God.

As they came nearer to Daddy, Sarah stumbling, feeling humiliated and wracked with apprehension, lifted her eyes to her husband. *He's thinner, his eyes more earnest like the Nathan I knew years ago.*

But he spoke to her in a warm voice. 'Hello Sarah, you're late.'

Acceptance. Sarah broke into sobs so loud it frightened the children.

'Sarah, I have to apologise to you too…' he began.

Then, in a moment they were all together in a heap hugging, kissing, laughing, crying, on the damp grass, not caring a bit. Meadow pulled Nathan towards her and whispered, 'Better late than never.' And struggled to wink with her overflowing watery eye.

Sarah, supported by Nathan's arm, apologising over and over again, was brought, shaking, distraught and tearful into her home.

Felix, with his lips firmly set, took a run at the heavy front door with both hands stretched out and he pushed with a groan and all his force until it shuddered, then slammed shut.